WILDE WAGERS

WILDE WAGERS

Elizabeth Caulfield Felt

OVERLEAF FORMATTING; INGRAMSPARK
DISTRIBUTION

Paperback Edition April 15, 2021
ISBN 978-0-9844507-3-2

for my mother

Cast of Characters

Mrs. Markby aka Mrs. M.....a writer
Miss Prism.....a friend of the Wildes
Miss Brooke Prism.....a friend of the Wildes
Mervay.....a friend of the Wildes
Hopper.....a friend of the Wildes
Dumby.....a friend of the Wildes
Dexter Baxter-Point.....a silly man
Dominic.....a friend of Oscar Wilde
Adele.....sister of Dominic
Adele's husband.....never properly introduced

In the Country

Archibald Bracknell.....the Admiral
Hortense Bracknell.....the Admiral's wife
Edith Bracknell.....the Admiral's mother
Peter Darlington.....nephew of Hortense Bracknell
Jane Darlington.....niece of Hortense Bracknell
Alfred Kelvil.....neighbor to the Bracknells
Dr. Gerald Goring.....neighbor to the Bracknells
Greenpin.....neighbor to the Bracknells
Frances Greenpin.....eldest daughter
Emily Greenpin.....a twin
Anne Greenpin.....a twin
Podgers.....a cheiromantist
Mrs. Hollis.....administrator at Kelvil's Hospital
Jennie.....Mrs. Hollis's daughter
Chiltern.....a butler
Abigail.....a servant
Dotty.....a servant
Foxmore.....a servant
Davey.....a servant
Gwen.....a servant

Prologue

Olivia had played many roles in her years as an actress but never before murderess. It was not a role she much cared for now. She had not killed poor Mrs. Bracknell and she certainly had not stolen that jeweled monstrosity, the Emrubdiam of Khartoum.

She sat in the back of a dogcart, wrists tied tightly together with linen strips that attached to the cart's iron ring that normally held a dog's leash, on route to whatever stood for a prison in the nearby country village. The dogcart was smelly, uncomfortable, and dangerously unsteady. Olivia sat awkwardly on the bare wood, arms tight against the ring in the corner, grimacing at every bounce and jolt.

The cart was meant to carry dogs to a race or a hunt, but with a belly laugh, the Admiral had compared her to a dog and commanded it readied. The groom who'd been ordered to drive had objected, citing the open back and his inexperience. Olivia would soon be grateful for the Admiral's theatrical rather than practical choice of transport.

The air was cool for a mid-August morning, patches of fog clinging to the fields. The sky was a dark steel grey and thunder rumbled in the distance, though it might have been the sound of railway cars banging at the station some three miles distant.

About fifteen minutes from Hudson House, the cart entered a thick but small wood, where the fog wrapped around the heavy-leafed trees. The wet cold air was hard to breathe. Olivia found the wood ominous. Having spent her life amid the cobblestones and traffic of London, she did not trust the English wilderness.

Faced to the rear and watching the road disappear in the fog, the actress did not see the sharp turn ahead. The cart tipped, angled sharply, and rolled briefly on one wheel before going all the way over. The wood panels of the corner in which she was tied split apart, and she was thrown into the brush at the side of the road. Her hands were still tied with the metal ring dangling from the linen strips.

The groom had also been thrown but landed on his feet, hands wrapped in the reins. Cursing and staggering, he tried to slow the horse who continued dragging the shattered cart down the road. Before he could look back and see what had happened to Olivia, she darted into the darkness of the wood.

It would only be a moment before the groom had the horse stopped and returned to find her. Olivia had little chance of out running him–her hands tied, wearing a thick skirt and slippers.

She dashed, her eyes searching for a place to hide. There. She dropped to her knees and crawled beneath a patch of thick, leafy gorse. Steadying her breath, she quietly cursed Oscar Wilde and his wager, Genevieve and Philip Lamb for being so charming, and herself for agreeing to a charade that might end with her head in a noose.

✍ First Chapter ✍

London 1881, three weeks earlier

"Papa is sleeping well," said Genevieve Lamb. "He's often criticized my conversation as being mindless and frivolous, but he's never called it boring. What do you think, Basil dear? Am I such a bore?"

Basil Daubeny lifted the corner of his mouth in a half-smile and twirled his pencil-thin mustache. "You know I find you the most engaging woman in London."

"Just London? I'd hoped you found me the most engaging woman in all the world. Shall I call for tea?" Without waiting for a response, Genevieve stood and waved her hand at a servant who seemed to step out of the wallpaper. "Geoffrey, tell Greyson we're ready for tea."

The footman nodded and left the room, leaving the door open.

Richard Lamb snuffled in his sleep, his head falling softly against the plush edge of his high-back chair.

"Clever to send him off like that," said Basil, standing and pulling Genevieve into an embrace. Just as his lips were about to touch hers, Genevieve giggled and pushed him away. "You are presumptuous."

"Can't blame a man for trying," said Basil, opening a gold cigarette case. He held the case out, offering her one.

She shook her head.

"Papa might wake up or–" a young man entered the room through the left-open door. "Philip! You're just in time for tea."

Two years older, six inches taller, and nearly as attractive as his sister, Philip Lamb held out his hand to Basil Daubeny. The two shook, barely containing their mutual dislike. They stepped apart as Greyson arrived with the tea cart.

Noticing the high-back chair, Philip asked, "How long has Father been asleep?"

"Not nearly long enough," said Basil with a smirk.

"About a quarter of an hour," answered Genevieve.

"Shall I wake him?" asked Philip.

"Let him sleep," said Genevieve, ushering her brother to the table. "I'll pour."

Basil remained standing. "Is that teacake?" he asked Genevieve, his voiced edged with disbelief.

"Yes?" answered Genevieve.

"You know I abhor teacake. I asked that muffins be served."

Genevieve waved her hands at the cake. "So you did. I utterly forgot. Shall I send Greyson to see if there are muffins?"

"Don't bother. I should be leaving." Basil crushed the end of his cigarette on a delicate china plate.

"Delicious teacake," said Philip, his mouth full of teacake.

Ignoring her brother, Genevieve said, "You're leaving? Without tea?"

"I have business in the city."

Genevieve frowned. "What a bore. Will I see you tomorrow?"

Basil nodded and crossed to the door.

"And don't forget, we have a box for the Regent on Saturday. It's it *A Midsummer Night's Dream*."

Philip slurped his tea.

Genevieve tossed him a sour look.

"I may not be able," replied Basil.

"Your aunt? Have you heard from her?"

"She claims to be better, but I want to see for myself and speak to her physician."

Basil kissed Genevieve's hand and infinitesimally tipped his head at Philip. "*A dieu,*" he said.

Au revoir," Genevieve called to his back.

"What a cad," Philip said, taking a large bite of teacake.

"He is not a cad. In fact, I think Basil Daubeny is planning to ask me to marry him."

Philip poured more tea into his cup, then looked at his sister and blinked twice. "You aren't thinking of accepting, are you?"

"Why shouldn't I?"

"How many reasons do you need? He's appallingly rude, he is obviously after your money, and you don't love him."

"Maybe I do love him."

Philip scoffed.

Genevieve pouted. "I might. What do you know about being in love? Have you been in love? No, you haven't." Genevieve put a small piece of cake in her mouth. "Mm. This is very good teacake."

"Yes, it is. Basil is a fool: reason number four." Philip lifted the teapot, examined its spout, and set it down. "I have never been in love, but I've watched mother and father, who are in love. I've read books about love. I'll recognize it when it happens. Lambs marry not for money, not for status, not for others. We marry for love, little sister. You must wait for it."

"Father likes Basil."

Philip shrugged. "Father likes everyone, and he knows Basil's father, doesn't he?"

"Basil's grandfather. They were at school together, I think." Genevieve licked crumbs from her fingers, thoughtful. "Basil isn't like my other beaux. He's different. This isn't like the silly crushes I've had before."

"That's because your previous beaux fell at your feet and answered your every whim. You've never been courted by a brute."

"Basil isn't a brute; he's just misunderstood."

"Misunderstood by you, my dear." Philip poured tea carefully from the pot, studying the spout and the angle of the flow. "Mother doesn't like him," he added.

"She doesn't?" asked Genevieve, surprised.

"Before she left this morning she told us to watch out for you. She doesn't trust Basil."

"He takes very good care of his sick aunt," said Genevieve.

"He may take good care of his aunt, but he will not take good care of you. I forbid you from marrying him."

Genevieve's eyes flashed. "You can't forbid me from marrying Basil."

"I can. You are not of age, and I have influence with Father."

She huffed. "You cannot, and I have more influence with Father." Genevieve stood, purposefully jiggling the table. Teacups clinked and tea splashed into saucers.

The disorder made Philip shudder. "Don't become emotional."

"I'm not emotional." Genevieve glared at him and shook the table. Philip grabbed the edge, trying to keep it still. Plates clattered, and the sugar bowl lid flipped off. The teapot, with its heavy flat base, Philip noted, merely slid a few inches.

Genevieve straightened, a determined gleam in her eyes. Before leaving the room, she turned in the doorway and declared, in a louder-than-necessary voice, "I love Basil Daubeny, and no one can stop me from marrying him."

Their father opened his eyes and looked about. "Teatime,

is it?"

Philip held up the teapot. "This is an extremely well-designed teapot."

Lily was late. She was never late. Olivia paced from wall to wall in her small dressing room at the Regent. Stopping, twisting, pulling at her arm sockets, she could not reach the buttons in the center of her back. Where was Lily? Opening the dressing room door, Olivia stuck her head into the corridor. Celia and Eliza, dressed in silvery fairy garb, were both hanging on some young toff that she didn't recognize. Eliza put on his silk top hat and Celia wound her fingers through his thick brown curls. Both girls laughed.

Where was Lily? Olivia took a step into the corridor and a young boy carrying a box rounded the corner at a trot and nearly ran into her.

"Sorry," he yelled over his shoulder as he headed toward the stage.

Two young men in makeup and tight breeches chased each other down the hall, fighting over a wig. Just behind them, the stage manager, Chester, a man in his middle years with a bulbous red nose, followed with another wig, offering it up. The men then argued about who should have which and disappeared into a room several doors down. Chester stopped by the girls flirting with the toff and told them to get ready. They waved him away.

"Chester," Olivia called, "have you seen Lily?"

He wrinkled his brow. "I think so. Maybe that was earlier."

"She went out for something. I need her."

"Have you asked Charley?"

Olivia shook her head. "I doubt he'll remember, but I'll ask. If you see her out front, send her to me."

"Right-o."

Charley was on his stool by the back entrance. He was an enormous lad with no neck and limbs as thick as the Elgin marbles.

"Charley!" Olivia shouted. "Has Lily come in your door?"

"Don't think so," answered the slow-witted but cheerful boy.

"If you see her, tell her I need her."

"Yes, ma'am."

Returning to her room and closing the door, Olivia sat at her dressing table, piled high with powders, balms, hats, gloves, a pair of scissors, and a wig stand covered in long golden curls. The lighting in the room was not good, so to examine her make-up, Olivia had to squint and bend toward the looking glass. The mirror was no longer reflective in its two bottom corners, a greenish-copper color growing into the glass. The Regent was a second-rate theater, but a step up from the music halls where she had been performing. Mr. Garrett, the Regent's manager, couldn't afford to pay for new productions, instead re-working Shakespeare and Goldman, reusing costumes and sets. The Season was nearing its end, and they had begun playing to full houses, having been "discovered" by the ton, the cream of London society.

Olivia put on a dab more lipstick, touched powder to her eyebrows to lighten them, and tried to keep calm. Staring at the mirror, she examined her eyes, made grey by her silver-grey gown. Pouring red powder onto a handkerchief, she pressed a comb into the powder and ran the comb through her long black hair. Streaks of red appeared, lightening the black and giving it a fiery glow.

"Sorry I'm late," said Lily, slipping through the door and shutting it quietly behind her.

Lily was small and waif-like, not much larger than she'd been five years ago when they'd first met, when Olivia's life had gone crazy. Lily had been twelve, following Olivia around, wanting a job at the theater. Although Olivia had ignored Lily at first, the girl had been persistent. Eventually Olivia had let her help as a dresser–fortunate, as Lily had ending up saving Olivia.

"Help me with these buttons," Olivia said. "I can't reach any farther, and we need to hurry with my hair. Did you get the necklace?"

"Here it is." Lily handed the box she'd been carrying to Olivia and stood behind the actress, fastening the buttons which ran up the back of her dress. The small silver buttons matched the diamond droplets that covered the grey velvet of the dress, giving it a magical shimmer whenever it moved. Olivia had been playing Hermia, in a blond wig and simple blue shift, but as the former Titania had run away to Paris with the son of the Duke of Dunstable, a new Titania was needed immediately. Olivia knew Titania's lines. She knew all the lines in A Midsummer Night's Dream; unlike some of the others at the Regent, Olivia paid attention to everything. Playing Titania excited her, the role, the lines, and the decadent dress. The skirt was made from yards of material and the form-fitting blouse with its long droopy sleeves made her feel like she had wings. Unfortunately, it was not a perfect fit.

"It's too tight on top," Olivia said, raising her left arm. "There's a rip. Can you fix it?"

"Oh dear!"

Lily hurried to the table in the back corner of the room and returned with needle and thread.

Olivia began to wriggle out of the dress, but Lily stopped

her.

"Don't take it off. I can do it like this," answered Lily.

"Good," said Olivia, sitting back and holding still. "There isn't much time and we need to put up my hair and get the crown to stay."

"We've plenty of time," said Lily, carefully drawing the needle through the material. "Guess who I saw at Butterfield's?"

Butterfield's was the shop that had repaired the paste necklace Lily had gone to fetch. Before Olivia could make a guess or even think of one, Lily answered her own question.

"The Earl."

"The Earl of Montmarch?" asked Olivia.

"What other Earl you think I'd be talking about?" asked Lily, pausing in her work to roll her eyes. "Your Earl. The Earl what has taken you to dinner after every performance these last two weeks."

"The Earl *who* has taken me to dinner. Go on. What was he doing at Butterfield's?"

"Shopping for a ring."

"And?" Olivia asked.

"And he says to the toff he's with that he's going to be proposing, so that's why he needs the ring."

Olivia bent her head forward, looking at Lily under a raised arm. "And what do you make of that, Lily?"

Lily took her eyes off the needle and thread and smiled. "He's going to propose to you tonight, don't you think?"

Olivia laughed. "Oh, Lily. He may be proposing tonight, but it won't be to me."

Lily gaped. "Of course it'll be to you. You haven't seen how he looks at you."

"Like a cat looks at a bowl of milk. He wants to taste me, not marry me."

"I don't believe it," Lily said, returning her attention to

the tear on the blouse. "Everyone knows your reputation. You aren't like that."

"It doesn't stop men from trying, Lily dear. I'm an actress which is not the sort of woman men like the Earl propose to."

Lily dropped the needle which hung by its thread from Olivia's underarm. "The Duke of Dunstable's son proposed to Maria."

"The Duke of Dunstable's son proposed that they go to Paris. He won't marry her."

Lily shook her head. "You don't know. They might get married–and the Earl might propose to you."

"And the Queen might dance in bloomers at Piccadilly Circus."

Lily frowned. "Then why have dinner with him?"

Olivia shrugged. "I suppose I hold out the hope that some day one of the men who ask me out will be honorable and old fashioned." She sighed. "Men like that don't chase after actresses."

Lily remained unconvinced. "I like the Earl. You might be wrong."

They were interrupted by a knock on the door.

"Come in," Olivia called out. Lily took the scissors from the dressing table and cut the thread beneath her underarm.

A man of about five and twenty entered the dressing room. He wore a top hat, which he removed to reveal dark wavy hair. His overcoat was of good material, but not new and his bright green waistcoat and extremely tight trousers marked him as a bit of a dandy. He had an open, cynical face and pouty lips.

"I'm sorry. I thought this was Miss Snow's dressing room."

"Come in, Mr. Wilde," Olivia said. "I've transformed from Hermia to Titania in less than twenty-four hours."

Mr. Wilde lifted an eyebrow. "Remarkable. I didn't know

you."

"A perfect compliment to an actress." Olivia turned to the mirror as Lily began work on her hair, weaving, piling, and pinning it in an elaborate coiffure high on her head. "I'm glad you are here. Now my day is perfect."

"What a lovely greeting, Miss Snow. I especially like meeting a woman who is happy to see me. It is so much better than meeting a woman who is apathetic about my presence, which is what I mostly find."

"I don't believe that for a moment, Mr. Wilde. You are deceived by the current fashion of pretending to dislike that which one most likes. The modern woman does not want to give away her cards."

"And are you not a modern woman, Miss Snow?"

"Heavens, no! I am terribly old fashioned. You tease me for it constantly."

"That must be some other gentleman. I do not believe in teasing. To tease is to show an interest in others and, as you know, my only interest is myself."

"I hope that's not true, as I have heard an interesting tale that is not about you."

"Just wait and hold still," said Lily, finishing with the high tower and pulling out several locks to fall and curl at Olivia's temples. She experimented with the placement of a heavy jewel-encrusted crown, the weight making it hard to secure on the delicate coiffure. The fake rubies on the crown pulled the red from the actress's hair, a nice contrast to the grey/silver of the rest of the costume.

Mr. Wilde sauntered to the small table in the corner of the room, leaned against it, and lit a cigarette. In the reflection of the mirror, Olivia could see the wisp of his smoke curling up toward the ceiling, but Lily's position behind her hid her view of the man. In a moment Mr. Wilde strolled back to the door. The two studied one another in the mirror.

"Before you tell me your tale, Miss Snow," began Mr. Wilde, "I must tell you why I have come. My mother is sharing my box. She admires you immensely and has asked me to invite you to her Salon this evening. It will be the usual types, talking about the usual things, which is why you must come. A virtuous, old-fashioned woman like yourself would add some scandal to the evening."

Olivia smiled. "Sounds wonderful." She looked at Lily who studied the crown in the mirror, nodded and backed away. Olivia turned on her stool to face Mr. Wilde. "I'm dining with the Earl of Montmarch after the show."

"Bring him along," said Mr. Wilde.

Eyes sparkling, Olivia glanced at her young friend. "Lily saw the Earl of Montmarch in Butterfield's buying a ring, and she overheard the reason for its purchase. Can you guess?"

Mr. Wilde raised his eyebrows but did not answer. "Can you not guess, Mr. Wilde?"

Again, Mr. Wilde remained silent, slightly shaking his head.

"Lily heard him say that he is proposing marriage tonight, and she believes he will propose to me. I, on the other hand, believe he will propose to someone else. What is your opinion?"

"If that man is proposing to anyone, he is making a grave mistake," answered Mr. Wilde. "Marriage is like the Matterhorn–beautiful from a distance but cold and deadly up close."

Olivia laughed. "I should have expected such a response from you. Well, in the event that the Earl asks for my hand, I don't imagine I will appear at your salon. However, if all goes as I imagine, I will be saying good-bye to the Earl early in the evening and would be happy to attend your mother."

Mr. Wilde bowed. "And now I shall leave you to your fairy kingdom."

As the door shut behind him, Olivia turned to Lily. "Tell Charley the same as usual. He can admit the Earl to the greenroom for me after the performance, but no one else."

Lily nodded.

Olivia stood and breathed deeply several times, gathering her character. Titania, confident queen of the fairy world, out to get revenge on her errant king.

❧ *Third Chapter* ❧

The marvelous thing about the dining room at Brown's was that you felt like you were experiencing the opulence of the royal family while being waited upon by your favorite uncle's steward. It was luxurious and comfortable, glamorous, and cozy. As a hotel, Brown's catered to London's wealthiest visitors: maharajahs from India, railway barons from America, Russian princesses, and South American diamond-mine owners. On Wednesday and Saturday evenings, the dining room at Brown's filled with the members of the ton, just out of the opera or the theater, who did not want to retire for the evening, and yet were not willing to submit themselves to a male-only club or a matron-overseen dinner party.

The food was extraordinary and one of two reasons Olivia continued to have dinner with Charles Poole, Earl of Montmarch. Olivia loved to eat, and Brown's provided the best food in London—quite possibly the best food in all the world.

So, it was with great disappointment that Olivia stepped out of the carriage in front of, not Brown's on Albemarle Street, but the Golden Bell, a little inn she'd never before seen.

"This isn't Brown's," she stated stupidly.

"You'll like this," he said, not meeting her eyes and guiding her inside.

The door opened to the taproom and the smell of stale

beer and old socks. Three older men, smithies or ostlers or some such occupation stared as they walked in. A group of younger men, less worn-weary but wearing the clothes and attitude of men who performed physical labor for a living, played darts in the corner.

Olivia wrinkled her eyebrows. "Why –"

The Earl pointed at a door on the far side of the taproom. As they crossed, the dart players halted their game to stare. The silence hung heavy in the room, interrupted only by the sound of Olivia's heels clacking on the well-worn wooden floor boards.

Charles opened the door to reveal a private dining room, as one found in many country inns: a respectable room where respectable women could eat while traveling with their respectable families.

The room was organized in such a way as to divide it into two. At the far side, a long divan and two plush arm chairs circled a tea table. The tea service was arranged neatly on shelves along a sidewall. Above the shelving was the room's only window, high on the wall, making it unlikely that any passing pedestrians could gawk at the room's occupants. The chairs looked comfortable, if well-used, but the divan, with its earthy brown and deep red upholstery, looked new. A faded Persian rug lay upon the floor and separated that part of the room from the dining area, where Olivia and the Earl stood.

The oblong table could have sat eight but was set for two. Sturdy bone china, dull silver, and a clear glass vase of yellow and red roses were laid upon a freshly laundered yellow linen cloth. A footman wearing the Earl's colors poured wine.

"Thank you, Ford," Charles said to the servant. "See if the cook has begun dinner."

"Yes, sir," said the young man, bowing out of the room.

"Brown's wouldn't give me a private room. Tonight is to

be special" said the Earl. "Please sit."

He pulled out a chair for Olivia and she sat. In the carriage ride, the Earl had told her how the carriage horses had been recently re-shod. How long their previous shoes had lasted, how well this new shoeing had been done by his man, an ostler he had brought with him from the country, the type of metal used, how long it had been pounded by the blacksmith, and so on. This was the second reason she dined with the Earl. He was the most boring person she had ever met. As a character-study, he was fascinating. She memorized his stories and studied the way he told them.

As she nibbled her beef and potatoes, he spoke of a haircut he had gotten that day, a topic that lasted through the first course. Olivia listened and watched, fully absorbed. She had been planning to be upfront about her knowledge of his purchase of a ring and his imminent engagement. Certain that the proposal was not to her, she had planned to stop seeing him. But she had envisioned one more meal at Brown's. They weren't at Brown's, and Olivia was having trouble imagining what the evening would reveal, so she kept quiet, and listened as he told her of a new type of snuff his brother was using, its ingredients and how that compared to the Earl's brand, and so on.

Her mind wandered. Why were they there? He obviously had something planned, and she was curious. Olivia smiled to herself. Curiosity may have killed the cat, but it was also responsible for cinnamon buns and an understanding of the orbits of the planets. One learns nothing by eschewing curiosity.

Despite anticipating the food at Brown's, Olivia was not disappointed in the food at the Golden Bell. When food was exceptional, she enjoyed it. That did not mean that she could not enjoy an overcooked beef roast, undercooked potatoes, and an excellent loaf of sourdough. Those who have gone through times without food learned to enjoy what is in front of them. Olivia was that sort of eater. The fact that things were not as good as they could have been did not affect her pleasure in the here and now. She took small bites and chewed for a long time, marveling in the textures and the flavors.

The slow and deliberate consumption of food was her way of not over-eating. As an actress, her beauty was important. She could not allow herself to become elephantine– which could easily be done. She did not have the figure of Lillie Langtry, but she was healthy and hoped there was a longer-lasting beauty in that. The wine was exceptional because Charles had brought several bottles from his own cellar. Why he thought the two of them would drink several bottles became evident as the meal progressed. He was trying to get Olivia to over-consume. The private room, the divan, the wine. So, thought Olivia, it was to be a seduction scene. How unlike the Earl.

Olivia sipped her wine slowly, pretending to re-fill her glass and encouraging Charles to finish his and drink more. Encouraging over-consumption could go both ways.

The footman removed their plates of Apple Jonathan, which she had enjoyed immensely, and left them alone in the private room.

"Let's us move to be more comfortable," stammered the Earl, standing and pointing awkwardly at the divan. "That's not a good idea," Olivia said, remaining in her seat at the table.

The Earl pulled out her chair, forcing her to stand.

Olivia frowned and turned to him. "A friend of mine was at Butterfield's today and saw you purchase an engagement ring."

A strong blush shadowed the Earl's cheeks.

"A toast?" Olivia poured him a new glass of wine, and

picked up the same glass she'd been drinking all evening. They clinked glasses and the Earl emptied his. Olivia wet her lips and returned her wine to the table. "In light of your recent engagement, I think it best that I leave now. We shouldn't have had dinner at all. I've always known you to be an honest man, Charles."

"But there's more wine!" said Charles, nearly spilling the wine as he poured himself another glass.

He drank the full glass, then put it on the table. Olivia watched as he wobbled. This was new. He didn't usually over-indulge. He must be nervous about the seduction. Had someone put him up to it?

"Did someone put you up to this?" Olivia asked.

The Earl took a deep breath. "Let's sit. Please?"

The politeness of the request won her over. Olivia followed him to the divan. He sat on one side and she sat on the complete opposite, twisting to look at him straight on. "Explain." She put on the face a mother wears when speaking to a naughty child.

"There is a wager," Charles began, "Do you know Jeremy Dottingham? Rodney Willes-Smith? Dexter Baxter-Point? Peter Darlington?"

"Some of the names are familiar," answered Olivia. Mr. Dottingham and Viscount Willes-Smith had each spent time in the greenroom trying to get her to dine with them. She hadn't liked the looks of either and had never accepted, though they had been persistent.

"They go to my club. We made a wager–a wager about you." Charles played with a loose thread on his jacket, not looking at her.

"A wager about me?"

"You are a virgin, yes?"

"I don't believe that is anyone's business," answered Olivia. She had worked hard to establish her virginal reputation,

27

but to talk about it! Even a total boor should know how inappropriate that was.

The Earl nodded energetically. "Quite right. Not our business–except our wager is about it. You don't go out with gentlemen, in the way that actresses do. It makes men want you. Everyone wants you."

He opened his hands to indicate that it was not his fault.

"And that's the wager?" asked Olivia, angry and aghast. "Someone wins money by stealing my virtue?"

Charles chuckled. "It isn't about the money."

"You can take me home now, because I refuse to help you win this wager." Olivia made to stand, but in a motion startlingly fast for the slow-moving Earl, he gripped her arm and pulled her back to the divan.

"Sorry," he whispered. "Refusal is not permitted."

"I don't have a choice in this?" Olivia asked.

"No. You don't have a choice," said Charles. "It must happen tonight. You see, I've never had a woman before and I'm going to be married soon. Ford is guarding the door. No one in, no one out, until I say so."

Olivia was irritated but did not let it show. She'd studied this man, understood him, and felt there was nothing to fear in this appalling situation.

"I see," said Olivia, nodding. "That makes sense. Is it to happen here, on this divan?"

Charles nodded. "They assured me a bed wouldn't be necessary. Would a bed be better?"

Olivia shrugged. "How should I know?"

"Yes! Exactly!" The Earl giggled, drunk.

Olivia smoothed the fibers of the divan upholstery, working up an escape plan.

The silence lasted a few minutes, until the Earl spoke. "You go first."

"What?"

The Earl blushed and stammered. "I don't know what to do. You should do something first. You must know something."

Olivia nodded. "Of course. Let's get you more comfortable." She tried to help him remove his jacket, which was awkward and caused them both to giggle. Olivia looked around. "Do you have the vinegar mixture? We should put that where I can easily reach it."

"Vinegar mixture?"

"Your friends must have told you about it."

He shook his head.

"So I don't get pregnant? You don't want a bastard by an actress, do you? I use it as soon as we are finished: vinegar, honey, bergamot oil, maybe something more?"

"Oh," said the Earl, looking abashed. "I didn't know. " After a moment, he looked at her askance. "How do you know this?"

"Just because I never have, doesn't mean I don't know what others do."

The Earl nodded in a jittery way, acknowledging that what she said must be the truth.

She patted him on the shoulder. "This is an inn. I'm sure they have some of the mixture at the bar or in a drawer or closet somewhere. Guests must request it."

Relief flooded the Earl's face. "Good. Yes. I'll ask for some."

"They might pretend not to know anything about it," cautioned Olivia. "Lawfully married couples do not use such a thing. The innkeeper might want to appear respectable."

The Earl hesitated on his way to the door.

"You'll need to keep asking," continued Olivia. "Don't believe feigned ignorance. Don't take no for an answer. Offer to pay well."

The Earl nodded and shut the door behind him.

Olivia was on her feet in a flash, pushing the plush chair against the shelves below the window. Climbing on the cushion, she was easily able to push up the window. Climbing onto the sill was more difficult. She stepped on the back of the chair, but the top of the shelving had decorative swirls and peaks that poked at her belly. Fortunately, her corset kept her skin protected.

Hands on the sill, she poked her head through the window, seeing an empty alley and cobblestones five feet below. The window was too small to turn in, and going feet first would be impossible. How to go head first without cracking her skull?

Pillows. Olivia grabbed two square back pillows and the two small round arm pillows from the divan and pushed them through the small window, careful to drop them directly below. Glancing at the parlour door, she saw the knob twist. She hoisted herself up, belly on the sill, and pushed through the window. Head down, arms flailing, she teetered, but did not fall. She maneuvered her weight outside the window, but some part of her clothing was caught. She pushed hard against the outside wall, pulling her legs through. She heard a rip, felt a tear, and tumbled feet over head, landing in a soft heap on the cushions.

"Olivia?" came from inside.

By the time she was on her feet, the Earl stood looking out the window, his eyes wide and confused.

"It isn't going to happen, Charles," she said, wiping dirt from her torn skirt, then looking at him with what dignity she could muster. "I do have a choice, and I refuse to participate in your wager."

"Stay right there," said the Earl, backing away. The rest of his speech was inaudible as he dashed away.

Olivia ran. At the end of the alley, she saw the Earl's carriage and driver along the street to her right. She ran left and turned left at the first intersection, hiding around the corner, and catching her breath. She had no idea where she was. There were no hackneys, no carriages at all, not even a policeman to ask directions. She walked to the next cross street and turned right.

She searched for a hackney or a policeman, but no help was to be found. She looked over her shoulder, but he didn't seem to be following. She heard a carriage up ahead, coming from a cross street. She hurried toward the sound, but when it appeared in the intersection, she recognized the Earl's colors. She flattened herself against a wall. The carriage continued straight.

Olivia breathed a sigh of relief. How was she to get home? Where was she?

From across the street, she heard a burst of laughter, then the quiet hum of voices. She looked up at the window of a townhouse . Shadows of people played across the curtains. Muffled laughter and conversation flowed from the open upstairs windows. She knew where she was. Olivia smiled.

The butler answered the bell almost immediately.

"I'm Olivia Snow. I was invited by Mr. Wilde."

The Wilde's parlour was just large enough to be called a drawing room. Mr. Wilde stood next to Philip Lamb, introducing guests and pointing out others scattered around the room. In one corner, a cigarette haze hung over the table of baccarat where, according to Mr. Wilde, "Giles Cheevely will lose his shirt and horses and probably his wife, if he can get anyone to take her."

Baron Von Dorfen, a stout balding man, sat beside Oscar Wilde's mother on the not-very-new divan. He spoke in a heavy German accent about Irish literature. On Lady Wilde's other side sat Mrs. Markby, the wealthy widow who penned erudite novels under the name Mrs. M.

In chairs at the end of the room sat Genevieve with her friends, Miss Prism and Miss Brooke. Philip tried to remember which girl was which. The one in the red gown was intelligent and well read and the one in grey had a terrible lisp and almost never spoke. He could never recall which name belonged to which girl. Mr. Wilde laughed in a strangely feminine manner at his own comment about one of the young ladies. Philip hadn't heard and smiled vaguely.

Philip turned his attention to a painting hanging on the wall behind the divan. It was of a giraffe. The use of colors was unusual, child-like, and yet the lines and precision were skillful.

"Tell me about that painting." Philip interrupted Mr.

Wilde who was gossiping about people Philip did not know. Mr. Wilde chuckled. "That was painted by a friend of mine, Frank Miles. He mostly paints portraits, but I asked for a giraffe and he was obliging. Do you like it?"

"No," Philip replied. His tastes ran more to the Italian renaissance. He continued to study the painting, thinking that there was something extraordinary about the complete lack of tradition or schooling. Philip looked down and discovered he was nearly on top of the people sitting on the divan. Before he could apologize, Mrs. Wilde spoke.

"Mr. Lamb, have you met Mrs. Markby and Baron Von Dorfen?"

Philip nodded politely at both. Mrs. Markby replied, "We were introduced when he first arrived. Were you at the theater this evening, Mr. Lamb?"

Philip shook his head. "My sister and mother were there."

"You missed a spectacular performance. Miss Olivia Snow was Titania. I first saw her as Kate in *She Stoops to Conquer*, perfectly performed. Miss Snow's a beauty with brains."

"A most talented and beautiful actress she is," said Baron Von Dorfen.

Lady Wilde said, "You invited her this evening, didn't you Oscar?"

"Indeed," responded Mr. Wilde. "I expect her later. She's having dinner with Montmarch. Her maid believes a marriage proposal to be imminent."

Mrs. Markby wrinkled her brow. "Montmarch has been courting the Delorme girl all Season. I hardly think he'll propose to Miss Snow."

Oscar corrected her. "His mother has been courting Miss Delorme. He'll end up married to her, but Montmarch will try to 'get' Miss Snow first–but not for marriage, if you know what I mean. I believe he'll plan his seduction this evening."

33

Lady Wilde grimaced. "That poor girl. Did you warn her?"

"Heavens, no," answered Oscar. "Bad news should always be delivered by the culprit. A friend who delivers bad news provides no good service. In one case, the offended party is likely to blame the messenger; in the other, the messenger is likely to laugh at the offended party. I like Miss Snow too much to protect her and too little to mock her."

"Oscar, sometimes you make no sense at all," answered Lady Wilde.

"As Mrs. M remarked, Miss Snow's got brains," said Oscar. "She's protected her virtue this long. I don't think a duffer like the Earl will be the one to break through the battlements."

The Baron fiddled with his pocket watch. "May I?" Philip asked, reaching for the watch.

The German glanced up. "What? Oh, ya. The time is not telling."

"I'm rather good at this type of thing," Philip said and took the watch. He found a seat near the card players and took a small screwdriver from his pocket.

The door opened and the butler announced, "Mr. Mervay, Mr. Hopper, and Mr. Dumby."

Oscar greeted the three, who stumbled into the room in a laughing bunch, followed by a strong reek of scotch and Cuban cigars. The newly arrived guests were loud.

Mr. Wilde exclaimed, "Good God, Dumby, what happened to your buttonhole?"

The gentleman in question, his face flushed with drink, looked down at his jacket to where a flower should have been. All sign of petals had vanished, leaving but a green stump and stem.

"Oh, my buttonhole," he said, befuddled. He looked up at his friends as if they might know what had happened.

Hopper put his arm around Dumby, saying, "A gypsy told

you that rose petals in scotch increase a man's masculinity, so you crushed your buttonhole, coated it in scotch and ate it."

Dumby shook his head fiercely, obviously trying to reactivate his cerebellum.

"I cannot speak to whether his manliness was increased," explained Mervay, "however, his ardor most certainly was. He stood and vowed to propose to Miss Delorme on the instant."

"At this hour?" asked Mr. Wilde.

Hopper shook his head. "Earlier, but still rather late. He got as far as the footman, whom he tried to bribe, only to learn that he was too late. Miss Delorme has accepted the offer of the Earl of Montmarch."

Oscar Wilde winced. "And then?"

"We returned to the club where he got himself into this state."

"Why on earth did you bring him here?" asked Mr. Wilde.

Hopper shrugged with nonchalance. "I wanted to come and Mervay didn't think we should leave Dumby alone."

Oscar pursed his lips. "Perhaps we can turn Miss Prism on him. It's doubtful she'll notice his lack of wit, but she'll spot his increased manhood, I dare say. Still, she is as yet unmarried. A young maid would not properly appreciate him, while a seasoned matron would be in a better position to recognize and compare."

Genevieve Lamb approached the group. "You are too naughty, Mr. Wilde. What would your mother say if she heard you?"

"Mama?" said Mr. Wilde. "She would pretend not to understand."

"She is a wise woman. I think that is the best course of action. I, too, will pretend ignorance," said Genevieve, striking a pose and looking off into the distance.

"That is the only way to get a reputation for being wise," responded Mr. Wilde.

Hopper took Genevieve's hand and kissed it. "I understand congratulations are in order."

Mervay frowned and took Dumby to an open chair across the room.

"What's this?" asked Mr. Wilde, extinguishing the remains of his cigarette in a gold-rimmed glass ashtray.

The young lady's eyes sparkled as Hopper explained. "Miss Lamb has accepted the hand of Basil Daubeny."

Mr. Wilde's mouth dropped. "Marriage? For you? I thought we agreed that marriage was for those with weak hearts and no imagination."

Genevieve lifted her chin defiantly. "I never said any such thing. Mr. Daubeny is handsome, charming, intelligent, and well-dressed. He will make a most excellent husband. I'm quite in love with him."

Across the room, Philip grunted unhappily, then noticed a small wire that jammed against the winding mechanism of the watch.

"You can't have known him for more than a week. He's barely just returned to London," Mr. Wilde replied.

Genevieve's response was drowned out by the butler announcing a guest.

"Miss Olivia Snow," he said.

Philip looked to the door and immediately regretted having not gone to the theater. Miss Snow was far and away the most beautiful woman he'd ever seen.

Olivia stumbled in her eagerness to enter the room.

"Good heavens! What's happened?"

A young lady caught Olivia and helped her to the divan. The people who were sitting there leapt up to vacate it. Relieved to be inside and safe, Olivia slumped onto the cushions, ignorant of her dangling coiffure and forgetting her ripped dress.

"I couldn't – find a hackney," she gasped, out of breath. "He was – ch-chasing me." Olivia paused for breath and Lady Wilde patted her shoulder.

"You're safe now, dear. Who was chasing you? Have you been robbed?"

"No, it was–" Olivia stopped. Wide eyes gawked at her. Mouths whispered into ears. She glanced at her torn skirt and felt her disheveled hair. In her hurry to get away from the Earl, she hadn't considered the impression she would make entering the Wildes' salon. This would not do at all. In the time it takes a note from a plucked violin to reach its player's ear, Olivia transformed herself. She hid her discomfort. She erased her weariness. She was instantly confident and serene.

"I apologize for interrupting. I really must be going."

Olivia attempted to stand, but Lady Wilde took her elbow and pulled her down.

"Don't be ridiculous," Lady Wilde said. "Harris, bring

Miss Snow a glass of champagne–or would you prefer tea, my dear?"

Olivia smiled and pulled out of the older woman's grasp. Standing, she said, "Really, I should not have intruded, I –"

Lady Wilde stood and, taking the actress by surprise, placed her hand over her mouth, stopping her speech. "Tea, Harris. Bring it to the Green Room. Miss Snow, come with me."

Though hardly more than a large closet, the Green Room lived up to its name. Apart from the two women, there was nothing in the Green Room which was not green. Wallpaper with a pale green background and dark green leafy vines covered the walls. The two plush chairs were upholstered in different patterns, but both featured green as the predominant color. The worn carpet was shades of green with green and brown vines decorating the edges. The single window was draped in a dark green curtain, and the desk beneath it held several potted plants.

Olivia laughed weakly. "This is your greenroom?" The term greenroom is used for a large room in a theater house which serves many functions, including being where the actors meet their admirers.

Lady Wilde chuckled while guiding the young woman to a chair. "Appropriate, isn't it?"

Olivia sat and studied the tear down the front of her skirt. A layer of petticoat had also been torn.

"I suppose I must do something about this," she said, fingering the fraying fabric.

"How can I help?" asked Lady Wilde.

"It's beyond the help of needle and thread," Olivia said, standing and examining the way the material fell from her waist. "If I had a bit of material to form an overskirt, that would hide the tear."

"And a shawl to cover you better," added Lady Wilde.

Her gown was an off-the-shoulder cut, with lace trim around the top. The lace must have snagged on the windowsill. Now several strips, one quite long, dangled from her chest. Olivia sighed as she realized the extent to which her dress had been ruined.

"Yes. A shawl would help."

Olivia ripped off the dangling bits of lace and tried to clean up the loose threading.

"I'll see to what you need," said Lady Wilde.

At that moment Harris entered with the tea cart.

Lady Wilde left in search of materials to repair the dress, and Olivia sat back and sipped a cup of strong black tea. It was quite reviving. By addressing the practicalities of her appearance, Lady Wilde had helped the actress recover her nerves.

She soon returned with a lovely grey and blue scarf and an old-fashioned brown overskirt.

"The colors and style don't match, but it should cover the tear."

"Lady Wilde, you are too kind."

Olivia tied the overskirt at her waist, the material falling in flounces atop the torn skirt, and she threw the scarf over her shoulders so that it covered much of her bodice. She would win no accolades from Beau Brummel, but she was presentable.

"You can return everything at your convenience," said Lady Wilde, plucking a loose thread from the scarf. "Shall I call you a hackney? I daresay our guests would love for you to join them, but I think everyone would understand if you didn't want to."

Olivia considered. She needed to manage this evening better than she had up to this point. These guests needed to see her in a better role than the one she had entered in. "I would love to join your guests," she said. "Did I see Mrs. M?

I've always wanted to meet her."

Lady Wilde smiled. "You young people have such re-markable recovery skills. Yes, let's see what everyone is doing. I imagine they've been talking about you this entire time."

✍ Sixth Chapter ✍

When the door clicked shut behind Lady Wilde and Miss
Snow, conversation exploded like a champagne cork.

"What has happened?" the Baron asked Mrs. M.

"I've no idea," responded the novelist, "but it was perfectly performed."

"What could have happened?" asked Miss Prism.

"She looked a mess," said Miss Brooke.

"Whom do you suppose she was running from?" Genevieve's question was voiced in a pause from the general tumult
and so was heard by all.

Mr. Wilde inhaled dramatically on his newly-lit cigarette,
paused, then said, "Most certainly the Earl of Montmarch."

"Montmarch?" said three voices in unison.

The man with the ruined buttonhole stood and shouted
"Stuff him!" He wobbled, then fell to his chair unconscious.

"Why on earth would the Earl of Montmarch be chasing
Olivia Snow?" asked Genevieve.

Except for the drunk man, asleep in his chair at the corner of the room, all the guests had gathered around the
Persian rug, sitting on the divan or the chairs or standing in
a circle. Mr. Wilde delayed in answering the questions as he
preened and feigned a theatrical countenance. He played
with his silver cigarette case, and just as his mouth opened
to answer the question, Mrs. M spoke.

"He was trying to seduce her."

All eyes turned to the novelist. "It was his last chance. Everyone knows of Miss Snow's virtue. Once she learned he was engaged to Miss Delorme, she would break off their relationship. But this evening Miss Snow thought Montmarch would propose to her. And, well, maybe he suspected that she might be a little more open to his desire." Miss Prism giggled and then covered her mouth.

"Clever chap," said a man with a bushy mustache, "although it would seem all did not go as planned."

Philip paced along the side of the room. The gossip annoyed him, but he wanted to learn more about Miss Olivia Snow.

A woman offered, "Montmarch is a monster."

Mr. Wilde responded, "He's not so bad. Has a fine cook, and that's really what matters."

"Miss Snow was lovely, wasn't she? Damsel in distress and all."

"She does know how to play a part."

"You don't think the Earl was chasing her?"

"Oh, does it matter?" sighed Mrs. M. "We've all been entertained, and we'll all have something to talk about tomorrow."

"You don't think it was real?"

Mrs. M laughed. "She is an actress. You saw what she wanted you to see."

"It was my impression that she did not intend for us to see her at all," responded Genevieve, waving her hand. "When she noticed we were here, she gathered herself and tried to leave. Her distress was real."

"Are you certain?" said Mrs. M and her eyes twinkled.

Genevieve wrinkled her nose. "I think . . . Perhaps . . . Well, I don't know."

"I am certain she was not acting," said Philip, moving into the circle.

The Baron chuckled. In his imperfect English, he said, "You haven't Miss Snow on stage seen, have you? She convinces. She's able any part to play. She could your sister imitate, and you confused become."

"Pardon?" said Philip.

"Do you have the same idea as me, Hopper?" asked Oscar Wilde, his eyes shining. "Perhaps a wager is in order."

"Miss Snow could pretend to be your sister," said Hopper walking toward Philip. "Somewhere she won't be recognized. In the country."

Heads nodded. Mrs. M rubbed her hands together.

"You would accompany her, of course, Mr. Lamb," said Oscar, "to be the one to judge whether or not she was able to fool the company."

Hopper nodded. "She'll fool them easily."

Mrs. M shook her head. "I disagree. On stage she's told what to say and given what to dress. Being a lady isn't as easy as one might think."

"Have you any invitations to the country, Mr. Lamb?" asked Mr. Hopper. "It would be nice to get this arranged quickly."

Genevieve jumped from her chair, hands flapping excitedly. "Remember, Philip? You got that invitation from Admiral somebody? He was on the ship with you when you traveled over? I've never met anyone in his family or crowd. He's invited you to his country place when the Season ends. It's perfect!"

Men crowded around the card table and money changed hands.

Philip kept his gaze on the pocket watch. The winding mechanism now turned smoothly. He carefully put the timepiece back together and considered the proposal. He found the idea of a wager revolting: the lying, the deceit, the manipulation of a poor actress. On the other hand, if he refused to participate, they might find some other man to pretend to be her brother. Someone not as honorable as he.

The door opened and Lady Wilde entered with Miss Snow. She was lovelier than Philip remembered.

Olivia felt everyone's eyes turn to her as she stepped into the room, and she loved it. She was beautiful, and in control of her audience. Lady Wilde introduced her to a German Baron, who kissed her hand, and to Mrs. M, who was as wry and witty as she had hoped. Olivia moved about the room, meeting people, chatting with old friends. She accepted a glass of champagne from Mr. Wilde who informed her of their wager. Olivia smiled but sighed inwardly. As if she weren't already in enough of a mess because of a wager.

As she worked the room, Olivia noticed a young man sitting by himself who looked at her only when he thought she wouldn't notice, refusing to make eye contact. She spoke with a Miss Lamb, some sort of minor European royalty, who delighted in the idea that Olivia would pretend to be her for the wager. The conversation moved to mutual acquaintances and then Olivia asked Genevieve if she knew the shy young man in the corner.

"Oh, that's my brother Philip. He's just back from Monaco and probably pining for the warm ocean air. Let me introduce you."

The two stood before Philip, who feigned interest in a gold watch.

"Philip, stand up. I want to introduce you to Miss Snow."

Genevieve made the introductions and explained that Olivia was the actress who would go to the Admiral's with him, but that he would not be allowed to wager on her performance. Olivia did not contradict her, though she had not agreed to the charade. This crowd worked fast. If she was going to disappoint them, she'd have to do it soon.

"I had no intention of wagering," he responded. "I'm not a wagering sort of man. It seems here in London everything is a wager."

Olivia raised an eyebrow and studied Philip. He had dark hair, and his warm brown eyes met hers directly. She had anticipated needing to draw him out of his shyness and was surprised by his sudden confidence.

Genevieve grabbed the actress's arm and nodded enthusiastically. "Last week I was at Lady Hampton's for tea, and she was expecting Mrs. Dalrymple. We bet a guinea on what color dress she would be wearing."

Mr. Wilde broke into the circle. "Yellow."

Genevieve's mouth dropped open. "How did you know?"

"Mrs. Dalrymple only wears yellow, my dear. You were had by Lady Hampton."

Genevieve pouted in a most charming way, Olivia noted. Playing the part of this effervescent girl might be fun. After all, she'd never been invited to leave London and spend the weekend at some rich man's estate before. Olivia tipped her head. Well, she had, but the expectations in that situation had been very different.

"If you are willing to play my sister, I'm willing to help you," said Philip, whose gaze had not left Olivia's face. "I've no doubt the charade will go your way."

"Well, I don't know–" Olivia began.

Mrs. M leaned toward Olivia and whispered in her ear. "I'll pay your fee. One doesn't hire an actress for free."

The money did make a difference. With the season at the Regent ending, she'd soon be scrambling for work. Olivia felt confident she could make a go of the charade. She didn't like leaving Etta with Mrs. Rambling for several days, but a paying job was a paying job. . . .

Genevieve said to Philip, "I've assured Miss Snow that you are a most excellent brother."

Oscar Wilde leaned toward Philip and said conspiratorially, "Every man in this room is jealous of you. A weekend with the lovely Miss Snow."

Slowly moving his eyes away from the actress, Philip turned to Oscar and tipped his head slightly. "That is to say, a weekend with my sister Miss Genevieve Lamb, as played by the lovely Miss Snow. I must act the part of the dutiful older brother."

Genevieve rolled her eyes. "It's a part he plays too well."

Olivia considered Philip. It was odd to think of him as an older brother. She was twenty-five and he looked at least two, possibly four, years her junior.

"And what sort of sister must I be?" Olivia asked.

Genevieve laughed. "If you are to play me, then you must behave badly. I never behave as Philip would have me. He is dreadfully old-fashioned."

"Then they are well matched," said Oscar. "Miss Snow is the youngest old lady I ever met." Turning to Philip he continued, "At the close of the weekend, you can admit who she is. I'm sure everyone at the Admiral's will find it quite the thing."

When Olivia took her leave of Lady. Wilde and her son Oscar, she found Mr. Lamb and his sister at her elbow, offering to take her home. She accepted. They made idle chatter on the drive, and exhaustion soon lay upon the actress like a warm, damp towel. It had been a long day.

The carriage stopped in front of Rambling's Apothecary on Bloomsbury Way. Olivia stepped out, turning to thank the brother and sister. Mr. Lamb was on her heels.

"Let me see you safely to your door," he said.

Olivia stood by the carriage and considered his offer. The Earl knew where she lived. She didn't expect him to continue his pursuit, but one never knew. It might be nice to have someone walk her through the dark alley to her door.

"Thank you," Olivia answered Philip and bent to the carriage door to say good-night to Miss Lamb. The young lady's return smile was warm and genuine.

As they stepped away from the carriage, Olivia said, "I like your sister."

"She is a good girl, though impulsive," he replied. "I worry about her."

"Like a good brother should." Olivia hooked her arm through his. "The entrance is in the rear."

She wondered again about his age. He was an older brother, but neither of them could be much older than twenty. Mr. Lamb escorted her through the dim alley which opened onto the small courtyard behind the building. The chickens kept by Mrs. Hadley were in their coop and quiet. Moonlight illuminated a row of nappies hanging on a line. Olivia pulled Philip toward her, saving him from walking into a crate of empty milk bottles. He smelled of brandy and something else, some exotic spice.

"You smell nice," Olivia flirted, "like brandy and something else, some exotic spice."

Philip may have blushed, but in the moonlight Olivia could not tell.

When they reached the door, Olivia took out her key. As often happened, it would not immediately go in. As she fumbled with the lock, Mr. Lamb spoke.

"I suppose I should have said something about how nice you smell. I'm not very adept at these sorts of things." Although his words were self-deprecating, they were spoken without the slightest hint of embarrassment.

Olivia laughed, softly, so as not to disturb her sleeping neighbors. "You are young. In years to come, I'm certain you will learn the words to praise the scent of a lady."

"You could teach me the words now."

The courtyard was without gas lighting, but the moon shone, giving Mr. Lamb a silver sheen and outlining his youthful features. His expression showed no flirtation, reflecting instead the gaze of a student to a teacher. Olivia stopped trying to open the door and leaned against it.

"It's true I was flirting, but what I said was true. You do smell like brandy and spice. If you wanted to flirt back, merely tell me what I smell like."

He shook his head. "I don't smell anything."

"Come closer."

She drew him close, bringing his face to her hair and then down so his ear was resting against her shoulder. She breathed him in again; he was a very pleasant-smelling young man.

He straightened and took a step back.

"Lilac," he said. "Champagne."

"Excellent. If I'd smelled like manure, you'd have had to make something up."

"Who's to say that I didn't?"

"Ha!" Olivia laughed, pushing playfully against his chest. "And you let me think you didn't know how to flirt!"

She shook her head and returned to the door lock. The key slid in and turned easily. Pulling the door open, Olivia turned back to Philip, but he had already stepped several paces away. He bowed formally and bid farewell. Olivia watched as he carefully made his way through the courtyard to the alley, grateful he hadn't tried to kiss her. The rear entrance was a storage area for the apothecary. Olivia and Etta lived in the garret apartment. Lily's family were on the first and second floors.

"Did he propose?" asked a voice from the inner steps.

Olivia jumped and would have screamed if she hadn't recognized Lily as the speaker. The actress stood in total darkness but could picture her young friend seated on the steps in front of her.

"Good Lord, Lily. You gave me a startle." Olivia held her hand to her throat where she could feel the pounding of her pulse.

"Sorry," she said, without sympathy. "I waited at Brown's to come home with you, but I never saw you. Did the Earl propose? Is that why you're late?"

Olivia shook her head, which was no answer in the dark. She reached for Lily, and feeling her arm, slid beside her on the step.

"He didn't take me to Brown's," Olivia explained, "and he didn't propose. He took me to some out-of-the-way inn where he tried unsuccessfully to seduce me."

"Bastard," Lily muttered under her breath. "Were you with him all this time?"

"I went to Oscar Wilde's salon. How's Etta?"

Lily yawned loudly and stood.

"She was looking at books in bed when I got home. She'll be asleep now."

"I should hope so," Olivia said, standing to climb the stairs. Lily grabbed her arm.

"I told her about the Earl. That I thought you were going to marry him."

Olivia sighed. "Why'd you want to do that? I told you he wasn't going to propose."

"I'm sorry," Lily said. This time her words carried regret.

"Oh, it's not your fault. I'll break it to Etta as well as I can."

Olivia kissed Lily goodnight and saw her safely inside her door before climbing the steps to the garret.

The moon was low in the sky and its light through the dormer windows gave only outlines to shadows. She undressed quickly and quietly, carefully laying Mrs. Wilde's dress over a chair and dropping her other layers of clothing onto a thin rug. When she was down to her shift, she sat on the bed and carefully slipped under the covers. It was warm where Etta's small body lay in the middle, curled like a ball.

Olivia gently pushed Etta over, so both their bodies could fit in the small bed. Putting her left arm around her, Olivia held the child tightly, drinking in the smell of soap and little girl breath. Etta wriggled, shaping herself to fit against Olivia, but did not awaken.

When Olivia awoke, Etta was no longer in bed; most likely, she was downstairs with Sam. Only half-awake, the actress stared groggily at the ceiling, slanting from its high point at the tip of the roof down to the floor boards. She gazed at the cobwebs in the upper corners and in the creases between roof and wall. Her eyes wandered to the dirty windowpanes. She decided to clean them today, to make the room warmer and brighter. The domestic chores she planned in the morning were rarely accomplished, but she still decided, daily, to do them.

The two dirty-paned large windows sprung out in gables from the roof, creating space where she could stand upright, which was not true in all sections of the room. From the window she could look out over the rooftops of London. They faced Bloomsbury Way, giving Olivia a view in the distant west of the grand Covent Garden Theater. Away to the east she could just see the spires of the Royal Courts of Justice.

That's what Olivia could see if she stood in front of her window. The other window belonged to Etta and was blocked by her possessions. The little girl had pushed an old wooden chair up to the boxy space, which she could climb atop if she wished to look out. Today, the seat of the chair was covered by a horse-blanket which fell to the floor on three sides to make a small cave-like house for her rag doll Esmerelda. Next to her chair was a small pile of magazines and books, including an illustrated *Alice in Wonderland,* Edward Lear's *Book of Nonsense,* and Routledge's illustrated Shakespeare. A wooden crate, its slats painted in alternating blue and pink, stood next to the chair in the remaining window-box space. The crate held Etta's prized possessions: her rag doll's clothing, neatly folded; a small glass bottle of rosewater which she had made herself with the tutelage of Mr. Rambling; a shining tiara Olivia had given her for her fifth birthday two months past, made from two combs glued together and decorated with bits of sequins and paste jewels from the Regent's costume room floor.

Olivia sighed and sat up, slowly turning her body so her legs fell to the cool floorboards. As she walked to the wardrobe, the blanket on the chair fluttered and a voice squeaked, "She's awake, Etta, we can come out now."

A small arm stuck out from behind the blanket, holding rag doll Esmerelda and dancing her about.

Olivia dropped to her knees and crawled toward the chair. "Have you been hiding from me?"

"Not hiding," said Etta's doll-voice. "Just being quiet so you could sleep. Lily said you got home late and aren't getting married."

"Are you disappointed?" Olivia asked, looking at the button eyes and the yarn hair of Esmerelda.

The doll twisted and turned as she answered. "No. I'm glad. I wouldn't want to live with a mean Earl who would make me scrub floors all day."

Olivia lifted a blanket corner so she could see Etta. The five year old barely fit beneath the chair, her back hunched and legs crossed awkwardly. Her mass of ginger curls hung loose in her face.

"Why would you have to scrub floors all day?" Olivia asked.

Etta crawled out from her hiding place and snuggled

into Olivia's lap. She played with the lace on the edges of Esmerelda's little dress. Esmerelda had five costumes, all designed by Etta and sewn by Olivia.

"Lily said the Earl wasn't Prince Charming. That he was more like Cinderella's evil stepmother. I'm glad you aren't getting married."

"Me too. You've had breakfast?"

"Mmhmm," she mumbled in the affirmative. She left Olivia's lap and knelt in front of her crate, holding the tiara up to Esmerelda's forehead. Etta's father's heavy signet ring dangled from a string around her neck.

"You're wearing the ring again?"

"Mmhmm."

Olivia sighed. "It's the only thing you have of his. If you lose it, you'll have nothing."

Etta kept dressing Esmerelda and didn't respond.

Olivia stood and turned to the wardrobe, noticing for the first time a tray containing a tea cup, saucer and small teapot on her dressing table. She had no dining table. Etta usually ate at the Ramblings, and Olivia caught meals wherever, whenever she could. There were no cooking facilities in the garret.

"Did Lily bring up the tea?"

"Mmhmm. I wanted to, but Lily said it was too hot."

Olivia poured a cup and took several long swallows. The tea was tepid, but the liquid refreshed her.

"Is it a piano day or a violin day?" asked Etta.

Olivia paused, trying to remember which day of the week it was. Last night was a Saturday. Today was Sunday with no performances on her schedule. "A violin day," she answered.

Etta grunted.

"What? You prefer piano with Mrs. Smith to violin with me?"

"Mrs. Smith gives me candy," said Etta.

"Gosh," Olivia said. "Do you think if I took lessons from Mrs. Smith she would give me candy?"

Etta giggled. "You could give Mrs. Smith the lessons. You play better than her."

Olivia finished tying the waist ribbon of her day dress and moved to Etta, tickling her in the ribs. "Maybe I could give Mrs. Smith lessons and she could pay me with candy."

The two rolled on the dusty floor, Olivia tickling Etta, the little girl wriggling and trying to push her hands away, until the door opened and Sam burst into the room.

"We could hear you was awake," the six-year-old Rambling boy said. "Can Etta come down and play?"

Etta escaped Olivia's tickling attack and went to stand by her best friend, with a pleading, expectant face.

Olivia stood, brushing away dust and dirt and straightening her skirt. "Only for a short while. After I've gotten dressed and had my tea, it will be time for Etta to practice the violin. You're welcome to join us, Sam."

The two turned on their heels and fled.

Olivia leaned out the door and shouted down the stairs. "I'll call you when I'm ready." Shutting the door, she sat at her dressing table and poured herself another cup of tea.

Genevieve carried her portable escritoire into the parlor where Philip sat with his friend James Berwick, reading and discussing *The Times*. The French windows were open, letting in the sweet smell of lilacs and the sound of the gardener cursing a squirrel, followed by the clank of a thrown trowel hitting a stone.

Genevieve made a big production of setting her writing desk on a small table by the window, turning it carefully until the light fell on her writing surface exactly how she wanted it. She removed the ink and two stylos, two sheets of paper and a blotter, and placed them with much care into a specific arrangement. Philip watched with annoyance.

"Writing your fiancé, are you?" he asked.

Genevieve moved the blotter so it was an additional inch from the edge of the table and straightened the sheet of paper in front of her.

Turning to his friend, Philip continued, "Basil Daubeny spends less time in London than any man I know. If he were truly enamored with my sister, you'd think he wouldn't shuffle off so fast."

"He is a busy and caring man," said Genevieve defensively, tapping her pen on the table. "I'm writing Miss Olivia Snow. It is a difficult letter, which is why I am here. I shall require your opinion."

James folded his section of the paper and turned his

attention to Genevieve. "Miss Olivia Snow? The actress? Why ever should you be writing her?"

Philip hid his head in *The Times.*

"You haven't told Mr. Berwick?"

Philip shook his head with a minuscule movement which neither his sister nor his friend could see.

Genevieve asked James, "He hasn't told you about last evening's wager?"

Philip took advantage of the loud curse and cracking noise that suddenly issued from the garden. He rose to his feet and crossed the room to look outside. Closing the French windows, he said, "I should have a talk with the gardener about his language."

Genevieve sat beside James on the dreadfully uncomfortable, intricately embroidered divan their mother had insisted stay in the London house, despite the fact that she never entered this room and certainly never sat on this particular divan.

"If Philip won't tell you, I shall," she said.

Philip sat on the desk chair in front of Genevieve's writing material and picked up the blotter. The blotting material was pulling away from the wooden base. He fiddled with the material while his sister explained last evening's wager in great animation, flapping her hands, shaking her head, and laughing more than necessary. James listened and watched and laughed. Genevieve was a charming storyteller.

". . . . and so, she and I are to switch places," finished Genevieve.

"That is not precisely true," Philip said, putting down the blotter and crossing to the divan. "Miss Snow is to be you, but you are not to be Miss Snow."

Genevieve stood and faced her brother, playfully grabbing his hands.

"*Eh, bien sûr,*" she admitted, "Daphne and I will stay

57

with Mrs. M while I am allegedly out of town."

Philip frowned. "Mrs. Markby would not be my first choice as chaperon."

"Well, she is my first choice," declared Genevieve. "I've already gotten Mother's approval. It isn't for you to decide."

Philip shook his head. Genevieve needed more watching than Mrs. M would likely provide. "You've got something inappropriate planned, I can tell. You'll remain at home while I'm away with Miss Snow."

"No. I won't be home. I'll be gone, just as if I were in the country with you. If anyone asks, Mother can say I'm staying with friends, and she won't be lying." Genevieve smiled haughtily.

"Not to worry, Philip," said James. "I'll keep a close watch on your sister while you are away."

Philip remained dissatisfied. James did not realize how ingeniously tricky Genevieve could be.

"Thank you, kind sir," said Genevieve lowering herself in a formal curtsy. "Now I must compose my letter to Miss Snow."

Genevieve returned to the writing table, followed by James who stood behind her and watched over her shoulder. "What shall you write?"

Philip shuffled to the bookshelves which comprised the entire northern wall and distractedly perused the titles. His mind was split between remembering the stunning Miss Snow and trying to discover what Genevieve was planning.

"I shall invite her to spend a few afternoons with me," answered Genevieve. "If she is to play me, she will need to understand my character and mannerisms."

Genevieve put the end of her pen into her mouth and pondered how to begin.

"She need only pretend to be a lady, isn't that so? She needn't pretend to be you," said James.

"Are you implying that I do not behave as a lady?"

James chuckled. "Not at all, as you well know."

Genevieve waved her pen in the air. "Nevertheless, I want her to be successful. If she can use me as a model, it will help her master the charade."

"Invite her to tea this afternoon," said James. "Then the two of you can decide how best to arrange the situation."

"Excellent, Mr. Berwick. This is precisely the sort of helpful advice I was seeking."

Philip snapped shut a book he hadn't been looking at.

"Today?" Philip asked. "I was to go to the Brumley's. I'll send my excuses."

"Don't do that," said Genevieve. "You needn't be here."

"*Au contraire,*" Philip responded. "I very much need to be here. I do not trust your modern sensibilities. James, can you join us?"

"I'd love to meet Miss Snow."

"As you wish," said Genevieve, blotting the paper before folding it. I shall have a servant deliver this immediately." With a sparkle in her eye aimed at James, she added, "And then the fun shall begin."

Sam sat in the chair by the window, leafing through a copy of Punch. Much of the humor in the magazine was adult, satirizing political figures and British culture, which the children did not understand, but there was enough childish humor to please them both and provide motivation for learning to read. Olivia never had to worry about anything inappropriate for children appearing in its pages; *Punch* was clean, old-fashioned fun.

Etta stood in the center of the room, her small violin tipped toward the floor, a frown on her face.

"Get into playing position, and this time when you play the minuet, think about keeping your bow straight."

Holding tight to her frown, Etta lifted the violin to a better angle and adjusted her stance. She began playing a simple Bach minuet, one she had learned months ago. The notes danced off the strings–she had a good ear and rarely missed a fingering. As Olivia watched the bow, it angled over the finger board.

"Straight bow," she said.

Etta stopped playing and glowered at Olivia. "It was straight."

"It was over the fingerboard."

"It was straight."

"Look at the rosin on the string."

Etta did not look where Olivia indicated. Instead, she

lifted the violin back to her shoulder and muttered. "I don't know why I have to learn this stupid thing."

"It's a good skill to have," Olivia said for the hundredth time. "When I was your age, I was making money playing the violin."

Sam looked up from his magazine. "You played for the Queen!"

"I was just a bit older than you, Sam."

Olivia had been six that summer, though she looked younger, which helped to mesmerize her audiences. With a violinist for a father, it was not surprising she'd taken to the instrument young. He'd begun teaching her when she was three, and by the time she was five she was performing for private parties. People called her, "Little Girl Mozart," a name she did not feel she deserved. She impressed people because she played, not with genius, but well, and looked much younger than she was.

Olivia performed at Buckingham Palace less than two years after Prince Albert had died, and the grieving Queen had shown little enthusiasm. The actress still felt the sting of her ambivalence. In addition to the violin, her father had taught her to sing and play the piano. These skills kept her and her mother in food and paid rent after her father had died.

Before Olivia could start Etta on the minuet again, a knock sounded on the door. Olivia opened it to find a young footman in exquisite powder blue and gold livery holding a letter to her.

"Miss Snow?"

"Yes."

He handed her the letter. "My mistress asked me to wait for your response."

"And who is your mistress?" Olivia asked, taking the letter and breaking the seal.

"The Princess Genevieve Lamb," he answered. His lip curled as he tried to maintain a stoic demeanor, but his eyes gleamed with pride.

Olivia cocked her head. No one had called her a princess last night. She raised an eyebrow and scanned the missive. "Princess" Genevieve Lamb and her brother Philip were inviting her to tea to prepare for the weekend in the country, where she was to play the young lady.

"Tell your mistress that I am delighted to accept," Olivia said to the servant.

"In that case," he responded, "A carriage will collect you at five o'clock." He bowed and turned toward the stairs.

Olivia shut the door quietly and turned to find Etta and Sam gaping at her.

Sam said, "You're gonna have tea with a princess?"

"It would seem so." She dropped the invitation casually onto her unmade bed. "Bach minuet, from the beginning. Straight bow."

A butler named Greyson, aged between forty and sixty, upright posture, neatly dressed, face empty of expression, that is to say a butler so perfectly like a butler should be that Olivia almost thought him an actor, led her to the first floor drawing room. Mr. Philip Lamb was dressed in beautiful, perfectly tailored clothes: light grey trousers, a pale blue waistcoat, a deep grey linen jacket and an old-fashioned Byron dark grey silk tie. He greeted her formally, kissing her gloved hand and introducing her to his friend, Mr. James Berwick, who also kissed her hand. Mr. Berwick had thick brown hair and an easy smile. He looked to be about Olivia's age, maybe a few years older. His waistcoat, jacket and trousers were of fine material, but not perfectly fitted or as obviously new as those worn by Mr. Lamb. Mr. Berwick wore an octagon tie of bright yellow silk, and maintained a neatly trimmed beard, in the current fashion. Mr. Lamb was clean shaven.

Olivia sat at one end of a Louis XVI walnut divan, the ivory cushion firm. Mr. Lamb sat at the other end of the sofa and Mr. Berwick sat on a matching Louis XVI chair at her side. Plates had been arranged on a table before them. The final Louis XVI chair beside Mr. Lamb was empty.

"I apologize that my sister Genevieve is not here," said Mr. Lamb. "I'm not certain where she's taken herself off to. She was extremely pleased you accepted our invitation, so I can only imagine she will arrive momentarily."

"Are you and your sister royalty, then? The young man who delivered the invitation called her Princess Genevieve."

Mr. Lamb pursed his lips in irritation and shook his head. "She is not Princess Genevieve, although I believe she does let the servants believe such. Our mother is a princess, but we are not."

Olivia raised an eyebrow. "How so?"

"Before Maman married our father, she was Camille Grimaldi, daughter of the Prince of Monaco. Her brother inherited the throne and our cousin will eventually follow suit. We are related to royalty, but not royalty ourselves."

Mr. Berwick chuckled. "In Britain, a relation that close to the crown would be called royalty. I don't know why you pretend otherwise."

Philip seemed uncomfortable but did not protest.

"And your father?" I asked. "Is he a commoner, then?"

Mr. Berwick's smiled deepened. "There is nothing common about the Lambs. Their family is intertwined with English royalty going back centuries. Lord Melbourne was Philip's cousin."

"Distant cousin," said Mr. Lamb.

"Lord Melbourne? The former prime minister? Confidante to the Queen?" Olivia asked. Last night she had been surprised by the young man's confidence, but now she understood. When one is the top rung on the ladder, it is easy to feel high up.

"As I said, a distant cousin," repeated Mr. Lamb.

The door opened and Miss Lamb burst into the room, removing her bonnet, and dropping it on a side table. The two gentlemen immediately stood, Mr. Berwick's eyes laughing at Miss Lamb and her brother's showing dismay.

"Please forgive me, Miss Snow," Miss Lamb said, gasping a bit for breath. "Mother made me stop by Mrs. Parquet's and her parrot was flying about, and I got distracted. I ran down our street which is why I've no breath. Oh, sit down, please! I've already told Greyson to bring the tea." She pulled off her long white gloves and threw them carelessly on the table by her hat.

Moving with exceptional speed to the vacant chair, Miss Lamb threw herself into it, nearly toppling the chair over backward. Her brother reached back to steady it, a look of outrage on his face.

The young lady laughed gaily. "Thanks, brother. That would have been embarrassing, wouldn't it?" She looked at Olivia. Both women pictured what almost happened: Genevieve, falling over backward, legs up in the air. Olivia laughed, though she could see that Philip was not amused.

"I'm sorry I'm late. Have I interrupted? I hope I haven't missed out on the plan. Have you been discussing how it should go?"

"I've only just arrived myself," Olivia said.

"Good God, Genevieve," said Mr. Lamb. "You enter a room like a thunderstorm. I can't begin to think what we were discussing."

Miss Lamb dismissed her brother with a wave. "Don't be ridiculous. I was hurrying to be on time. Oh, wonderful, here's Greyson with the tea."

The butler entered the room, rolling a cart filled with an extraordinary tea. Olivia watched as he set eating plates and serving dishes onto the table in front of them. There were a half dozen different platters holding tiny sandwiches, sweet breads and exquisite pastries. Trying not to drool, Olivia studied her cup and saucer. The china was sturdy with a delicate pattern of violets. The tea was black and strong. Miss Lamb poured and the group spent a moment gathering food onto their plates.

"What were we saying?" asked Miss Lamb. She had just

taken a bite of something, but somehow managed to speak without showing what was in her mouth. Olivia wondered how she did it. The manners of the aristocracy were indeed hard to imitate.

Mr. Berwick smiled at his friend's sister. "The planning has not yet begun. We were waiting for you, my dear." Genevieve clapped her hands. "Good! I haven't missed a thing. Oh! Cucumber sandwiches!" She helped herself to two and insisted Olivia try one.

She did, marveling at the thinness of the bread.

"What sort of advice can we give Miss Snow about being a lady?" asked Miss Lamb, taking a bite from her sandwich. Her brother cleared his throat and spoke. "I've been thinking of that which makes a proper lady, and I've three things that Miss Snow can consider. First is a high moral character. Good Christian behavior is the duty of a lady, for she is a role model for all other women. Second, she puts others before herself. This is most readily demonstrated through the way a lady behaves with her closest associates: her family and dear friends. Finally, she must be reserved but not aloof. Idle chatter does not–"

"Stop, Philip, please," interrupted Miss Lamb. "You're describing a nun, not a lady." Mr. Lamb frowned. "I'm a lady and I'm most certainly not like that. What are your ideas for Miss Snow, Mr. Berwick?"

Mr. Berwick blushed slightly. "I'm not certain my ideas will help. I believe much of what makes a lady is her education. Ladies of the aristocracy are educated so much differently than other women. A lady will know and be able to converse about the classics, art, music–can you play the piano, Miss Snow?"

Olivia nodded but did not elaborate.

Miss Lamb leaned across the table and squeezed Olivia's hand. "You're bound to play better than me. I'm terribly undisciplined, though I do love to sing. We must open our conservatory to you so you can practice. Ladies at a country weekend are always being asked to perform for the gentlemen." She rolled her eyes. "It's such a bore."

"I think I would enjoy playing music," Olivia said honestly.

"Perhaps you and Philip could work up a duet," said Mr. Berwick. "He's known for his musical talent."

"Are you?" Olivia turned to Mr. Lamb, curious.

In a movement meant to garner everyone's attention, Miss Lamb dropped her napkin on her empty teacup, saying, "James is earnest in his advice, which I admire. Philip is stuffy like normal. Morality and education, pooh! The men have missed the most important part of being a lady."

Miss Lamb artfully paused, letting all eyes rest on her. She held her hands in front of her, palms upward. "Clothing, of course. If a woman is wearing the right gown, hat and gloves, there will not be the slightest question of her status. She can behave in any manner she pleases, and still no one will doubt she is a lady."

Olivia smiled, her fondness for the girl growing.

Miss Lamb stood. "Come, Miss Snow. We will visit my dressing room and see what will work for you."

"You can rely on a man to offer you an opinion, even if he knows nothing at all about the subject," said Genevieve, leading Olivia into a large, well-lit dressing room. The walls were papered in a bright floral pattern, with vines of gold that glittered in the light from the lamp hanging from the ceiling. A full-length mirror was bordered by two more lamps. Dresses, gowns, and cloaks were laid out upon every piece of furniture.

Olivia gazed with wide eyes, reaching to touch an ivory chenille evening gown. An inner door opened and Genevieve's maid appeared, carrying a box full of shoes.

"Betty, bring my traveling dress and all that goes with it."

Genevieve chose a delicate brown slipper from the box and held it out to Olivia. "I'm sure the gowns won't be a problem as we are so near in size, but shoes may be an issue. I've quite a large foot, as embarrassing as that is to admit."

Olivia took the slipper, sliding her fingers along the supple leather. "It does look a bit large for me," she said, sitting on the edge of a plush chair heavily laden with skirts. Without removing her well-worn boot, she sized her foot against the slipper.

"No, that won't do at all," said Genevieve, grabbing the slipper and shoving it deep into the box of shoes. Genevieve moved the box to an empty corner of the room and dropped it noisily. "I'll buy you some nice slippers. If you wear a boot like that, the game will be up before it begins. The key to passing as a lady is money. And the key to showing that you have money is fashion."

Olivia nodded, running her hand along the cotton fabric of a long lavender skirt. The weave was so tight it felt like silk.

"Do you prefer the loose skirt with large bustle or the newer, narrow skirt?" asked Genevieve.

Olivia tilted her head. "The narrow skirt is more attractive, but it restricts movement."

Genevieve nodded vigorously. "Exactly." She held up a skirt of emerald green silk, with a bodice patterned in black and dark green velvet. The matching mantle lay across a chair behind her. "If you want this, it's yours. I've only worn it the once, but when dancing was proposed and tables moved to the walls, I had to sit out as I couldn't make any of the steps."

Olivia moaned softly and took the dress, lifting it to her face, sliding the silk against her cheek. "I vowed never to wear a narrow skirt again after a similar mishap, but this is lovely. I cannot say no. Thank you." Genevieve rummaged through a pile of dresses.

"Your eyes are green?" asked Olivia.

Genevieve straightened and leaned toward Olivia. "Yes. What color are your eyes?"

"Well, that depends on what I'm wearing," answered Olivia. "My mother had green eyes and my father blue. My eyes are changeable; they match the color I wear: green, blue or grey."

"Is that possible?" asked Genevieve, examining Olivia's eyes. "Show me."

Olivia held the green silk skirt to her neck. "What color are my eyes?"

"Green. Very green."

Olivia turned her head and wrapped a peacock blue scarf around her neck. "Now what color are my eyes?" Genevieve gasped. "Blue. Utterly blue. *C'est incroyable.*"

Olivia unwrapped the scarf and held a grey jacket against her chest.

"Now they're grey. What fun! I wish my eyes could do that."

Olivia laughed. She tried on several of the gowns, enjoying the feel of the cloth, the cut, the way she looked in each.

The door opened and Betty entered with the traveling suit.

"Here, Betty," said Genevieve, thrusting the dress and hat into Betty's already full arms. "Wrap these and the green dress in a box for Miss Snow. She'll be taking them with her."

Olivia carefully folded the green skirt with its chemise and mantle and awkwardly traded it for the traveling suit that Betty had brought.

"Thank you," the actress said, smiling at the maid.

When the door had shut behind the servant, Genevieve frowned at Olivia. "It's more than the clothes, isn't it?" she said, half to herself. "If you're going to be a lady, you'll have to watch how you treat the servants."

Olivia cocked her head.

"You thanked her in the same manner that you might thank me. It's a subtle thing. Noticeable. You didn't seem like a lady talking to a servant."

"Didn't I?'

"And you helped her with the task."

"Her task?"

"You folded the skirt."

"But I –" Olivia began.

"The best thing would be to ignore the servants completely. It shouldn't be difficult. A good servant fairly melts into the walls. The maid you'll be assigned at the Admiral's will do her best not to attract notice."

"I'm not going to ask for a maid. I'm bringing Lily. I can trust her not to give me away."

Genevieve laughed. "I'm sorry. I didn't realize you had a lady's maid. Will she keep the secret?"

"She isn't a lady's maid; she's my friend. But yes, she'll keep the secret. Lily already knows about the wager." Genevieve frowned. "Has she worked as a lady's maid?"

"No."

"Has she been in service in any position?"

Olivia shook her head.

"If she hasn't, she won't be able to pretend. There's a whole social order. As a child, I spent most of my time with the servants. People make the mistake of thinking that because they are quiet or invisible that they're stupid. They aren't. Well, not the good ones. They'd spot a fake lady's maid in an instant. You'll have to say that your maid is ill and that is why you didn't bring her."

"I was hoping to have Lily with me. She's my companion, a sort of young chaperon of sorts."

Genevieve laughed. "Believe me, my brother will be a better chaperon and much stricter than your Lily, no doubt."

"That would work if he were my brother, but he isn't, is he? Who's to chaperon me and him?"

Genevieve laughed so violently, she had to sit down. "Oh, Miss Snow. You couldn't possibly be safer. Philip is strict and old fashioned. Every mother in society trusts Philip. That is another thing about being a lady. A lady knows intuitively which men she can trust and which she cannot. Perhaps other women have just not been born with that skill."

Olivia raised an eyebrow at Genevieve's naiveté. "You have an intuitive understanding of which you can trust?"

Genevieve nodded, waving her hand. "Take, for example,

Mr. Wilde. He's great fun, but he isn't a man a lady should be alone with. If I were to walk through Hyde Park with Mr. Wilde and no one else, my reputation would be damaged. On the other hand, my friend Phoebe can walk out with Philip and there is no stain on her reputation. Philip is safe; Mr. Wilde is not."

What Genevieve said was true, Olivia knew, but because of social status, not because one man was more trustworthy than the other. Oscar Wilde did not have Philip Lamb's money or title.

Olivia said, "As an actress I study character. But with such a short weekend, how can I know with whom I can walk in the garden and with whom I cannot?"

"Well, for me, it is intuitive," said the wealthy young lady. "I can feel a man's character as soon as I meet him. Like my fiancé, Basil. He can seem a bit cold and rough to some people, but I can sense he's a pure soul. As you don't have my intuition, I suppose you will have to rely on Philip. He will know some of the people, and you'll just have to be careful around the others."

"I will be exceptionally careful, as it would be your reputation at risk."

Genevieve's eyes sparkled, her laughter full of fun. "It would, wouldn't it? What a lark!"

She laughed again, softly, and then picked through the clothes beside her.

"Here, try this," she said, holding up a patterned blue skirt with an enormous bustle. "We need to start choosing what to pack. With a visit of only three days, you can't wear anything more than once, and you'll need something for breakfast, a nicer dress for lunch, a tea gown and something special for dinner. You should take my tennis dress and a riding outfit, and we mustn't forget to shop for slippers and maybe a few more hats."

ᰚ *Fourteenth Chapter* ᰚ

Thick fog rolled down Albemarle Street, giving a dream-like quality to the pedestrians bustling to shops and businesses. A thick pane of glass separated Olivia from the muffled cries of hawkers and the clip-clop of horses' hooves. Carriages seemed to appear from nowhere and disappear just as quickly.

Olivia turned her head toward the brightly lit dining room and her companion of the day, finding it strange to be dining in Brown's in the afternoon. The clientele was more open and friendly when the sun was up. Gone was the competitive attitude of the evening, where men showed off the women on their arms, and women showed off their jewels and their men. Instead, dowagers ate with grandchildren, country cousins met with city cousins, foreign tourists regrouped and relaxed, an actress took tea with the daughter of a princess.

Sipping her tea and nibbling her fairy cake, Genevieve Lamb talked and gesticulated and laughed in great bursts as she had done the full three hours the two had been together. She had taken Olivia to all her favorite shops, and the actress was now outfitted for the weekend. In addition to the clothing loaned from her own wardrobe, Genevieve had purchased for Olivia evening slippers, morning slippers, traveling shoes, riding boots, three pairs of gloves, several caps, and a bonnet.

They had worked up a wardrobe in shades of green. Gowns in emerald green, light sea green, and earthy olive green were accompanied by clothing that was neither blue nor grey. The brown traveling suit needed only a deep green scarf; the scarlet and black evening gown was accompanied by a black cap sporting red berries and large green leaves.

Miss Lamb paid for everything and Miss Snow allowed it. The actress was hesitant to be beholden to a man, there being certain expectations when a man bought a woman expensive items. With Miss Lamb, none of that existed.

"I'm simply awash in money," Genevieve had said, "and I love to shop. You are doing me a favor by letting me buy what I want without bringing home that which I have no space for."

As they sat across from one another at Brown's, Olivia studied Genevieve with a skilled eye. Miss Lamb's youthfulness was fresh and energetic. She could talk and eat and gesticulate all at once with perfect table manners. She never choked, never slurped, never showed a mouthful of food. At first, it seemed like magic, but the more she watched, the more she realized how studied the young lady's manners were. Genevieve was careful about how she handled her food, what sort of food it was, and how much she placed in her mouth. The slight movements were each made perfectly and nearly unconsciously. The actress finally decided the young lady had been forced to practice this choreography hours upon hours to allow for such casual grace while eating.

"Don't you love the fog?" asked Miss Lamb, her face flushed with delight. "When I view the fog, I get all tingly inside: I'm here, in London!"

Olivia smiled and nodded, choosing not to disagree. Damp. That's what the fog made her feel. Not tingly, but damp.

"You'll need to know my background." Miss Lamb finished her tea and lay the empty cup on its saucer. "I was born in Monaco. Although we visited family in England every few years, I lived there my entire childhood. When I was seventeen, I was enrolled in the *Institut Villa Mont Choisi* – do you know it?"

Olivia shook her head. Genevieve fluttered her hands as though it were unimportant.

"It's a Swiss finishing school. Which is ironic, because I needed much more than finishing. My parents had not paid much attention to my education. With only brothers, I'm afraid I ran a bit wild, trying to be like them. I sat in with their tutor, so I got a good education, but not a young lady's education."

Olivia nodded and studied Genevieve as she spoke. Her voice was quite beautiful, her aristocratic English fluent with a musical lilt. As she spoke, her eyes lit and her hands moved, waving and pointing to expand her words.

"That's why they sent me to school in Switzerland."

"Was school awful?" Miss Snow asked, having no trouble envisioning Genevieve as a child running wild down the beaches of the Mediterranean, climbing olive trees with her brother, and spitting pits at people passing below.

"Oh, no! I loved finishing school. There was studying, of course, but mostly they taught us social niceties. Isn't that a funny phrase? Social niceties."

"And that wasn't difficult?"

Miss Lamb nodded with great exuberance. "Oh, yes! It was horribly difficult. But I was seventeen, and I could see the advantages to behaving as a lady. I wanted to be a lady. A part of me had always wanted to be like my mother – I'll never truly be like her; she is so quiet and elegant. I admire her more than anyone. I have the names of Grimaldi and Lamb to live up to. And, really, finishing school was amusing. We practiced walking properly, eating properly, conversing on appropriate topics, dressing for any occasion. Most girls stay at the *Institut Villa Mont Choisi* for one year, but I had so much to learn, I stayed for two. And now I'm here." She opened her arms to indicate Brown's, London, England, the world. "Do you have any questions?"

Olivia smiled, charmed. A wild child turned elegant lady.

"How much older is Philip than you?"

"Three years. I'm twenty and he's twenty-three. John-Robert is the baby at eighteen. He's at Oxford, though he traipses into London when the mood suits."

"How long have you been in London?"

"I came last fall, to get settled before this year's Season."

Miss Snow nodded. "Your parents want you to marry an Englishman?"

Miss Lamb sat up straight and shook her head with energy. "Oh, no. Mother was against the whole idea. At twenty, I'm rather old for a debut, but Daphne Prism and I had talked so much about The Season at finishing school, that I just couldn't wait to come and experience it. I can usually talk Mother and Father into anything, so we took a house in Grosvenor Square."

"Tell me about your fiancé," Olivia said, taking a small bite of spice cake.

Miss Lamb's green eyes lit, and she smiled widely. "His grandfather knew my father at Oxford – my father is quite old, old enough to be my grandfather, really. The Daubenys go back very far, like the Lambs. Basil is handsome and charming. He missed most of the Season, but we met at a ball given by Mrs. Houseman – do you know her?" Olivia shook her head and Genevieve waved away the question. "Basil took me riding, and we had him to dinner twice, and then he asked me to marry him."

Olivia remembered the nice-mannered gentleman from their tea. She hadn't remembered the name Basil Daubeny.

She said it to herself again. Basil Daubeny. She would need to remember that name.

Miss Lamb held out her hand and showed off her engagement ring. "It's hard to believe that was less than a week ago."

Her fingers were long and thin, her light olive skin, making the round emerald in its silver setting look like a magical green gem.

"It's gorgeous," said Olivia. "Did Mr. Daubeny know your brother first? Are they good friends?"

Genevieve pulled her hand back. "What? Basil and Philip? No. Philip doesn't like him at all, but that's just Philip being annoying."

"Really? I'd have guessed the two had been friends for years. They seemed so relaxed in each other's company."

"You've met Basil?"

"At the tea. He worried about my education being less than that of a lady."

Genevieve giggled. "That was Philip's friend James. You haven't met Basil, although you should. When he's next in London, I'll introduce you. He's so fine!" Genevieve blushed. "Mama pretends not to like him, but that's because she thinks I'm too young to marry, which is hypocritical and silly. She was married to her first husband at seventeen."

Olivia watched a cart go past with an array of delicate pastries.

Miss Lamb said something about her ring and extended her arm, fluttering her fingers. The green gem sparkled. In less than a moment her face turned from utter joy to a masked horror. Her voice cracked as she asked, "Do you think I should give the ring to you for the weekend? If you're pretending to be me?"

Olivia shook her head immediately. "Heavens, no. I wouldn't want the responsibility of it. If anyone asks about it, I'll say the setting is being fixed."

Relief swept Miss Lamb's face. "Thank you," she said. "I don't want to take it off."

Olivia smiled. "You shouldn't have to."

When Olivia's father died, she and her mother had made ends meet with her mother's sewing and Olivia's music hall performances. Life hadn't been too bad. But when Olivia's mother died, leaving the actress alone with a small infant, Olivia life's had been difficult indeed. Fortunately, darling Lily told her of the inexpensive garret apartment, and Lily's nosy, nagging mother was willing, for a small sum, to help care for Etta. Five years later, many of their neighbors didn't even remember that Etta wasn't a Rambling, which was just fine with Olivia. Gossip had nearly ended her career, once.

Lily opened the door that led to the stairwell just as Olivia reached the bottom step. "Mum wants to talk to you. She isn't happy about the wager."

Olivia sighed. "Where is she?"

"In the shop."

The two young women walked through a short hall and pushed aside the curtain that separated the apothecary from the living quarters.

Several customers stood in a queue and a small group were at the counter. Olivia did not see Mrs. Rambling, but the kindly apothecary was easy to spot.

Benjamin Rambling was a tall, bone-thin man. His thick grey hair was short and always combed and clean. His clothes were nothing special, but always clean. His pudgy hands were calloused from work but well scrubbed with clean, trimmed fingernails. Mr. Ramblings had a great love, bordering on obsession, of cleanliness, and his apothecary showed it as well. The glass of the large windows that looked out onto the street were so clean, Olivia feared someone would one day attempt to walk through them. The long wooden counter that spanned the room glowed from its constant scrubbing.

Olivia saw Mrs. Rambling by the apothecary window. She noticed them and roughly maneuvered through the line of customers. She had a broom in one hand and a dust tray filled with shards of glass, dust, and powder. Ruby Rambling was as short as her husband was tall. Olivia stepped aside so that Mrs. Rambling could pass by. Lily and her mother were the same height, neither of them much higher than Olivia's shoulders. But whereas Lily was seventeen and still waif-like, Mrs. Rambling was full-chested, making her look larger than she was. Her personality did that too.

"You, with me," she said, nodding her head at Olivia. Flipping her head between Lily and Mr. Rambling, she said, "You, stay and help."

Mrs. Rambling walked backward through the curtain so as not to spill the dust tray. Olivia followed and waited while she dumped the contents of the dustpan into the hall bin. A baby whined, then began to cry. Mrs. Rambling put the broom and tray into a closet and motioned toward the kitchen.

Sam and Etta crouched in the corner, trying to calm baby Theo, to no avail. Etta was singing softly, and Sam waved a sock-baby.

"Put the kettle on, would you?" Mrs. Rambling said to Olivia as she pushed the children aside and picked up the baby from his basket. "He's hungry, he is. Not much you lot can do for him. Go on upstairs and to your chores."

"My bed's made and the floor's swept," said Sam inching

toward the back door.

"Me too," said Etta, although Olivia doubted the truth of it. The actress wasn't as strict as Mrs. Rambling, and Etta often got away with not doing her chores.

"Out to play, then," said Mrs. Rambling. "I need to talk to Olivia. Stay in the courtyard. I'll need your help with the bread in a bit."

The door slammed shut before she had finished speaking.

Theo stopped screaming about the time that the kettle began to scream. Olivia brought two mugs to the table where Mrs. Rambling sat with the baby at her breast. His head was covered with an old tea towel. The mother leaned back in the chair with her eyes closed, but she opened them when Olivia put the mug by her elbow and sat down. Mrs. Rambling adjusted her position, so the baby was as far as possible from the hot mug. After blowing on the tea and taking a sip, she said, "Lily tells me you've got yourself messed up in some toff wager."

"That's one way to put it. You could also say that I've been hired as an actress for a weekend."

"Hired? How much?"

Olivia paused. It was not Mrs. Rambling's business, but she knew from experience that Mrs. Rambling would keep at her. Besides, she needed Mrs. Rambling to watch over Etta while she was gone. It was no use alienating the woman, so she told her the amount.

Mrs. Rambling nodded. "Reasonable. What exactly do they expect of yeh?"

"I'm being hired to pretend to be Miss Genevieve Lamb. That's all. Her brother Philip Lamb and I will attend a weekend at Admiral Bracknell's estate. Some people have wagered that I will not be able to fool those attending the party; others are wagering that I will fool everyone. Obviously, I will do my best as an actress, but I will be paid either way."

Mrs. Rambling put down her tea. "Who makes up the party?"

"Besides Philip Lamb, Admiral Bracknell and his wife, I don't know who will be there."

"And this Philip person? What's to keep him from putting you into a situation and taking advantage?"

Olivia was surprised. Mrs. Rambling usually only cared about the money. "I'll be careful. As you know, I'm famous for my virtue. I've made certain Mr. Lamb is aware of this." The thought of the Earl of Montmarch and the Golden Bell and the failed seduction flashed into her mind. She'd been careless that night, but nothing very bad had happened. She would be more careful.

Mrs. Rambling nodded. "I expect Etta will stay with us?"

"If you don't mind."

"What's one more?" She lifted the rag on her shoulder and moved Baby Theo to her other breast. "At least I get paid to care for that one."

Olivia didn't mention that she felt unusually uncomfortable leaving Etta. She pictured bringing the little girl with her and nearly laughed aloud. That would give the whole charade away. The Princess Genevieve Lamb, bringing her mystery child along.

"Anything else?" asked Olivia, standing.

"Call in the tykes," said Mrs. Rambling, moving to the cradle where she lay the baby down. "They can help with the bread."

Olivia called out the door. When she turned, Lily was behind her. "Pa said to give you this." Lily handed Olivia a folded apothecary envelope.

"What is it?"

"Cloves. He said you're probably out."

Olivia put the envelope to her nose and smelled. Her

mother had sometimes suffered from toothache and took clove to relieve the pain. The strong spicy scent always conjured up visions of her mother, so beautiful, so gay. When her tooth had ached, her mother was always extra cheerful, trying to hide the discomfort by pleasing others. After her death, Olivia had found a few cloves left in a paper pouch in her dresser. She took to sucking them, enjoying the sharp taste and the odd way they made her inner cheek feel. Mr. Rambling had noticed and kept her supplied. Cloves reminded her of happier times. They were also an excellent breath freshener.

Before they left for the country, Olivia brought Lily with her to the Lambs'. The actress wanted to make sure that Genevieve would know Lily and take her seriously if anything should happen to Etta. Not that anything would. Still, Olivia had a niggling feeling about the weekend. She'd feel better with a plan in place. If something happened with Etta, and the Ramblings needed to contact Olivia, Lily could call on Genevieve.

Greyson the butler showed the two young women into the morning room.

"Lily, sit down and stop touching everything," said Olivia, grouchy with nerves.

Lily ignored her, moving from table to mantle to cabinet, examining the ivory figurines, lace antimacassars, porcelain clocks, and little china knickknacks. She picked up a carved wooden elephant, painted in bright colors, and ran her finger along a delicate ivory tusk.

Hearing the click of heels in the corridor, Olivia grabbed Lily and pulled her onto the divan beside her. The door opened and Miss Lamb swept into the room.

"Miss Snow! So wonderful to see you. Philip will be ready in a moment. Your trunk is already loaded onto the carriage. Oh! You have someone with you. Greyson didn't say."

As Miss Lamb crossed the room, Olivia stood, pulling Lily to her feet. Lily still held the little wooden elephant.

"I apologize for arriving early, Miss Lamb, but I want to introduce you to Miss Lily Rambling, my neighbor and dear friend."

The two politely greeted one another.

Olivia continued, "If you remember, Lily is the one I wanted to come with me to act as a lady's maid and chaperon. Instead, she'll stay in London. This works well because if there are any problems that require my immediate attention, any emergencies or such, Lily will come to you, and you can get word to me in the country."

Miss Lamb nodded slightly, gazing at Lily, then turned to Olivia and wrinkled her brow. "What sort of emergency could possibly happen over the weekend that would require you?"

"One never knows," Olivia answered vaguely.

A deep smile slowly grew upon Genevieve's face. "And if there is anything to relay the other direction? If I should need to contact Lily for anything, how shall I do that?"

"Why ever should you need to contact Lily?" Olivia asked.

"One never knows," laughed Miss Lamb.

Olivia returned a half-hearted smile. She had no wish that Miss Lamb start snooping around the Ramblings. When she'd worked at the music hall, a rumor had started about her being pregnant out of wedlock. Olivia had managed to silence the gossip and over the next few years had created an honorable reputation for herself.

Lily, however, had no thoughts of secrecy. "You can send word to Rambling's Apothecary, Bloomsbury Way. I'll come directly."

"Wonderful!" said Miss Lamb, clapping her hands and smiling. "Now I'll just be a moment and see what's keeping Philip."

After the door had shut behind Miss Lamb, Olivia turned to Lily. "Don't let her know anything about Etta. I want to keep my private life as private as possible, do you see?"

Lily nodded. She knew the story. "Etta's my sister. It's what everyone thinks anyhow. I won't say different." Lily laughed. "Did you see her face when I told her where to find me? She must have some sort of plan for when you and her brother are gone, don't you think?"

"I fear so."

Lily smiled broadly. "Naught to fear. You can trust me."

Olivia hugged Lily. "Of course I can."

While Olivia and Philip sorted the bags and got them loaded on the carriage, Genevieve pulled Lily aside.

"What did you say your name is?"

"Lily."

"Lily, would you come to dinner tonight?" Genevieve handed Lily Mrs. Markby's card and address. "It's such a bore to be alone, and I can't go out for risk of spoiling the wager. Will you come?"

Lily looked uncertain. "Dinner?"

"Seven o'clock. Shall I send a carriage for you?"

Lily's eyes were sharp.

"My mum won't like it."

"Would it help if I spoke to her?"

Lily laughed. "That'd be worse, most likely. She don't trust you toffs. But don't worry, I can tell the straight from the crooked, and you're all right. I'll figure out a way to come."

Genevieve flapped her hand. "Marvelous!"

Philip and Olivia were nearly done loading. Genevieve leaned close to Lily and whispered. "I don't see why the two of them should have all the fun. But we can't talk now; Philip would never approve. I'll see you tonight."

Philip sat with his back to the direction of the train. Olivia gazed out the window. The browns and crowds of London slowly transformed into the greens and pastures of the countryside. She turned to study her traveling companion, to find him studying her.

"It's an odd position we find ourselves in, isn't it?" asked Philip.

"Not as odd for me as for you, I suppose," Olivia answered.

"Are you often hired to pretend to be someone you aren't–outside the theater?"

"This is the first time. Although as a child I often performed in posh sitting rooms. I made up a pretend-self for those events."

Philip wrinkled his brow. "As a child?"

"I play the violin, started at an early age."

Philip nodded absent-mindedly. "My plan is to avoid acting. I intend to treat you as though you are my sister. I imagine you will be less trouble than Genevieve; you strike me as a reasonable female."

Olivia kept herself from laughing.

"Although you are not truly my sister, I want to make it perfectly clear that I consider you under my protection."

"Thank you," said Olivia.

Philip opened a brown leather satchel and pulled out

several sheets of paper and a ring. "Genevieve's signet. She thought you could wear it."

Olivia took it from his palm. The ring was small and silver with an awkward etching of a little dog, similar to the symbol on the ring Etta wore around her neck.

"This is your family ring?" asked Olivia, skeptical. It looked like something sold three for a tuppence at a fair. "I know someone who has a ring with the same little dog."

Philip looked offended. "It is a lamb, not a dog."

Olivia laughed and looked at the ring closely. "A lamb. I suppose it could be. I guess it looks more like a lamb than a dog. I always thought the dog was poorly carved."

Philip frowned. "I cannot comment on your friend's ring, but this signet has been in my family since the middle ages. Every Lamb gets a signet for his or her fifteenth birthday. It's tradition."

Olivia smiled out the corner of her mouth. The lamb looked like it could have been carved thousands of years ago by a caveman. "That's a very nice tradition," she said, slipping the ring onto her left pinkie finger. It was a little loose but not a bad fit. "So, what is in the papers? You were going to tell me about your family."

Philip straightened the papers against his thigh. "I've charted a family tree and some descriptions of our home in Monaco, our estate in Devonshire. This sheet is about Genevieve, her education, her friends, that sort of thing."

He held the paper toward her, but she folded her arms across her chest.

"I'd like you to tell me."

"Excuse me?"

"You can read through the sheets, if you wish, but I want to hear it from you."

Philip looked at the sheets in confusion. "Are you saying that you cannot read? Because–"

"I'm saying nothing of the sort. Of course I can read. I want to study your voice, its inflexions, its intonation. I want to study the way you move when you talk. Now that I've told you, I know you'll be self-conscious, but I need to study you. You are an aristocrat who grew up in Monaco, speaking French and English. I am pretending to be an aristocrat who grew up in Monaco, speaking French and English."

"Do you speak French?"

"I can follow it well enough. If anyone wants to speak French with me, I'll tell them that we are in England and should speak English."

Philip nodded. "The British aren't much interested in things not British. But why study me? Haven't you done this with Genevieve?"

"Yes, but I want a larger pool of mannerisms to choose from."

"I see." Philip crossed one leg over the other, flattened one of the sheets against his thigh, and began to read. "Miss Genevieve Camille Marie Lamb was born May 21, 1861 in Monaco–"

Olivia listened to his words, memorizing the facts, but also studying his posture. He held his chest straight with shoulders back, and yet his movements were relaxed: the way his neck moved, and his chin came down and up as he looked at the sheet and looked at her. His eyebrows were haughty and his eyes arrogant or perhaps just overly confident. His nose was small and straight, and his thin lips moved with assurance as he spoke. He didn't seem in the least self-conscious, as she had feared. His dark hair was combed back, and his face was clean shaven. His clothes fit perfectly, were fashionable and expensive. She found him adorable.

Olivia closed her eyes to concentrate on his voice. There was a trace of an accent, very slight. A certain tightness on his th's, a smoothness to his r's and his vowels were sharp and clean. His accent wasn't noticeably French. In fact, it wasn't noticeably not British. It would be fun to imitate and would certainly make her seem like his sister.

He told her of how his parents had met: it was a second marriage for each. Both had been recuperating at a spa in southern France mourning their first spouses. Their first marriages had been love matches and neither thought they'd love again. They had been wrong, finding comfort in each other, then friendship, then love. There was a great age difference between the two; his father was twenty years older than his mother, but it was a love match.

"Lambs marry for love," Philip said, thoughtfully twirling a ring on his finger.

He told her of his childhood. He, Genevieve, and their younger brother John-Robert had run wild in Monaco. He had an older half-brother, the son of his father, who went to school in England and visited from time to time. Philip greatly admired him. The entire family was devastated when he'd died a few years ago in an accident.

"I'm sorry."

Philip nodded and continued with his story. Genevieve had been the wildest of the three. He had no idea how the *Institut Villa Mont Choisi* had turned her into a decorous lady.

"At least on the outside," he said. "Her wildness is still there, and more dangerous for all that she hides it. Nobody but me seems to realize the trouble she is always on the verge of causing."

Olivia raised an eyebrow, but Philip didn't notice. He told her of a trick that Genevieve had once played on their cousin, Albert Grimaldi who would one day be Prince of Monaco. Apparently, Albert was obsessed with everything to do with the ocean. Genevieve pretended to find an unusual fish fossil on the beach. Albert spent weeks trying to find one of his own, until Philip realized what he was doing and told him that Genevieve's fossil had been found in England, given to Genevieve by their older brother.

"–and now you know all about me, my sister, and our family. More than you would ever want, I should think." He folded the papers he'd brought and put them into his jacket pocket. His warm brown eyes took in Olivia's face and roamed her person. "I must say," he said, "you look remarkably like Genevieve, dressed in her clothes as you are, but as of yet you haven't captured her personality at all. I'm curious to see that transformation."

Olivia shook her head. "At first, I thought I'd try to 'play' her, but I've decided against it. Your sister lives to be the center of attention, and I think it is in my best interest to garner as little attention as possible. I will pretend to be Miss Genevieve Lamb, but I will be a quiet, modest Genevieve."

Philip laughed. "I don't think 'quiet' and 'modest' and 'Genevieve' belong in the same sentence," he said. "I must say, this is unexpected. I've imagined you performing as my sister, attracting the eyes and ears of everyone all weekend long. Just thinking about keeping you in line was exhausting. I like it. I approve."

Olivia laughed to herself. As if she needed his approval.

Philip drummed his fingers on his knee. "But I don't see it working. You are too beautiful." He spoke the words not as compliment, but as acknowledged fact. "The men will encircle you. I will do what I can as your brother, but you'll garner attention. No way around it."

"I'm a better actress than you guess," Olivia said. "If I want to melt into the woodwork, I will melt into the woodwork." She rose, her bag in hand. "Excuse me for one moment."

She exited the train compartment and steadied herself

against the narrow corridor wall. The train seemed to rock and bang much more here than when she'd been seated. A porter was immediately at her side, offering to help, but she sent him on his way. From her bag she removed a simple wool scarf in olive green and wrapped it around her shoulders. From a side pocket in the bag, she extracted a set of wire-rimmed spectacles and put them on.

Walking back down the corridor, Olivia knocked at their compartment door. Philip pulled it open. In a quiet, humble voice, Olivia said, "Excuse me, sir, is this seat taken?" She kept her eyes mostly down, darting nervous glances at him.

His laughter was loud and deep.

"Sit, please, modest young lady of indeterminate means."

Olivia sat carefully, her eyes looking to the left of him.

"Well?" she asked in a timorous voice, pulling her shawl tight.

"You've hardly changed at all–glasses and a shawl."

"And?" she probed, still not meeting his eyes.

"Yes, well, you don't fool me. You are still beautiful, but I will grant you that others might be fooled."

"Thank you, Mr. Lamb." She brushed away her veneer of shy young lady and met his eyes.

They smiled at one another comfortably.

"That won't do," he said. "I should be 'Philip' from here on out. You need to think of me as a brother and address me as such."

"Of course," she said. "Philip, my older brother."

She said the words, realizing that it would be impossible to think of him as a brother. He was charming in a way that was new to her. She appreciated his morality and old-fashioned good sense. The gentlemen who mixed with actresses were not usually of his caliber.

She looked out the window and imagined what it would be like to have a man who cared for her. A brother. A father.

A husband. She wouldn't have to worry about money, or leaving Etta with the Ramblings, or what aging would do to her career. She sometimes dreamed of having someone she could talk to at the end of the day. Someone who understood her. Someone who loved her. But it was just a dream.

Philip stared out the train window and tried to understand what was happening. Miss Snow did not appear to be interested in him. He was used to young ladies who flirted, young ladies whose mothers flirted, young ladies who blushed and left the room when he entered, young ladies who asked for instruction on how best to sit a horse, young ladies who begged him for a bit of handwriting in their scrapbook. They were annoying, but as the son of a princess he knew that was to be expected. What mother did not want her daughter to marry up? What young lady did not seek the same for herself? Philip was disconcerted by this young lady who asked questions, who studied his movements like a doctor studying a skeleton. Her lack of romantic interest in him was both freeing and offensive.

While she gazed out the window, Philip studied her more closely. On the surface she resembled Genevieve. Both women had dark hair and were of a similar size. The actress's skin was paler than Genevieve's who had a light olive complexion. His sister's mouth was smaller, with thin lips. Miss Snow had rosebud lips and a dainty nose.

He leaned back and breathed deeply. Miss Snow was incredibly attractive, but he was not here as her suitor. He was to be brother and protector. He had no difficulty with the idea of protecting her. He wanted very much to protect her.

She turned to him. "Tell me about this Admiral person who will be hosting us. How did you meet?"

"We took the same ship from Marseilles."

"And?"

Philip blushed. "Genevieve didn't tell you?"

"No. Is it embarrassing? All the more reason for me to know."

He tapped his thumb and forefinger several times. "No, not embarrassing. Not exactly. It was five or six months ago. We were on the steamer *Ville de Naples.* Mother wanted me to take the train, and a ship to Dover, but you should know this about me: I believe that choosing the easy option is for the weak-hearted. I am often seasick, so to avoid the sea would be to submit to this weakness."

Olivia laughed. "You chose to go by sea because you have a tendency for seasickness?"

Philip nodded. "I'll never conquer seasickness if I avoid the sea. Additionally, I wanted to try my astrolabe. Do you know what an astrolabe is?"

Olivia shook her head.

"It's what the ancient mariners used to navigate, what allowed Columbus to cross the Atlantic and discover America." Philip's eyes lit with the unadulterated excitement of a little boy. His fingers moved, as though he held the instrument. "Mine is a five-inch diameter bronze wheel with graduated degrees scratched along its rim. The alidade, the dial, is attached to the hub of the wheel and when sighted along the sun at noon should designate latitude. I haven't it with me now, but I'll show you when we return to London. I found it in a pawn shop in Nice."

"And did it work?"

Philip shook his head and tapped a finger and thumb. "A complete disappointment. Wholly inaccurate. The sextant was far better–the Admiral had its navigational charts."

"So that's how you met? By navigating the ship?" Olivia's eyes sparkled with mirth.

Philip shook his head, not noticing her quip. "Not exactly. We met at the Captain's table. The Admiral was sitting to my right. He and his wife were returning from Egypt; he'd been at some excavation. We talked for a while about Egyptian antiquities and such. I mentioned my astrolabe and sextant. We agreed to meet later, so he could show me how to use them. Then his wife choked on her steak and I saved her."

Olivia startled. "You what?"

"I'm quite good in a crisis. My thoughts sharpen; I remain calm. Many people become foolish and helpless."

"You saved the Admiral's wife?"

"I stopped her from choking, got her to regurgitate the morsel of meat."

"She was choking?"

"The others were pounding on her back, which was having no effect. It occurred to me to use gravity as an aid. I put her over my shoulder, head down, and bounced until the meat came out."

"Good heavens!"

"I lost a ring in the process, which was a pity." Philip held out his left hand for Olivia to see. A golden ring with an intricately carved coat of arms gleamed from his left pinkie finger. "This is the Grimaldi family signet. I lost my Lamb ring. It must have fallen off when I helped Mrs. Bracknell. I couldn't find it after."

"Remarkable. You saved the Admiral's wife. Tell me more about the Bracknells."

"I don't know much. I'd brought a sextant and astrolabe for the voyage. The Admiral and I met that evening to use the sextant on deck. Wondrous invention. Have you seen one?"

Olivia shook her head.

"I'll show you both the sextant and astrolabe when we return. If you'd be interested?"

"Indeed." Olivia doubted he would remember and doubted even more that he would have anything to do with her when the weekend was finished. But it was nice for him to suggest a future friendship. Philip was an odd and interesting mix of little boy and old-fashioned gentleman.

The air was warm, the breeze fresh, and a clear blue London sky hung above them. Genevieve skillfully managed the horse who pulled her phaeton through busy Hyde Park. Mrs. Markby waved to a pair of elderly ladies hobbling arm in arm on the walking path.

"It's much nicer to enjoy the park from a moving carriage," said Mrs. M. "My legs are not what they were."

Genevieve snapped the reins and the horse moved into a trot. "Marzi needs the exercise. I don't take her out as often as I should." After passing a slow-moving landau. Genevieve returned the horse to a fast walk.

"Tell me again about Oscar Wilde's wager," said Mrs. M.

"It isn't his wager; it is our wager. A private one–so don't tell Philip." When Mrs. M had nodded in agreement, Genevieve continued. "I told Oscar that I could fool people in London into believing I am Olivia Snow. He doesn't believe I can, and we've put money on it."

Mrs. M laughed. "That's not a wager you can win, my dear. London is agog for Miss Snow; she's been seen by everyone."

"On the stage, but not up close. We look a great deal alike. Also, I met with Miss Snow's young friend, Lily. She's going to help."

Mrs. M squinted at her companion. "I don't see how Lily can help you win the wager."

"She will be by my side for the charade. Just as she is normally by Miss Snow's side. With Lily, and with everyone calling me Miss Snow, I should fool a good many people."

"Where will you go? Who will you fool? Who will be the judge?"

Genevieve waved the hand that did not hold the reins. "It hasn't been decided. We can talk tonight at dinner."

Genevieve giggled. "Perhaps Lily can be the judge. She doesn't know anything about the wager yet."

Mrs. M said, "I'll lay a bet that you fail."

Genevieve mock-gasped. "I'll take your bet. Why does nobody believe in me? I'm going to play Miss Snow beautifully."

Mrs. M smiled and the two ladies shook hands.

"Your brother asked me to invite his friend Mr. Berwick to dinner," said Mrs. M. "I believe he is there to keep you out of trouble. I don't suppose he will care for the wager or your play-acting."

Genevieve shrugged. "Probably not, but we can go out after he leaves."

"Not me. I'm not going out. Late nights give me the headache. You young people can have your fun and tell me about it in the morning."

The carriage ride from the railway station to Hudson House took less than a half hour. The Admiral's driver turned onto the long drive that led to the manor house. People milled about on a side lawn. A group of young men and women played croquet, while others walked about a small sculpture garden, and some older people sat in lawn chairs and chatted. Everyone paused to look at the carriage, creating a lovely tableau. When the horses halted, activity burst forth. Servants hurried to unload baggage, a footman opened the door to help Olivia out, and an elderly couple left their place in the garden to come greet them. The woman leaned heavily on a cane as she walked. A small terrier followed at her heel.

Philip shook the man's hand and kissed the woman's. "Wonderful to see you. Mrs. Bracknell. Admiral. I'd like you to meet –"

"Is this your sister?" interrupted Mrs. Bracknell, looking at Olivia sideways. The Admiral's wife was a thin woman of about fifty, with graying brown hair, and small hard eyes. "I would never have guessed. She doesn't look a thing like you, Mr. Lamb." She squinted as she studied Olivia's face.

Philip said, "She takes after my father, or so everyone says."

"Well, then he must be a beautiful man," said Mrs. Bracknell, looking at the actress askance. Olivia managed a slight blush.

"Did your brother tell you how we met?" the Admiral said. "Saved my wife, he did. He hit her on the back, while I turned her upside down. Jolly good!"

Olivia looked to Philip, who cocked his head.

Mrs. Bracknell shook her head. "Pay him no mind. My husband likes to re-arrange the past." More loudly, she said, "It was Philip who saved me, dear. While you stood about spluttering."

"What? What?" said the Admiral, blinking several times.

The Admiral's wife said, "We've been having games on the lawn now that yesterday's rain has passed. I expect sunshine for tomorrow's hunt as well." She indicated her guests with a wave of her arm while leaning on her cane for balance.

Her husband spoke, "You'll join us with the hounds, what? We all know about the Lambs and their horses."

Olivia, not being a Lamb, knew nothing about horses. Philip, being a clever boy, put his hand on her shoulder and laughed. "I will ride out, but not my sister. She can't abide to see anything injured. If she came out with us, it would be to rescue the fox, I'm afraid."

"Hunting is such a cruel sport," Olivia whispered, keeping her eyes modestly down.

"Oh, and here's Mr. Kelvil," said Mrs. Bracknell to Philip, "He's been telling us what great friends he and your sister are."

Olivia's stomach clenched. She watched the man apprehensively, her mind a whirl. He walked with an eager step, was well-built and dressed in fashionable attire. His dark hair was thin, and he had a mustache.

"Alfred Kelvil," said Philip in a cool voice. "I had no idea you knew the Bracknells."

"This is my home county. We are fortunate to have them move into the neighborhood."

"Mr. Kelvil was one of the first to welcome us, and we wanted to do the same for young Goring who has arrived so recently," said the Admiral. "Do you know Dr. Goring?" the Admiral asked Philip. At the brief shake of his head, the Admiral continued, "He's resident physician at Mr. Kelvil's spa, but a gentleman for all that. Well, you'll meet him soon enough."

"I don't wish to be impertinent," said Mr. Kelvil, "but I hope you'll introduce me to this young lady. I was under the impression Mr. Lamb had brought his sister, but I see he's brought someone even lovelier."

Olivia managed to blush again.

Mrs. Bracknell pursed her lips and threw her a scornful glance.

The Admiral showed his confusion by being incoherent. "What? What? What's that what?"

Mrs. Bracknell interrupted, "My dear, stop spluttering. You're making a fool of yourself."

The little dog at her feet yipped several times.

"What?" asked the Admiral again.

"Well, you see–" Philip paused, having no idea how to continue.

Still not making eye contact with anyone, Olivia offered her hand to Mr. Kelvil and said in a timid voice laced with irritation, "If no one will introduce me, I'll do it myself. I am Miss Henrietta Lamb. I assume you expected my sister Genevieve, but she is yet in London."

Olivia glanced up and caught Mr. Kelvil's eye, dropping her own quickly. He took her gloved hand and brought it to his lips.

"A pleasure to meet you, Miss Henrietta. Your siblings should be chastised for making no mention of you."

Philip spoke. "This was Genevieve's Season and Henrietta must wait for next year. She is shy, and I thought a small gathering such as this would help to prepare her for the rigors she'll be forced to endure next year."

"Yes, yes," said the Admiral, slapping his hands together.

Olivia aimed a small, friendly smile at Mrs. Bracknell, who merely glared at her. At the edge of her vision she could see Mr. Kelvil studying her. She pulled her shawl tight.

Mr. Kelvil offered his arm. "Would you care to join us in some lawn games? Or perhaps you would prefer a walk through the garden?"

Olivia kept her eyes down and let her protective older brother speak. Philip responded, "We need to clean the road from our clothes." He wiped at his sleeves, coal soot from the train dusting the air.

"Of course, of course," said the Admiral. He offered Olivia his elbow.

"I'll let my husband walk you to the house. I've injured my knee, you see." Mrs. Bracknell waved the cane a few inches above the grass. "Archie, have Chiltern show them to their rooms." Mrs. Bracknell said to Philip, "We've managed a guest room for the young lady, but we've had to convert my husband's sitting room for you, Mr. Lamb."

"That will be lovely," answered Philip.

"Your things should be in your rooms. You must let Chiltern know immediately if you need anything." Mrs. Bracknell waved them off and hobbled awkwardly toward her other guests, leaning on her cane, her little dog following faithfully.

As they climbed the front steps, the Admiral said, "Dinner's at eight, but drinks before." He turned to Olivia and winked.

The entrance hall featured a rich cherry wood floor, a diamond-sparkling chandelier nearly as large as Olivia's garret apartment, mirrors along one wall, and a grand staircase reaching up to the first floor. An immaculately dressed, middle aged male servant greeted them.

"Chiltern," said the Admiral to the butler, "please show Mr. and Miss Lamb to their rooms."

Philip and the Admiral barely regarded Chiltern, but Olivia had to work not to stare. He reminded her of her father, although she wasn't certain why. Her father had never worn a butler's coat and was more balding than this man. She wondered if it was the way he held himself, a sort of confident and dignified subservience.

"This way, please." His smile to her was warm and kind, and he actually made eye contact. Was that normal? Did he already suspect? Was her acting so poor? Olivia stumbled on the first step, and Philip caught her by the elbow. They followed Chiltern up a flight of stairs and were shown into adjacent rooms on the first floor.

When the door was firmly shut behind Olivia, she let out a deep breath. This was going to be exhausting. It was much more difficult than playing a part in a play. Here, there were no lines to fall back on. Everything was extemporaneous.

Sitting at the edge of the bed, she removed her boots, stretching her ankles and toes. She walked to the wardrobe, taking off her traveling jacket. A single loud knock sounded, the door flew open, and Philip stepped into the room, slamming the door behind him.

Olivia smiled. "That went well, don't you think?"

He glared at her. "Henrietta? How could you?"

Olivia wrinkled her brow. "I thought it was rather clever. That man obviously knew Genevieve."

Philip waved his hand in a strangely Genevieve-like way, but his movement was less endearing, filled as it was with annoyance or frustration at Olivia.

"What's wrong?"

He took a breath and let it out slowly. "Why Henrietta? If you had to pretend to be a different sister, why did you pick the name Henrietta?"

Olivia knew why. Etta's full name was Henrietta. It was the first name that had come to her, but she wasn't about to tell Philip that.

"What's wrong with the name Henrietta?" she asked.

Philip shook his head. "Didn't you listen on the train? Didn't you note the Lamb family history?"

Olivia rolled her eyes. "Yes, I listened. You're angry because I solved the problem and you didn't. You were speechless when–"

Philip stepped closer. "I had an older half-brother named Henry. He died when I was eighteen, remember? He lived most of his life in England. Many people knew him. All in my family's history, and a good reason not to have a sister named Henrietta."

A knot grew in Olivia's throat. She remembered the story about his half-brother, who had died in an accident. Philip had never mentioned his name. She was certain of it. However, it would have been labeled on the papers, which she had only glanced at.

"I'm sorry. I should have remembered. But it seems to have worked. The people here didn't know Henry. Nobody suspects."

Philip frowned. "You should have paid more attention."

"I'm sorry," Olivia said, apologizing for a second time.

"Right," said Philip, "no harm done."

Olivia asked, "You know Kelvil?"

"At university. He's a bad sort; I don't like that Genevieve has been running with his crowd."

"He seemed nice enough."

Philip scowled. "Well, you're wrong. He's not nice at all."

Olivia nodded and agreed she'd be careful around Kelvil, although personally she felt the man was harmless.

"If you're done warning me about the guests, you should

leave my room," Olivia said. "We must change for dinner."

Philip looked around, seeing the situation for the first time: her empty boots and stockinged feet, her jacket on a chair.

"You shouldn't let men into your room when you are undressing," he said.

She threw a boot at him but missed. He gave her a cheeky smile and a wink before closing the door.

Mrs. Markby's rooms were modest but comfortable. Although Genevieve had told her brother and Mr. Berwick that Daphne Prism would be staying with her, the truth was that Daphne was visiting her sister and new nephew in Gloucestershire.

The guest chamber was small with barely room for the wardrobe and a small dressing table. The bed sat under a window and was crisply made with lavender scented cotton sheets and a hexagon quilt. A trundle bed, also neatly made, peeked out from under the larger bed. When it was pulled out, there would be no open floor space in the chamber. Of course, when the bed was out, she and Lily would be sleeping. Genevieve smiled and her heart soared. It was a small room, but it was perfect.

When Genevieve explained the charade and wager to Lily, the actress's young friend hesitated.

"I don't think Olivia would like it."

Genevieve frowned. "It's fine for her to pretend to be me, but not fine for me to pretend to be her?"

"Olivia is an actress. It's what she's paid to do."

"Is that your only objection? That I'm not an actress?" Genevieve paced the room, waving her arms. "Nobody thinks I'll be successful! But I'm very good at pretending, and Miss Snow and I don't look so very different."

Lily began to speak but Genevieve interrupted. "You

don't have to decide yet. Wait until after dinner. Give the idea a chance to steep." Genevieve grabbed Lily's hand. "Come see our room."

Lily let herself be dragged while explaining, "I can't stay the night. My mum would send out Scotland Yard."

Genevieve hesitated, chewing her lip, then smiled, her eyes sparkling. "Well, if you can't borrow a bed, you can borrow a gown. Come and see what I brought."

Lily tried on several dresses, Genevieve finally settling on the pink taffeta.

"It's so fine," Lily said, nearly frozen in her discomfort.

Genevieve laughed. "Not so fine as you, my dear. Now, let us see what we can do with this hair."

Pushing Lily into the chair of her dressing table, Genevieve unwound the girl's simple plaits, brushed out her hair, and pinned and twirled it in the current fashion.

The pins scratched Lily's crown and the weight of her hair felt awkward atop her head. When she looked at her reflection, she wrinkled her brow. "I don't look like me."

Genevieve frowned. "I hadn't thought of that. You need to be Lily, to make the charade work."

Lily stared at her reflection. Making a decision, she pulled pins from her head and said, "I'll put my hair back to normal and wear the gown. It's nicer than my rags."

Genevieve clapped her hands. "So, you'll do it?"

"Maybe." Lily had the feeling Genevieve would pretend to be Olivia, no matter what she, Lily, did. It would be better if Lily were there to keep an eye on her. It might even be fun.

When James Berwick and Oscar Wilde arrived, Genevieve presented Lily Rambling, in simple plaits and pink taffeta.

"We are old friends," said Oscar, kissing her hand. "You look ravishing this evening, Miss Lily." Lily giggled.

"Where is Miss Prism?" asked Mr. Berwick, as he, Lily,

Mrs. M, Oscar, and Genevieve took their seats in the dining room.

Oscar answered, "Run off to Gloucestershire on some nonsense."

"It isn't nonsense to visit a newborn nephew," Genevieve said. "If a child were born to my brother, I would waste no time in being by its side. I daresay, I'd be there for the entire confinement."

"If a child were born to your brother, I might stay to watch myself," said Oscar Wilde.

Mrs. M and Genevieve laughed, but Lily had been sipping water as he spoke and ended up spluttering and coughing. Oscar apologized and patted Lily on the back.

"So, Lily," asked Genevieve, "How do you think the charade will go? Do you think your sister will fool the company?"

"Oh, she's not my sister," said Lily, "but Olivia will win. She's the best actress in England."

"Not your sister?" Genevieve frowned. "I thought she introduced you to me as her sister."

Lily shrugged. "Might have done. We do that sometimes."

"You pretend to be sisters?" asked Mr. Berwick. "Why so?"

A footman served a soup of steaming onions and herbs. Lily sat stiffly as the soup was poured. She shrugged, not wanting to explain. "The soup is really good," Lily said, looking at Mrs. Markby.

"Thank you, dear," said Mrs. M.

"Wasn't Mr. Daubeny to have dined with us?" asked Mr. Berwick.

Genevieve sighed. Her fiancé was nearly never in London. "Yes, but his aunt is in poor health, so he went to see her."

"Aunt Agnes?" asked Mr. Berwick.

"Do you know her?"

"I've heard of her. Philip tells me she is often ill."

"Yes, she is often ill. I think it shows remarkable compassion that Basil is willing to forgo entertainments such as this to rush to the side of a sick, elderly aunt." The words sounded more defensive than Genevieve meant. She took a sip of her wine and considered the soup.

"Is this a rich aunt?" asked Oscar.

"No," Genevieve said, putting down her spoon. "She is not rich. In fact, she lives almost entirely on Basil's income. It's his great love of her that takes her to him, and not any hope at inheritance."

"Sentiments that mark him as an honorable man," said Mrs. M.

"And what does Aunt Agnes think of her nephew's fiancée?" asked Mr. Berwick.

Genevieve's cheeks flushed, and she took another sip of wine. "I haven't met her. We are waiting until she is well. Her health has been delicate since our engagement."

"Sad. Very sad," said Mrs. M. "Lily, tell us something new and interesting."

Lily's eyes opened wide and her face paled.

Mrs. M laughed. "My apologies, dear. I didn't intend to put you on the spot. I'm merely hoping to change the conversation. Mr. Berwick, can you tell us something new and interesting?"

"I read today that the French have taken over Sfax, which portends–"

Mr. Wilde waved his hand for Berwick to stop. "Politics are worse than sick aunts. I have it from my cook's daughter's cousin that the Chadwicks have fallen victim to that clever jewel thief."

"Helen Chadwick?" asked Mrs. M. "I was at her gala a month ago."

"That appears to have been when she was hit," answered Mr. Wilde.

My mother doesn't believe in a jewel thief," said Mr. Berwick. "She says Madame de Beurry, the first 'victim' probably misplaced her necklace – she's always misplacing something – and servants across London are taking advantage of the talk to steal from their employers."

"Your mother would say that," replied Mrs. M. "She views every disagreeable occurrence as the fault of the victim."

Mr. Berwick could not disagree.

Genevieve had been quiet during the talk of the jewel thief, hardly listening. She wanted to suggest her charade, but the conversation never got to an appropriate place to introduce the topic. Now that the conversation paused, she spoke. "I think we should go to the Alhambra tonight. Everyone will call me Miss Snow, and Lily, my sister, will be by my side to finish the charade. We can wager on how successful I'll be at fooling the people we meet. Who wants to come?"

Mr. Berwick opened his mouth, but Lily spoke first. "Not the Alhambra. Olivia used to sing there. Everyone'd know you weren't her."

"Is there some place you think would be better?" Genevieve asked.

Lily spoke, but Mr. Berwick was louder.

"I forbid it."

"You can't forbid it," Genevieve answered.

"I agree with both of you," said Mrs. M. "Mr. Berwick, you cannot forbid this young lady. Genevieve, it is a terrible idea. I've promised both your brother and Miss Snow to hide you from society. Going out is out of the question." When she finished speaking, she wagged her eyebrows at Genevieve, who almost laughed. Mr. Berwick did not notice.

"Well, if you think it's not a good idea, then I won't go

out," Genevieve said, winking at Lily and Oscar. They winked back, and Mrs. M winked once or twice herself.

Oblivious, Mr. Berwick said, "Good. I'm glad that's settled.

Olivia wore the emerald green silk with the slim skirt that
Genevieve had given her. It was a gorgeous gown, and she
felt gorgeous in it. Although she had decided to play small,
she couldn't resist the dress. She wore the wire-rimmed
spectacles and would be quiet and shy.

As she entered the drawing room, Philip moved immediately toward her. When he noticed what she was wearing,
he raised one eyebrow but did not comment, instead saying, "I've met everyone, and there isn't a one who should
suspect."

He proceeded to introduce her to the company:

First were the Admiral's wife's nephew and niece, Peter
and Jane Darlington. Jane seemed friendly; Peter did not.
Both were short and stocky, a body type that worked better
for Peter than for Jane. Her delicate lemon cuirass bodice
and tight skirt made her look like a children's bulldog dressed
for a tea party.

Olivia was reintroduced to Mr. Alfred Kelvil and met his
friend Dr. Gerald Goring, the physician-gentleman. Goring was bookish and pale with impeccable manners. She
learned that the doctor had moved from London recently to
help at Kelvil's Sanctuary for the Elderly and Infirm. When
Olivia explained that Mrs. Bracknell had called it a spa, Mr.
Kelvil smiled and smoothly changed the subject to spas on
the Mediterranean. Philip's dislike of him was nearly palpa-

ble. After a few minutes of conversation, Philip ushered her away to introduce her to other guests.

The Greenpin family consisted of Mr. Greenpin, a vacant, balding man, and his three daughters, Frances, the elder, and the twins Emily and Anne, mirror images of loveliness with blonde ringlets, blue eyes, and dressed in matching Princess-line dresses. Emily wore yellow and Anne wore pink. Anne seemed the more forward, flirting with Philip, while Emily shyly stood off to the side. Philip handled the flirting awkwardly, answering silly questions seriously, asking boring questions about family and houses and horses, and trying to include the shy sister in conversation. Anne did not relent, laughing and touching his shoulder his arm, his waistcoat. He stepped away several times. Olivia watched him quietly, charmed by his confidence, awkwardness, and impeccable manners.

Frances spoke to Olivia. "Coming here was Father's idea. I hope we don't stay for the whole hunting season. He's always dragging me away from London when I have work to do."

Frances wore a loose-fitting Liberty silk dress, her voice heavy with annoyance.

"What sort of work do you do?" Olivia spoke with the forced strength shy people manage when they are trying to socialize.

"I'm active with the Union of Women's Suffrage, the Married Women's Property Committee and the Workhouse Improvement Society." Miss Greenpin gave Olivia a critical look. "Someone like you could make a difference. Women are not treated fairly by society–poor women more so than the rest of us."

Olivia pondered how a lady such as Genevieve might react to this female radical. Her dress was horribly ugly, the cloth hanging loosely about her, her movements enough to indicate that she wore no corset beneath. Olivia tried to admire her for the boldness it took to wear such a robe but could not help being repelled by its hideousness. Her ideals were much more attractive. But what would Genevieve think?

"Indeed," Olivia said with a muted Genevieve-like enthusiasm, even daring to wave her hand a bit. "I have often thought how unfair it was that I was born female. Men have complete control over their lives, while we have almost none. Philip can come and go at his whim, but I am constantly chaperoned. I appreciate the bold statement you make with your dress. I daresay I should like to have one made myself. I can barely move in this tight skirt."

Miss Greenpin frowned. "I'm not talking about fashion," she said. "I'm talking about unfair laws. Do you realize that regardless of how much money your brother inherits, you could be left penniless? If you marry a wealthy man and he dies, you have nothing. Any money your family gives you doesn't go to you; it goes to your husband. Women have nothing of their own, and when those who support them die, they are often left destitute."

Although Genevieve would probably wave her arms and respond energetically to Frances, the quiet and shy Henrietta would not.

"It's a tragic situation," she offered, not making eye contact. They were interrupted from speaking further by a bell-like ringing. The Admiral tapped a table knife against his empty whiskey glass, trying to garner his guests' attention. The room quieted.

"Today is our fifth wedding anniversary," he said, smiling at his wife.

Mrs. Bracknell sat on a sofa, the small terrier on her lap. She smiled at her husband and held her hand out to him. He kissed it with affection.

"So, of course, I have a gift for my wife. Chiltern?"

The butler appeared beside the couple, carrying an ivory case about the size of a large scrapbook. Chiltern opened the lid, showing the interior to Mrs. Bracknell. Because the case was facing the couple, Olivia could not see the gift, only Mrs. Bracknell's reaction to it. Her eyes widened and her face lost all its color. Then, rapidly, her color returned, redder than before. She smiled and appeared to be pleased. The Admiral removed the necklace from its case and fastened it on his wife's neck. A quiet murmur ran through the room as everyone saw what had been hidden.

The necklace was a wide band of what looked, at first, like intricate bead work, in three bands—but the beads weren't beads, they were gems. The inner and outer bands were alternating emeralds and rubies. The inner band, three or four rows thick, were diamonds. Olivia gasped.

The Admiral spoke, his face ruddy with pride. "The Emrubdiam of Khartoum, an old treasure found in a pharaoh's tomb. I saw you looking at it, my dear. Wanted to surprise you. Snuck out and bought it at night, what." Mrs. Bracknell laughed. "Is that what you did? How extraordinary. What a lucky woman I am."

The twins moved straight to Mrs. Bracknell who kept bringing her hand to her throat, making it hard for the twins to get a good look. Mr. Kelvil and the doctor clapped the Admiral on the back and all three moved to the sideboard to refill their drinks. Frances Greenpin and Jane Darlington moved past Olivia, and she heard Miss Greenpin say, "All that money put to so little use."

Olivia sought out Philip, wanting to ask his opinion. Had he ever seen anything like it? Could all the jewels be real? The design was simple, elegant and, to her eyes, thoroughly Egyptian. Philip was standing near the door, talking with an elderly woman who had just entered the room.

"Oh, dear," said Mrs. Bracknell loudly, with anguish. Olivia turned. The Admiral's wife held her new necklace which was no longer around her neck. "The clasp has broken," she explained. "It must have been very old. Not worn for thousands of years. Chiltern, will you–no, I'll take it to my chamber myself." She turned to the guests nearby, "Please excuse me."

Olivia watched Mrs. Bracknell leave. The woman seemed unnerved by the gift which was understandable. Olivia would be nervous to wear or own something worth so much.

A few minutes after Mrs. Bracknell had returned, dinner was announced. Her little dog skipped over to a little pillow-bed in the corner of the parlour. The guests filed out to the dining room.

Olivia was seated between Dr. Goring and Mr. Greenpin. She turned to the doctor, but before she could say anything, a footman appeared between them, discretely whispering in the doctor's ear. Although he spoke quietly, she could hear him clearly.

"Sir, your hospital has requested your speedy return."

Dr. Goring leaned toward the servant and said quietly, "What is the emergency?"

The footman shook his head. "A carriage was sent. The driver might know."

"Thank you," said the doctor. He stood, carefully placing his napkin beside his plate, and cleared his throat. "Mrs. Bracknell, Admiral, I apologize for missing dinner and the evening, but there is an emergency that I must attend to."

Mrs. Bracknell appeared irritated. "Must you leave? Surely there is someone else who can handle the matter?" Dr. Goring replied, "That may be so, but I won't know until I see what the problem is. I would not feel right enjoying myself while those in need waited."

"Yes, yes, I see," said Mrs. Bracknell, sighing.

"I'll walk you to the door, Doctor," said the Admiral, following the doctor and the footman out of the room. When the door shut behind them Mrs. Bracknell shook her head in exasperation. "This is what comes of inviting a doctor to dinner. Our numbers are thrown off now."

"Quite the good luck, I say," said the elderly woman who had been sitting on Dr. Goring's other side. This was the woman Philip had been conversing with before dinner was announced. She slid out of her seat and onto the chair next to Olivia, just vacated by the doctor. "Now I can talk to someone I'd like to talk to."

Mrs. Bracknell's face grew crimson and she glared at the elderly lady. Philip, sitting to the hostess's right, said something that Olivia could not hear. The anger left her face and she turned to give better attention to Philip.

The lady now seated to Olivia's left introduced herself as Mrs. Edith Bracknell, the Admiral's mother. "That doctor's a ninny," she said. "I'm glad he's gone. What's your name?"

Olivia replied, studying her with hidden amusement. The woman's grey hair was curly and unkempt, and there seemed to be a smudge of dirt upon her cheek. As soon as her wine glass was filled, she took it up, drained it, and signaled to Chiltern for more.

"Pardon my thirst. I came straight from the garden," the Admiral's mother explained. "That damned gardener my son hired doesn't know a dog rose from a dogcart. I just finished in the west gardens and I'm as thirsty as a camel in the desert. Make that a horse. I don't suppose camels get thirsty."

After Chiltern had refilled her glass, the widow nodded to Olivia and took another long drink. "This is a good year. My son may not know gardening, but he knows his wine."

Olivia took a sip of the wine, enjoying the full, heady flavor.

"Yes, very good," she said, smiling shyly at the elderly woman.

The widow wasn't listening. Scanning the guests around the table, her eyes fell upon her daughter-in-law. Leaning toward Olivia, she said more loudly than their proximity warranted, "Never marry for love. A man will never forgive you for it."

Olivia looked across the table as the Admiral returned to his place. "They were a love match?"

The widow Bracknell's laugh was like a crow cawing. "Hardly. I was talking about me. I married for love and had a miserable, poor existence."

Olivia thought of her own mother and father, who had married for love and been extremely happy. She said, "My parents . . . That's to say, my friend's parents married for love. They were very happy."

A slight curve lifted the corner of the widow's mouth and she lifted one eyebrow. "Were? They are not happy now?" "They both died young," Olivia answered idly, as if the deaths had not devastated her.

"Ah, well then," answered the widow Bracknell, "an early death is the secret to everlasting love. It is the living that spoils the loving." She paused in her speaking only a moment as she buttered a roll. "My son made his fortune in the navy, traveling, exploring, stealing from the natives. He chose to marry for status and a happier man you won't find anywhere."

Olivia watched the Admiral, smiling between drinks, chuckling with his neighbor, nodding cheerfully to those seated farther away. If he wasn't a happy man, he was playing the part well.

As she studied the Admiral, she felt the widow's gaze. Olivia turned to face her as the widow asked, "You look familiar. Have we met?"

Olivia shook her head in small movements. Quietly, politely, she answered, "I don't believe so. Have you been to Monaco? I have spent most of my life in Monaco."

"Monaco? I don't know where Monaco is." She looked across the table at her son and yelled, "Archie, have I ever been to Monaco?"

The Admiral looked at his mother. Several seats over, his wife flinched at her mother-in-law's manners. The Admiral responded as if it were perfectly natural to shout across the table. "Have you ever been to Monaco? I hardly think so. You've never left England, Mother." A far-away look appeared in his eyes. "I've been to Monaco, though. Fought some pirates just off the coast. Dreadful battle." He paused. "We rescued their captives. A countess and her three children. Mighty grateful, they were." His eyes kept their dreamy focus, but he stopped talking. Most of the other guests had continued in their own conversations, paying him no mind.

"Ha!" cried the widow loudly. Turning to Olivia, she said, "My son has a vivid imagination. He uses it to overlay the past. Gets an idea in his head, and suddenly believes it is what really happened. Been like that since he was a boy. Can't believe a word he says."

Olivia remembered how the Admiral had taken credit for saving his choking wife. How annoying it would be to live with someone who incorrectly remembered the past. Could someone truly live that way? She studied the Admiral. The glaze over his eyes had disappeared and he chewed his food happily, nodding.

The widow Bracknell said to Olivia, "If you aren't English, where's your accent?"

Olivia smiled shyly. "I grew up bi-lingual. My father is English, perhaps you know him? Richard Lamb? I'm told I look like him." When the widow didn't respond, Olivia continued. "My mother is from France," Olivia's pulse quickened when she realized she'd made a mistake. "South of France, Monaco." She corrected as smoothly as possibly.

The widow didn't seem to notice anything amiss.

"Well, that explains your reputation, although now that I've met you, I cannot believe a word of it."

"I have a reputation?" Olivia asked, her voice quiet, her eyes wide.

"Oh, just the garden gossip. Mind you, nobody tells me anything, but I hear just the same. You're supposed to be a big flirt, an attention stealer, spoiled and beautiful."

Olivia blushed. "They must have been talking about my sister Genevieve. She's a bit like that, but kind and generous. Much nicer than they made her sound." Olivia looked at her plate, fish in a thick cream sauce and potatoes with green beans and small pieces of bacon. The smell was heavenly.

The widow pointed her fork, which had a chunk of fish on its tines, and said, "Oh, you can't trust gossip entirely, but there's usually some truth in it. Take the twins down there. One seems forward, and one seems shy–but it's the shy one who's forward."

Mr. Kelvil sat between the twins, near the end of the other side of the table. He and the outgoing twin were talking and laughing, but his seat was unusually close to the shy twin. He was eating with just one hand, his other beneath the table. Could they be holding hands–or something else?

Olivia glanced back at the widow who nodded her head and lifted her eyebrows. "See what I mean?"

Olivia did not respond.

"She's got a wild side to her, that one," she continued, "and I didn't learn that from gossip, but from catching her with a footman in the bushes. Try the fish, it's quite nice."

Olivia made a sound that could have been a gasp of shock or a giggle. She would let the elderly woman think whichever she pleased.

The widow focused on her meal, and Olivia savored small bites. Looking around, she saw Philip chatting with the Admiral's wife. He seemed interested in their conversation, his attention fully focused on her, his kind eyes sparkling, his mouth slightly curved in an unforced smile. His two hands were above the table, one holding a fork and the other a knife. No hanky-panky there. Olivia giggled to herself and then made a note not to drink too much of the wine. Scanning the other guests, her eyes caught those of Mr. Darlington and they both looked away, embarrassed.

The widow Bracknell spoke, unhindered by the fact that her mouth was full of potatoes, "I'll need your help when we move into the drawing room after dinner. I've a surprise sent up by a friend, a cheiromantist."

"A what?"

"A cheiromantist." The widow Bracknell repeated the word slowly and more loudly, thinking Olivia had not heard. The actress had no idea what a cheiromantist was, but it might be something that a lady would know.

"His name is Mr. Podgers," the widow continued. "I haven't told my daughter-in-law. She can't say no in advance to what she doesn't know is coming, can she? Nevertheless, she has a way of stopping anything entertaining. So, if she tries to turn him away, promise me you'll show interest and let him do you first."

"Do me?" Olivia asked, alarm written plainly on her face.

"Thanks, darling. I knew I could count on you. Well, I'm done with this slop and ready for my cigarette in the roses," she said, draining her glass and standing from the table. "Lovely dinner, Hortense. I must refresh myself before the evening entertainment. See you in the drawing room."

Olivia glanced at the Admiral's wife, who smiled with difficulty and then glared at her husband. Olivia hid a smile behind her napkin. The widow Bracknell was odd, but she liked her. The elderly lady was the kind of crazy character crucial to modern comedies. Olivia's eyes moved from the offended hostess to Philip. Perhaps he could tell her what a cheiromantist was before she embarrassed herself. Philip looked up and their eyes met. She winked at him, and he smiled back.

The women gathered in the drawing room and waited for the men, who had remained in the dining room to smoke. Miss Greenpin, the radical feminist, and Jane Darlington, the Admiral's niece, sat together on a small sofa, talking quietly. Mrs. Hortense Bracknell, despite the need for her cane, moved speedily about the room, rearranging knickknacks, chastising servants, and worrying antimacassars while her little dog, Crumpet, followed at her heels. Olivia watched as she opened two large French windows, closed the windows, then opened them again. Olivia was glad to see her leave them open. The room was stuffy and certain to get stuffier as the evening progressed.

The twins stood by an elegant end table, one of them idly paging through a scrapbook, the other gazing about the room. As her eyes approached Olivia, the actress dropped her gaze in bashfulness. The twins crossed the room to her.

Olivia smiled shyly and the one dressed in pink spoke, "I was hoping to meet your sister and talk to her about Basil Daubeny. Is she really to marry him? He spent summers with an aunt near us, so we know him a little. We haven't seen him for years."

Olivia spoke in a voice shy but friendly, imitating Philip's slight accent. "The engagement happened very quickly. I've only met him once; I wasn't in London for the Season, you know. He's very handsome and very nice."

A strange gleam flicked in the eyes of the quiet twin and then was gone.

"Please, tell me your names again," Olivia said. "You look so much alike."

The talkative twin giggled. My name is Anne. I'm in the pink. I always wear pink, even if only a ribbon. My sister is Emily. She'll wear whatever color suits her mood, but never pink. So, there you are. You'll always be able to tell us apart."

Olivia offered them a mostly genuine smile. Now that she had paid attention to them, it would be easier to tell them apart, with or without the pink. Anne was not only talkative, but genuine. There was kindness and interest in her eyes. It was impossible not to like her. Emily, on the other hand, did not appear silent from shyness but from a complete lack of interest in what anyone might say. She also seemed conniving, as though there were a plan going on in that quiet head of hers. Olivia reconsidered. Her perception of the girl might be influenced by the widow Bracknell's story.

Before Olivia could say anything further, the widow and all the men walked into the room, including the doctor, whose medical emergency must have been short-lived.

Olivia glided toward the side of the group, hoping to reach Philip and learn what a cheiromantist was, but Mr. Kelvil got between them.

"Miss Lamb, I haven't gotten the chance to say how lovely you look this evening. The color of your dress brings out your eyes."

"Thank you, Mr. Kelvil. I hope you enjoyed dinner." Olivia glanced hopefully toward Philip, who was with the twins. He talked to Anne, while Emily stood inappropriately close to him. Was that her hand brushing against his pant leg? A flutter of surprise passed across Philip's eyes and he took a sudden step to his right.

"I see you've noticed the lovely Emily-Anne," said Mr. Kelvil. "A dangerous combination for any man. The one will distract him with her charm and innocence while the other moves in to take what she can. Still, I'm sure your brother can handle the situation. Oh, I am sorry," he said, noticing the deep blush that spread from Olivia's face down her neck.

Blushing on command was a skill Olivia had learned years ago. If an actress can fall deeply enough into her character, she will find herself outraged and embarrassed by the very things that would outrage or embarrass her character. Shy, innocent Henrietta, not yet out, would be shocked by Kelvil's story.

"It is hot," Olivia said, feigning embarrassment at her feigned innocence. "Could you get me a glass of lemonade?"

"Allow me," said Mr. Kelvil.

The widow Bracknell climbed atop a hard-back chair located near the center of the room. She'd removed her slippers but still seemed unsteady atop the cushion and at such a height. The Admiral's wife scowled, and her little dog yipped and jumped up at the woman on the chair. Mrs. Bracknell pushed her husband toward his mother. He tried to get her off the chair, but she slapped at him.

"Everyone's attention, please," said the widow. "I would like to introduce to you Mr. Podgers." She pointed to a short, balding man standing to her right. He looked very embarrassed to be so addressed and tried to get her to come down from the chair. "Just wait, will you?" she answered. "Mr. Podgers is my good friend and cheiromantist and has come to entertain us this evening. Miss Lamb has kindly agreed to go first. Miss Lamb." She gesticulated for Olivia to come closer. Olivia step forward hesitantly. The Admiral helped his mother down from the chair.

The widow Bracknell had managed to turn all the room's attention to them. Olivia pretended to cringe at all the eyes upon her. The widow took Olivia's hands and pulled off her gloves. The actress stood still, not having to pretend to be nervous. When the gloves had been removed, the widow turned the young woman's hands palms up. "Podgers, please. And speak loudly so everyone can hear."

The company gathered around in a tight circle. Mr. Podgers' hands were soft and warm. He gently traced the lines on Olivia's palms with his left pinkie, all the while humming and making unintelligible whispering noises. With relief, Olivia realized a cheiromantist was a fancy name for a palm reader. She'd had her palm read several times, but only by gypsies at festivals. She'd heard there were respectable, professional palm readers who served the London elite. Mr. Podgers must be one of those.

"Well?" said the widow, losing patience. "What can you tell us about her?"

Mr. Podgers brushed his fingers swiftly along Olivia's palms, as though brushing off breadcrumbs. He put her hands together and pushed them gently away, smiling kindly at her.

"This is a woman with a pure heart and a devotion to honesty. She is good at deception but never tries to deceive. She has a secret which will turn out to be a secret to her as well. She will marry for love in the not-too-distant future." He blinked several times, nodded, and smiled.

"Marry for love?" cried the widow. "But I specifically advised her against it!" She gave Olivia a fierce glare as though the young lady had expressly defied her. Turning toward the guests, the widow asked, "Well, then, who's next?"

Olivia pushed her way through the crowd, ending up by Mr. Kelvil who handed her the glass of lemonade. "So, you have a secret, do you?" he teased.

Olivia sipped the cool lemonade. "I can't imagine what Mr. Podgers means."

"Secrets are such fun," said Mr. Kelvil, leading Olivia toward the French windows at the rear of the room. They were ignored by the others, who were focused on Mr. Podgers and his fortune telling.

The two went through the French windows and onto a small balcony. The air was cool, a relief from the hot room. The gardens were invisible in the darkness and to her light-blinded eyes. Olivia glanced upward and froze, awestruck by the beauty of the night. It was clear, with stars spread from horizon to horizon, sparkling like freshly polished diamonds. Olivia gaped. She'd never seen the like in a London sky.

"Ah. The cool air is such a relief," said Mr. Kelvil, stepping a little too close.

Olivia shook her head. She couldn't let the stars distract her. She needed to be the modest Miss Lamb, not the brain-addled Olivia. She took a small side-step and said, "The stars are beautiful tonight."

"Not as beautiful as you," said Mr. Kelvil.

Olivia rolled her eyes in the darkness, and offered the embarrassed giggle of her character, expecting she would soon need to send him on his way. However, Kelvil did not step toward her again and made no movement to touch her. Instead, he tilted his head and looked at the sky too.

"Do you know the constellations?" he asked. With a sudden nervousness, he chattered about Libre and Virgo and Orion, the big and little dippers, and the North Star. Kelvil pointed as he explained, and Olivia tried to follow the line of his arm without getting too close. She was interested but unable to draw lines to form the pictures he and the Ancient Greeks could see. To her, the stars were a million diamond pinpoints. Lovely and mysterious.

Deciding she would never see what he saw, she stepped away and asked him what he thought of the Emrubdiam of Khartoum.

"Pretty spectacular, isn't it? Not that I pretend to know anything about jewelry. The Admiral is a serious collector, though. Egypt, the Orient, the Seven Seas. He's traveled everywhere and brings home the best artifacts he can find, as I understand it. I've only traveled a little, Scotland, France, Italy. Never Monaco." Kelvil coughed awkwardly. "I'm talking too much, aren't I? I suppose I'm just nervous at being, well, you see –"

Olivia felt an arm on her shoulder and jumped.

"I couldn't find you inside," said Philip, his face tight.

Mr. Kelvil tipped his head ever so slightly to Philip and said, "Your sister was over heated from the hot room and the excitement of the cheiromantist, so we came to get some air."

"I see," answered Philip. "Thank you, but I can care for her now."

Mr. Kelvil tipped his head, stepped past Philip, and went inside.

"You shouldn't be alone with him," Philip scolded.

"It was innocent enough."

Philip crooked his head and gazed into the room, watching Mr. Kelvil. "There's nothing innocent about that man. I don't trust him. You need to be more careful."

Philip was leaning against the balcony rail. The yellow haze from the interior gas lights shone upon his face, illuminating his air of bold superiority. Olivia rethought her earlier dream of having a man to protect her. Did he think so little of her? She wondered if this were a performance, or if he really thought her a foolish child? She followed his gaze into the house. The pink twin laughed gaily at something said by the doctor.

"And you should be careful of those twins," Olivia answered.

Philip blushed but gave no verbal response.

"Have you had your palm read?"

"No, I don't–" she grabbed his arm firmly and pulled him inside.

"Mr. Podgers," Olivia called, "Mr. Podgers, you must do my brother."

The circle which had formed earlier to observe the palm reading had broken up, with people chatting in small groups. Mr. Podgers stood talking to the Admiral.

"Mr. Podgers," Olivia said, "Please read my brother's palm."

"No, thank you," said Philip wresting his arm away. "I'd rather not."

"Yes, yes, Mr. Lamb," said the Admiral. "You must. I'll be after you."

Over his objections, the Admiral pulled Philip's hands toward the palm reader.

Mr. Podgers immediately turned them over and studied the palms. They were clean, soft hands, Olivia noticed. The hands of a man who had never done more than study.

Out of the corner of her eye, Olivia noticed the Admiral's nephew staring at her. When she turned toward him, he looked away.

Mr. Podgers made the brushing movement along Philip's palms and released his hands. "There is a strong bond between this man and his sister. They have much in common: a love of honesty, and two secrets: one they both know and one they neither know." He finished with the blink, nod, and smile that he had given Olivia.

"Is that so? Astonishing. Thank you," said Philip with an artificial smile. He turned his back on the cheiromantist and whispered to Olivia, "What were you thinking?"

"Well, there was hardly anyone around to hear," she said softly. "Besides, nobody believes that stuff and nonsense: a secret known isn't even a secret. It's just a game, for entertainment."

"My turn," said the Admiral. His face held a child-like excitement, and he spoke more loudly than necessary. Philip and Olivia were the only ones near as Mr. Podgers began his study of the Admiral's palms. The cheiromantist ran his pinkie finger along a line, then flinched. "I'm sorry," he stuttered, dropping the Admiral's hands, "I don't see anything."

The Admiral took a step forward him, pushing his hands at the palm reader. "Try again. It's my turn, man. You've got to read me. I own this place, what."

Mr. Podgers offered a sickly smile and once again took the Admiral's hands. He cleared his throat, "You are a man of great wealth and influence."

The Admiral beamed.

He stared at the palm, moving his pinky finger but not saying anymore.

The Admiral harrumphed. "Tell me more. Something about my future."

Mr. Podgers frowned. "There will be many unexpected changes for you, in the near future. Involving your family. I can't say-see anymore." He dropped the Admiral's hands, slowly backed away and dropped into a chair, exhausted.

The widow Bracknell approached him and they spoke quietly. Mr. Podgers shook his head several times then stood. The two left the room.

"How mysterious," said Jane Darlington, the Admiral's bulldog of a niece, moving herself between Olivia and Philip. "Both brother and sister with secrets. Isn't that what the palm-reader said?"

Olivia giggled and Philip frowned.

Miss Darlington continued, "I won't pretend to believe in fortune telling, but that man told me I'd soon find the solution to my problem. A vague prediction, but one that just might come true. I have a sick horse, and I understand you are an expert on horses. Can we sit for a moment?"

As Philip and Miss Darlington sat, Peter Darlington spoke to Olivia. "Have you seen the Admiral's collection?"

"No, I haven't. What does he collect?"

Mr. Darlington's eyes darted around as he spoke, looking everywhere but at Olivia. "Everything. The more expensive and rarer the better. Let me show you."

"Certainly," Olivia answered, placing her hand on his offered elbow, and following him. Near the door stood the Admiral and his wife, arguing in hushed voices. She held her little dog in her arms, scratching his ears.

Peter Darlington interrupted them. "Aunt Hortense, Admiral, I've offered to show Miss Lamb the collections from your travels. Would you care to join us?"

Mrs. Bracknell and her dog glared at Peter. "Can't you see I'm hosting a dinner party?"

Mr. Darlington flinched, and a red rash of embarrassment climbed his neck.

The Admiral responded to his wife's words by patting her on the shoulder and saying, "He's helping to entertain the guests, my love." Turning, he said, "Jolly good, Peter, show Miss Lamb the antiquities. But hurry back for the charades!"

Mrs. Bracknell pursed her lips. "Your mother has ruined the evening. I'd planned the charades for as soon as the men came in. Now everyone is distracted and moving about. These two are leaving. How do I gather everyone together without seeming controlling?"

The Admiral clucked at Mrs. Bracknell, telling her the charades were certain to go off fine, just give it a bit of time. The guests were enjoying themselves and when they became bored, she could step in with her game.

Olivia looked at Mr. Darlington, trying to decide if they should offer to stay for the charades or to leave and come back. Shy Henrietta would certainly let Mr. Darlington be the one to speak. They stood for another awkward moment–awkward for them, if not for the Admiral and his wife. Mrs. Bracknell continued to complain about his mother, and he continued to try to comfort her. Mr. Darlington took a step toward the door and Olivia followed.

Meanwhile, in London, Mr. Berwick left Mrs. Markby's shortly after dinner. Genevieve, Mrs. M, Lily, and Oscar Wilde plotted in the parlour.

"Where shall we go?" Genevieve asked.

"I have a previous engagement," Oscar said, crossing his legs and exhaling a long stream of smoke.

"Cancel it," said Genevieve. "It can't possibly be as entertaining as this evening is going to be."

Mr. Wilde puffed thoughtfully on his cigarette.

"Be that as it may, I committed to this engagement several weeks ago. It would be terribly inconvenient to my friends to shake it off at such late notice."

"Why, Mr. Wilde," Mrs. M said in a mock-shocked voice. "Think of your reputation. People will start calling you responsible and reliable. Caring even."

He smiled out of the corner of his mouth.

"No one will be at the Eagle much before midnight," said Lily. "Couldn't you do both?"

Genevieve's eyes sparkled and she nearly bounced in her chair with excitement. "Could we come with you? Tell your friends that we're going to the Eagle and invite them to come? Does anyone there know Miss Snow?"

Oscar put out his cigarette on a glass ashtray and cleaned his fingertips with a handkerchief. "I can't very well escort you to a gentleman's club. I shall leave my apologies on the way to the Eagle."

Genevieve jumped to her feet, grabbing Mr. Wilde's hand and shaking it. "Thank you! You won't regret it!"

Mrs. M stood. "Off to bed for me. Remember, I'm wagering against Miss Lamb. Someone will point out that she isn't who she says she is. Stick by her side, Lily dear. I'll trust your report."

Miss Darlington was not an attractive woman, but when she began speaking, her eyes lit with intelligence and worry. "I apologize for bothering you, but you have a reputation for understanding horses."

"Of course," said Philip with real interest. "Any way I can be of service. Is it an injury?"

"Not an injury. She's stopped eating and drinking, and–"

"For how long?"

"Two days. I found her late morning yesterday lying in the Admiral's pasture."

"Was she still or rolling around?"

"Rolling around."

"Any changes in her breathing?"

"Not that I've noticed."

It sounded like colic to Philip.

"Has the horse been anywhere recently?"

"I had her with me at Brighton. We returned to Hudson House last week."

The problem sounded like sand colic, which could be serious. Philip explained that when a horse ate grass from sandy soil, sand could enter and get trapped in its stomach. He recommended regular but easy exercise which would hopefully force the horse to drink water. Water was key to flushing its system. He suggested a bran mash.

"I'll look in on your horse in the morning, before the

hunt."

"I'll order the bran mash immediately," said Miss Darlington, standing, "and tell them to keep trying water. Thank you."

Philip watched Miss Darlington leave, impressed with her devotion to her horse. When he looked for Miss Snow, he couldn't find her. She had once again disappeared. Philip sighed. Scanning the room, he saw Mr. Kelvil chatting with the doctor and Mrs. Bracknell. At least she was safe from him. Kelvil turned away from the conversation and moved to renew his drink. Philip approached the small group, planning to ask Mrs. Bracknell if she knew where his sister had gone. Dr. Goring was speaking.

"It isn't an asylum at all. It's something between a hospital and a hotel, you see. A retreat for the elderly who need the extra attention of a physician and a large nursing staff."

Mrs. Bracknell finished her drink and signaled for another. When she again held a glass, she returned her attention to the doctor. "Do the elderly bring themselves to you, or do the relations?"

Dr. Goring picked at his jacket nervously. "Most of our clients come because they want the retreat; however, there have been a few severe cases where the client has memory loss or is otherwise incapacitated, and it is the relations who initiate the visit."

"This is what we need for my mother-in-law. You must speak with my husband."

Searching the room for the Admiral, Mrs. Bracknell emptied her glass in one swallow. The Admiral was nowhere about. Philip scanned the room and saw the Admiral's mother seated nearby, easily within hearing distance. The older woman held a cigarette in one hand and glared at her daughter-in-law with a hatred not usually seen outside the theater.

Mr. Darlington's earlier bashfulness and silence was replaced by the drone of a whiny five year old. He complained about the food and the guests, the country, and the weather. He and Olivia walked down a long corridor lit by gaslights. At the end of the passage, they turned to the right to follow another long corridor, this lit by candles in wall sconces. Mr. Darlington complained about his uncle's inability to modernize. Midway down the second corridor was a small flight of stairs going up to the right. Mr. Darlington took a candle sconce from the wall and ushered Olivia up the stairs. She climbed into the darkness to a small landing with two doors opposite one another.

"Here we are," said Mr. Darlington, choosing the door on the right. They stepped inside to near complete darkness. The candle he held gave off a dim glow, illuminating only his face and making the rest of the room seem eerie and dangerous.

"Ridiculous," said Mr. Darlington, walking around the room and using his candle to light other candles, on tables and wall sconces. "He says he's installing gas lights, but I haven't seen anyone working on it."

"He hasn't been at Hudson House very long, has he? Oh, my!" The light had increased, and Olivia could see the marvels of the Admiral's collection. Objects of all sizes and colors and materials were laid out everywhere. Chinese screens, chunks of walls with age-old carvings, marble sculptures, and tables artfully arranged with smaller items: jewelry, figurines, scrolls. It was a bit like the prop room at the theater, and yet utterly unlike that room. Both were crowded with curiosities, but whereas the props were cheap and damaged, these objects were gorgeous and historical and obviously expensive.

"He's an ass, but his collection is prime, isn't it?" said the ungrateful nephew, moving to where Olivia stood by the door.

"It's amazing."

First, she explored a table of Chinese artifacts: large porcelain vases decorated in intricate designs. Some vases were sketched in all blue, some all red, and others with a multitude of colors. There were older pots, too, made of a heavy metal, with odd curving handles. The table next to this held Oriental statuettes, in jade, ebony and gold. Each statuette had a human form with Oriental characteristics, holding their hands at odd angles and sitting with their legs crossed in uncomfortable poses.

Olivia next examined parchments, letters, writings on silk. The script was elegant, the Chinese characters beautifully drawn, more like a work of art than a letter. She bent closely to study the fine lines on the paper.

"Can you read any of these?" she asked, straightening and turning toward Mr. Darlington.

He brushed his hand against his hair nervously. "No. That's my aunt. She has a gift for languages. She's the one who collects the books and letters and such. The Admiral prefers larger, ostentatious items."

"Like the Emrubdiam," Olivia noted.

"Exactly. He's very rich and wishes to show people how rich he is through his collection."

Olivia admired a screen depicting a brightly colored, fearsome dragon swooping upon a village of pagodas. The Oriental screen was set to the side of a large fireplace, clean and empty. The stone mantle above the hearth displayed an array of jade and ivory carvings.

"Can I touch?" Olivia asked.

"I'd give them to you, if they were mine," said Mr. Darlington, in a pinched voice. He picked up a jade statuette of a young woman wearing a strange hat and holding her hands above her head. Handing it to her he said, "None of this is mine. The Admiral is much better at getting than giving."

The jade felt smooth and surprisingly warm. She placed it back on the mantle.

"Should it be yours?" Olivia asked.

"Aunt Hortense is the only living relative that my sister and I have. She's my father's sister and helped to raise us after our parents' deaths. Uncle Wilbur, her first husband, treated us like his own children. He died of consumption five years ago."

"I'm sorry," Olivia said, scrunching her brow and doing the math: uncle dead five years, aunt celebrating a five-year wedding anniversary.

"She married the Admiral a few months after his death, saying grieving periods were old fashioned."

"That must have been hard for you," Olivia said.

"Harder for my sister," Mr. Darlington answered. "I was away at school. She was at home, nursing Uncle Wilbur. After his death, she was moved from house to house wherever was most convenient for aunt. We have no money, you see. There is an income that should have come to us from my father when I reached majority, but it seems to be lost. I believe the Admiral talked my aunt out of giving it to us."

"Is that legally possible?"

He shrugged. "We can't seem to find anything out. It appears to be gone, spent, and we're here living off the crumbs of a very rich man." He spread his arms about, showcasing the Admiral's collection and wealth.

"Why doesn't he display these throughout the house?"

"He intends to. He's had everything brought to this room because a man is coming to catalog and appraise them. Or so he says. There's been no sign of such a person."

Olivia scanned the treasures, wondering whether to stay and study them with the peevish Mr. Darlington. If his story were true, one might feel sorry for him, but his petulant manner made sympathy difficult.

Olivia walked to a small table which held jewelry: thick gold bracelets made to look like lions kissing; a golden cap or crown, made for a small head, with primitively carved flowers and what might have been angels; a shimmering tiara. She picked up a bracelet to better see the engraving. It seemed too large and heavy to be worn comfortably. She returned it to its place on the table.

The next table was mostly empty, with one wooden box, about the size of a large book. The top was decorated with a tree, its streaked bark and golden leaves all made from different colored wooden chips, sanded smooth and made shiny with lacquer. Olivia picked it up, turning it over and over. "How does it open?" she asked.

Mr. Darlington took it from her. "This is one of my aunt's puzzle boxes." He scanned the table. "I wonder where the rest are. She has more than a dozen. She collects them. Each has a secret way of maneuvering a splinter or sliding a panel or pushing a button." He ran his fingers over the box, but nothing happened. He put it down. "I don't know how to open it."

Olivia ran her fingers over the tree and its golden leaves, but the box felt smooth. She could see no way to open it.

"Why did you want to show me the Admiral's collection?"

"I wanted you to know what kind of man he is." The

bitter edge to Mr. Darlington's voice was grating. He took a step toward Olivia, standing uncomfortably close. He didn't look at her, instead fingering a small stone carving.

"I didn't want you fooled by his gift to my aunt of the Emrubdiam. He is not a generous man."

Before she could respond, there was a sound behind them, and the Admiral entered the room with the twins. The older man's voice was loud and friendly, "Jolly good! Still here, are you? The charades have been canceled, and these lovely young ladies want to view my collection. Impressive, what?"

"It's amazing," Olivia said.

"I was fortunate to travel as a young man. Always had an eye for the collectible. In Africa, in '72–"

The pink twin gave out an excited shriek and the Admiral's attention was taken. He turned to Anne, chuckled, and began speaking to her about something on a table. He lifted a piece and moved to the corner of the room and a large armchair. "Let's look at this here," he said, sitting on the chair. To Olivia's surprise, Anne walked over to him and sat on his lap. She took the figurine from him, examining it closely and saying something the actress could not hear. They both laughed.

Olivia stared at the scene. Emily continued to admire pieces on a table and even looked up to ask the Admiral a question. He responded to her as though he did not have a young woman sitting on his lap. The young woman on his lap held out her arm, admiring a golden bracelet she'd slipped onto her delicate wrist.

"Seen enough?" asked Mr. Darlington.

"Yes," said Olivia. "My brother will be wondering where I am."

As they exited the room, she saw that the candles in the corridor had been extinguished. Irritated, Mr. Darlington said it was a common joke of the Admiral. He returned to the collection room to get a candle. They walked down the corridor, the way dimly lit by the candle. He stopped beneath the first wall sconce, but instead of lighting it, he turned and grabbed Olivia by the wrist, bringing her hand to his mouth and drenching it with open-mouthed kisses.

Olivia pulled her hand from his grasp, saying, "Sir!"

"I've never felt like this before," said Mr. Darlington. The candle trembled in his hand. "Please, say I may come to your room tonight."

"Of course not!" Olivia was appalled. Could he tell she was an actress? Would he have made such a request to the daughter of a princess? Was this how men treated all women?

He mumbled something incomprehensible and tried to move closer. She pushed him away. "No! You may not. Leave me alone!" Olivia hurried down the dark corridor, knowing that it was only a few steps to the passage with lamps. She could hear him stumbling behind her.

After a few steps, she saw a light approaching. Mrs. Bracknell, Mr. Darlington's aunt, was walking along with a candle. Her steps were not straight, and this was not only because of her limp and cane. An odor of alcohol preceded her. The little dog made a soft growling noise.

The admiral's wife didn't seem to notice Olivia in the darkness. The older woman stumbled, and Olivia reached out to steady her.

"Are you all right?"

"I've the headache and an idiot for a husband," said Mrs. Bracknell. She held the candle up better to see Olivia's face. "Oh, it's you. You look just like your mother."

Earlier, Philip had claimed she looked like their father. Was this a trick? "I didn't realize you know Maman. Most people think I look like Papa."

"I knew them both," she said, waving the hand that held her cane, throwing off her balance. She staggered and the candle slipped out of her hand. It made a small thud, and they were thrown into darkness. Olivia wondered where Mr. Darlington had scampered off to.

"Damn," said Mrs. Bracknell. Her little dog barked.

"Let me help you." Olivia put her arm around the older lady and led her back toward the drawing room.

They staggered around a corner to be met by the gas lighting. They must have been near the drawing room, but Olivia had lost her bearings. She reached another hall and was unsure which way to turn. Mrs. Bracknell seemed befuddled.

"Crumpet, come to Mama," she said, leaning her cane against the wall. As she awkwardly bent to pick up the dog, she slid down the wall and sat gently on the floor.

Olivia crouched down. Philip and Mr. Darlington arrived at the same moment from different directions.

"Is she all right?" asked Mr. Darlington.

"What happened?" asked Philip.

Olivia started to explain, but Mrs. Bracknell, who was being lifted by the men, spoke first. "Where's the Admiral? With the twins?"

Mr. Darlington smiled mischievously. "Yes, he's with the twins," he answered. "They're looking at the collection. Shall I take you?"

"Maybe you would prefer for me to help you to your room?" Olivia suggested.

Philip said, "Perhaps we could ask the butler to find her maid?"

Mr. Darlington laughed. "Oh, no. I think it would be better if we found what the Admiral and the Greenpin twins are doing, don't you Auntie?"

Mrs. Bracknell harrumphed, shaking off Peter and Philip

who were both holding her elbows, ready to escort her. "I'm not an invalid, and I'm not deaf. I can find my husband on my own." She hobbled down the corridor, the others watching her go.

"She won't have a light for the dark corridor," said Olivia.

"I'll go with her," said Peter, who held a candle.

Philip and Olivia watched him walk away, then Philip asked, "What happened?"

Olivia shrugged. "She was acting cantankerous and fell, maybe drunk, maybe not. She said I looked like my mother and that she knew both my mother and father. It was unclear if she meant your parents or my real parents."

They stood quietly.

"Is the charade over, then?" asked Philip.

"We'll have to see what happens in the morning." Olivia yawned, suddenly overcome with fatigue. "I'm knackered," she said. "Do you suppose it's too early to retire?"

"Knackered?" laughed Philip. "I hope you haven't been talking thus to the gentry."

She shook her head. "Only for you, dear brother."

"As host and hostess are otherwise engaged, I suppose we can show ourselves to our rooms." Philip offered his arm and Olivia took it gratefully. They walked up the stairs.

Philip asked, "What did you think of the Admiral's present to his wife?"

"The jewels are beautiful, but as a necklace it is . . . ostentatious."

"Too large for your delicate neck."

They paused outside her door.

"You shouldn't flirt with your sister."

"Did that sound like flirting? Saying my sister has a delicate neck? It is true, you know. As do you. Most young ladies do, unless they are overweight or have some sort of physical deformity."

Olivia's eyes sparkled. "I see. You weren't flirting, merely being precise." She wondered if he would try to kiss her and realized he would not. The thought was such a relief, she felt a tightness in her shoulders relax.

"Lock your door tonight," Philip said. "This is an odd crowd, and I don't trust a one of them."

Olivia debated whether to tell him about Mr. Darlington and his request to come to her chamber. She decided not to. Philip would only worry or get angry. He was right. This was an odd crowd, and she didn't trust a one of them either. Except Philip. And that was nice. She said good-night and closed and locked her door.

The hackney dropped Genevieve, Lily and Oscar Wilde off at Shepherdess Walk. Despite the late hour, people milled about in front of the music hall, including a boy who couldn't be much more than seven chasing a ball around. Mr. Wilde led the ladies through the Eagle's grand entrance and into the tighter crowds inside. They acquired a box on the ground level, and Genevieve rushed to the rail to look about.

A man danced on the stage and maybe sang; it was hard to tell from the noise of the crowd. Nobody appeared to be watching his performance. The floor of the theater was a crush with people sitting, drinking, and talking, and throngs maneuvering between the tables. A cluster of three women stood chatting and smoking. A boy sold nuts out of an open box he carried with straps around his neck.

A man at a crowded table directly in front of them turned and winked at Genevieve. She blushed and drew back, but he stood from his table and came right up to the box.

"Two lovely ladies come to sit by me." He took off his top hat and made a farcical bow, then grabbed Genevieve's hand and kissed it. "Mr. Baxter-Point. Can I offer you champagne? burgundy?"

She was speechless at his boldness.

Mr. Wilde leaned over the edge of the box and said, "Hallo, Dex. Who's on stage tonight?"

The man glanced over his shoulder at the stage and

shrugged. "No idea. Who's this?"

Genevieve raised an eyebrow at being called "this." Mr. Wilde answered without hesitation.

"The beautiful and clever Miss Olivia Snow, with her young protégée, Miss Lily Rambling. May I present to you Mr. Dexter Baxter-Point, who is certainly the slowest-witted man of my acquaintance."

Mr. Baxter-Point smiled and tipped his hat at the introduction, ignoring or unaware of the insult.

"How do you do?" Genevieve said.

"Oh, look, there's Dominic," said Mr. Wilde, leaping the rail and disappearing in the crowd on the floor.

"Miss Snow? You that actress lady everyone talks crazy of?" asked Mr. Baxter-Point.

Before Genevieve could answer, Lily said, "She's an actress, but she ain't crazy."

"Yes, yes. Do you mind?" he said, pulling himself up by the rail and clumsily rolling into the box. He landed in a heap on the floor, then stood and brushed himself off as though it were the most natural thing in the world.

"Great pleasure! Meaning to meet you. Here you are. Do you mind?" he asked, pulling a chair and sitting so close that he and Genevieve were practically touching. She tried to move her chair, but he grabbed her hand and kissed the buttons on her glove.

Genevieve gaped. Lily covered her laughter by coughing, then said, "Champagne would be lovely, don't you think, Olivia?"

"Champagne? Oh, yes! Or ratafia. I'd prefer ratafia," Genevieve said, pulling her hand away and placing it on her lap.

Mr. Baxter-Point grinned stupidly and stood. "Ratafia? Don't know. Try. Do you mind?" he said, disappearing out the back of the box.

When the door shut, Lily erupted into giggles.

"What an odd man," Genevieve said, examining her pearl buttons for saliva.

"He thinks you're Olivia," Lily said. "Men are like that with her. You best be careful. She bein' an actress they think she's fast. Most women who come to a place like this are. What's ratafia?"

"A drink that was popular ages ago. Miss Snow said she is known for being old fashioned so I thought ordering ratafia would be like her."

Lily shrugged. "I never heard of it, but that don't signify."

Genevieve dragged her chair away from Mr. Baxter-Point's and closer to the rail. The male singer was no longer on stage; instead, there was a girl, who couldn't be much more than fifteen, singing a song about being seduced and abandoned while winking at the men in the audience. Her voice was only passable, but it was loud, and she engaged well with the crowd, who paid her more attention than they had the male performer. A man at a table near the stage stood and yelled. The singer laughed and tossed her head in his direction. The people nearby laughed in response.

Genevieve leaned farther out, trying to hear better, when she was grabbed by the shoulders, rolled over the rail and into the arms of an extremely large man.

She struggled briefly and the man, as hairy as a bear with breath like a tavern floor, set her down. "Careful little lady," he said, slurring his words. "I was just helping yeh, so yeh didna fall."

"How dare you! I wasn't going to fall!"

"Yeh're a lively one," he said and before she knew what was happening, he put his hands over both her ears and pulled her head toward him, smothering her lips with his tangled beard and noxious breath. Before Genevieve could even struggle, he'd let her go and turned his back, walking away and laughing deeply.

"Here, get back in the box," said Lily from the box, pointing to the short corridor which led to the back of the boxes. Wiping her mouth on her sleeve, Genevieve stumbled against another man, who ignored her. As quickly as she could, she dashed to the box door, keeping her head down. Trembling, she sat in her chair and pushed it well away from the rail.

Lily said, "I told you to be careful. Well, no harm done."

"No harm done! How can you say such a thing?" Genevieve objected. "That man, that bear, that ogre. He kissed me. Oh, it was revolting!"

Lily only laughed.

Before Genevieve could say more, the door opened. Mr. Baxter-Point entered with a bottle of ratafia and three glasses.

Genevieve drank swiftly, the strong fruit flavor doing much to hide the repulsive taste of the bear-ogre-man.

They watched the various performers and chatted with Mr. Baxter-Point, who could not move his chair closer to Genevieve because of a small table she had maneuvered between them and which now held the ratafia.

Mr. Wilde returned with his friend Dominic, Dominic's sister Adele, and Adele's husband, whose name neither Lily nor Genevieve caught because none of the newcomers were properly presented. Genevieve realized that a lack of introductions was probably for the best as Mr. Wilde might well have forgotten she was Olivia Snow. He was on his way to being foxed, drinking directly from a bottle of champagne and obsessing on Dominic's hand-bag.

"I don't believe there's nothing in it," Oscar said "Why would you bring a hand-bag to a music hall if it were empty?"

"Because it's such a lovely hand-bag," answered Dominic.

Mr. Wilde nodded. "It is a lovely hand-bag: large, black leather, handles. Why did I not think to bring my hand-bag?

It's a bold statement to carry an empty hand-bag."

"It isn't his hand-bag," Dominic's sister offered.

Dominic tried to hush her, but she continued, "It was given to him at the cloak room at Victoria Station instead of his own bag, but he didn't notice."

"Not at the time, I didn't. It's a much nicer bag, but it doesn't contain the things I took on my travels."

"Whose things does it contain?" Lily asked.

Dominic frowned. "It doesn't contain anything. Given to me empty. But it is so much nicer than my hand-bag that I've decided to keep it."

Mr. Baxter-Point studied the bag carefully and declared that it had been manufactured in Birmingham. "Says right here," he said, pointing to an inscription that said it had been manufactured in Birmingham.

Another bottle of ratafia was brought in.

"What on earth are you drinking?" asked Mr. Wilde, making a show of looking around. "Is my grandmother here?"

"The ratafia is for me," Genevieve said proudly. "I'm a very old-fashioned woman."

Mr. Wilde met her eyes and laughed. "Yes, yes, so you are, Miss Snow. I'd almost forgotten."

"Old fashioned?" Mr. Baxter-Point opened his eyes wide. Raising his arm and pointing his finger to the ceiling, he proclaimed, "The berlin!"

Before anyone could ask him what he meant, a disturbance at a box directly across from them captured their attention. A tight crush hid what was happening, but then a man tumbled backward, opening the crowd. Another man shook his fist at the fallen man.

"Did you see that?" asked Dominic's sister's husband. "He knocked Eddie the Giant a facer. I wonder how many he got."

The fallen man stood and wobbled away from the crowd.

He was the bear-ogre-man.

"Is that Eddie the Giant?" Genevieve asked, pointing at the staggering man.

Mr. Baxter-Point answered. "Kisses ladies. Gets slugged." Turning to Mr. Wilde, he asked, "Number?"

Mr. Wilde shrugged. "I got here too late."

"I wagered fifteen. Best see if I've won anything," said Dominic's sister's husband, holding up a slip of paper and exiting the box.

"He kissed Miss Snow," said Lily, "but he didn't kiss me."

"Huzzah!" cried Dominic.

Dominic's sister laughed shrilly, and everyone congratulated Genevieve, for being kissed, and Lily, for not being kissed. What had seemed traumatic to Genevieve earlier now seemed droll.

Dominic's sister's husband returned with the information that he had wagered too high. Eddie the Giant had only kissed eight girls before being slugged.

By the time they left their box, the crowd had thinned to nothing, the stage performers long finished. They stood outside the Eagle, looking for a hackney. There were several on the street, but others were climbing in. Soon the street was empty and quiet except for the low chatter of the Eagle's last patrons walking away. Mr. Wilde offered to walk to the corner, in search of a hackney.

A gilded berlin carriage, much like Cinderella's transformed pumpkin, turned the corner and stopped in front of them. Mr. Baxter-Point opened the door. Genevieve giggled, realizing this was what he'd meant when he'd shouted "old fashioned" and "berlin."

"Do you mind?" he asked. A strangely worded request, but the invitation was obvious, and the berlin would easily fit them all.

"Why, thank you," said Genevieve, taking his hand and

climbing the steps into the carriage. The impression of beauty was not replicated inside. The interior needed refurbishing. The cushioned seats were flat and threadbare, the window curtain hung at a crooked angle.

"Do you mind?" Mr. Baxter-Point said to Lily, pushing her back. He quickly pulled the steps into the carriage, shut the door, and banged for the driver to go.

"Wait," said Genevieve, "you've closed the door on Lily." She glanced out the window to see Mr. Wilde's friends smiling and waving, but she couldn't see Lily or Oscar. "I can't leave Lily behind. And I certainly can't be here without her."

Mr. Baxter-Point shook his head. "Don't want her." Pointing his finger at the ceiling, in the same ridiculous way had earlier in the evening, he shouted, "Abduction!"

This time, the meaning was clear.

With his ersatz sister safely locked in her chamber, Philip returned to the drawing room. Kelvil's presence bothered him. He had known him at Oxford; they had stayed at the same boardinghouse for several months, Kelvil eventually leaving, but not before disrupting the establishment. He was sly and slippery with no moral sense.

Kelvil had gotten their maid pregnant. A girl not much older than fifteen, sweet and cheerful. She left biscuits out after each cleaning, her mother being the establishment's cook. Philip imagined that Kelvil had tricked her into the relationship, possibly even forcing himself on her. As the one who cleaned their rooms, she would have been conveniently available, alone, with no protection. One day, the girl's mother came to Philip's rooms and begged him to tell her where Kelvil had gone. At first Philip didn't understand why she wanted to know, but when he realized her daughter's condition he understood. Kelvil was allegedly traveling with his family on the Continent, but his departure coincided so perfectly with the girl's pregnancy, there could be little doubt that he'd fled. Philip offered to use his connections in France to find him but saw little chance of success.

Term ended, Philip traveled to Monaco, making inquiries but finding no trace of Kelvil. When he returned to England in the fall, the mother and daughter were no longer employed by the boardinghouse. Rumor was that the girl had killed herself.

The only guests who remained in the drawing room were Mr. Greenpin, Miss Greenpin, Miss Darlington, and the Admiral. Mr. Kelvil and Dr. Goring were present but had ordered their carriage and were saying their *au revoir*'s.

The Admiral was trying to convince them to stay the night, ensuring them that chambers had already been arranged for their comfort.

"I'm afraid I must be available to my patients. It is in the darkness of night that many find themselves needing attention."

"Quite. Quite," said the Admiral, "but there is no such call for your time, Mr. Kelvil. Surely you can stay?"

Mr. Kelvil laughed. "I have my own responsibilities to return to, Admiral, as you very well know."

"Come early for the hunt, then. You are both riding out, yes?"

They agreed, and the Admiral placed his hand on Kelvil's back, moving with the men to the door.

Philip turned his attention to Mr. Greenpin who sat in a chair in a far corner of the room, talking to himself. Philip hadn't spoken with the older man and had nearly forgotten his presence. He'd been told by the widow Bracknell that Mr. Greenpin fancied himself a poet, with his head in the clouds and his eyes lost in some otherworld fog. She believed it was a pity his wife had died after the birth of the twins, as she might have been able to control them more effectively. After trying to converse with Mr. Greenpin, Philip agreed with the widow. The man smiled often but was difficult to talk to. He mumbled in rhyme and never made eye contact. Philip was uncertain that Mr. Greenpin recognized his attempt to start a conversation.

The eldest Miss Greenpin had been watching the exchange. She apologized to Philip, explaining that when her father was working on a poem he often found it difficult to focus on anything else. She convinced her father to retire and left with him.

Those left in the drawing room soon agreed that the morning would arrive before they were ready for it and bade one another *bonne nuit.*

Mr. Baxter-Point shouted, "Abduction!" again.

Genevieve frowned at him. "Stop saying that." She wondered if he knew she was Genevieve Lamb and planned to ask for a ransom. His dull eyes wandered over her, and she remembered that he was a very stupid man.

"What can you mean by abducting me?" Genevieve asked. "You can't expect to receive a ransom for an actress. Besides, everyone at the Eagle saw me leave with you."

He nodded happily. "Witnesses."

In spite of the seriousness of the situation, Genevieve couldn't bring herself to fear Mr. Baxter-Point, a man who couldn't talk in complete sentences. There was no way he could bring this off, yet here she was in a fancy berlin carriage with him, bound for . . . .

"Where are you taking me?" Genevieve asked.

"Home."

"To meet your mother?"

Mr. Baxter-Point guffawed.

"Where do you live?" she asked, not expecting an answer but getting a full explanation from the dullard about his rooms in London and his family's estate up north and his favorite place of all, a little hunting lodge in Leicestershire, where he was taking her. Genevieve racked her brain trying to remember where Leicestershire was but could not place it on a map.

"Do you think we could stop at my home so I could pack a trunk or, at least, a few bandboxes?"

This made Mr. Baxter-Point guffaw again, an annoying sound and a singularly unpleasant sight.

"Why have you abducted me?"

"The wager. I'm going to win. Nobody thought I'd win, but I'm going to win."

Genevieve wrinkled her brow. "What wager?"

"Jeremy Dottingham. Rodney Willes-Smith. James Blacknell. Peter Darlington. Earl of Montmarch. We wagered for Olivia Snow's virginity. I'm going to win."

Genevieve gasped. He thought she was Olivia!

Looking quite pleased with himself, Mr. Baxter-Point leaned back in the corner of his seat, stretching one arm along the top cushion and stretching the other along the door, resting his forearm on the door handle.

The carriage hit a bump and jolted, causing Genevieve to fall back in her seat. Mr. Baxter-Point's weight fell against the door, where his arm leaned on the door handle. The door flew open and, with a screech, he tumbled from the carriage.

Genevieve's laugh came out as a snort. She slid to the window and looked out. The bright moonlight revealed his body in a heap at the side of the road. Mr. Baxter-Point rolled over, stood, and brushed himself off, much as he had earlier when he had fallen into her theater box. Confident he was not injured, Genevieve saw no reason to alert the driver of the missing passenger, at least not until they were a good deal beyond where he had fallen. She giggled and watched out the window. The moonlight washed the countryside in silver. Soon the sway of the carriage and the several glasses of ratafia had their effect. Genevieve closed her eyes and slept.

The ceasing of the carriage woke Genevieve. They were

at an old posting inn. She wondered how far from London they'd come. She opened the door and leapt out, not bothering with the steps. The driver was handling the horses and paid her no mind, so she looked about. A sign indicated The Benbow Inn. It appeared respectable, from what she could tell by moonlight. The yard was neat and well groomed and flower baskets hung beneath each front window. Several of the upper rooms still showed light. Noise and light flowed from the downstairs windows.

The berlin's driver called out. "Where's the sir?" He had the carriage door open and was looking around the yard.

"He tumbled from the carriage just outside London," Genevieve replied.

"He never!"

"He did."

"Where are we?" The sound of Oscar Wilde's voice behind her made Genevieve jump. Her jaw dropped to her silk slippers at the sight of him and Lily climbing out of the berlin's small back seat.

"Lily! Oscar! However did you get there?"

Lily said, "When that cork-brained fellow shut the door on me and started up the carriage, I realized what he was about, so I grabbed Mr. Wilde and we ran after. When you slowed at the turn, we jumped up back."

Genevieve stared at the seat and the unguarded back wheels of the berlin. "While it was in motion? You could have fallen under the wheels!"

"That would be a stupid thing to do," said Lily.

"Pushing Dex out was brilliant," said Oscar. "Quite the funniest thing I've seen in years."

"I didn't push him. He leaned on the door handle and fell out."

Lily and Oscar looked at each other with wide eyes and laughed.

"No man can escape his own intelligence," said Oscar.

Looking around, Genevieve asked. "Where do you suppose we are?"

Lily shrugged.

"I've no idea," replied Oscar. "I fell asleep ten minutes into the journey."

"I fell asleep too," said Genevieve. "Well, join me inside the carriage and we can pick up your friend on the way back to London."

They turned, but the carriage was no longer behind them.

"No, wait!" shouted Lily, running toward the berlin which had left the inn's yard and started down the road. Lily yelled and ran, stopping when she realized it was no use.

"I can't believe he's left us here," she told the other two when she had returned, out of breath.

"He's Dex's man. Probably gone to find him," said Oscar.

"How will we return to London? My mum will roast me if I'm not back soon. She's probably pacing the kitchen right now."

Genevieve sighed. "There's naught we can do. I'll talk to your mum tomorrow and explain. We'll have to spend the night here and take a train in the morning."

"I wonder if they have champagne," said Mr. Wilde. "The road has given me a thirst."

Lily shook her head. "Can't we find a carriage or wagon? I can't stay here. My mum will be frantic."

"We can ask," said Genevieve doubtfully.

The inn's front hall was clean and tidy. Despite the late hour, they could see through a door that the tap room was busy. A woman descended stairs and startled at the sight of them.

"Our carriage broke down and we need to get to London," said Genevieve. "Is there someone who could drive us?"

The woman looked shocked. "At this hour? London? We don't have nothin' that would take you that far in the dark. We're no longer a posting inn since the railway. You could take the morning train. The nine o'clock."

Lily covered her face. Oscar patted her back and made supportive noises.

Genevieve asked, "That's what we'll do then. Do you have rooms?"

"I've just the two left."

"Wonderful," said Genevieve. "Lily and I will share, and Mr. Wilde can take the other."

They signed the register, Genevieve remembering at the last moment to be Olivia Snow, and the innkeeper's wife led them to the stairs.

"I'll stay here and make some friends," said Oscar, indicating the tap room. As the two women began to climb the stairs, Oscar grabbed Genevieve's arm. "A wager for you. I bet that I can befriend every man here before I go to bed."

Genevieve looked through the tap room door. She could see about half a dozen or so men of varying ages. "That's a foolish bet," she answered. "If you buy a man a drink, he will call you friend."

Oscar's eyes sparkled. "I like that. Like a proverb. If you buy a man a drink, he will call you friend. No, I have it: If you give a man a drink, he will be your friend, but if you teach a man to drink he will be your husband."

"I don't understand."

"See, a wife makes a man drink, teaches him to drink. So, if you teach a man to drink, then you are married to him. He is your husband."

Genevieve shook her head. "You'll need to work on that."

When Olivia awoke, the loneliness of the bed frightened her. Etta's warm little body was missing–where was she? This confusion and worry pumped adrenaline, bringing clear understanding followed by a wakefulness she could not subdue. Olivia lay in the darkness, missing Etta and the ease of a day spent at home. Today she must don the cloak of Miss Lamb and pour all her energy into being someone else.

The comfort of sleep moved farther and farther away. She turned from left side to right side, but the room was stuffy and hot. Her nightgown tangled around her legs, becoming damp with sweat. Reluctantly, she slipped out of bed and drew back the heavy curtain shielding the window. The sky was white with dawn, the early autumn sun not yet visible above the trees. She opened the window to let out the stale night air. Leaning on the sill, Olivia marveled at the freshness of the country. The air felt light, redolent of grass and wood and flower, so much nicer than the coal-smoke weighted fog of London. Etta would like it here.

Her window looked upon the back of the house, a wide lawn extending off to a wood in the distance. Directly below the window was a brick terrace, bordered by tall red flowers and thick shrubbery. She could hear the distant sound of voices. Beyond the garden, figures moved about the carriage house and stables, getting the horses ready for the hunt. Elbows solidly on the sill, Olivia took in all there was to see and unconsciously twirled the ring on her pinkie finger.

As she pulled herself back into the room, the ring spun loose, dropping to the ground below. Olivia gasped. Miss Genevieve Lamb's ring. Not the engagement ring, thank God, but the Lamb signet ring. The family tradition. Olivia watched as the silver circle rolled across the terrace bricks, off the side, and into the hedges. She stared, heart pounding, memorizing the location.

Quickly throwing on a day dress and slippers, she donned a light mantle for more modesty and left her chamber. The manor was dark and quiet. Servants were certainly up and busy, but Olivia neither heard nor saw anyone. Her chamber was near the end of a long corridor, and she debated which way to go. The main staircase would take her to the front entrance hall. She had no idea how to gain a door to the back of the house and walking entirely around Hudson Hall was out of the question. There was a servant staircase at the end of the corridor just down from her chamber. She dashed to it.

To her great relief, the stairs opened onto a small hall where boot brushes, mops, buckets, and other supplies were neatly arranged. Across the small hall was a door leading to the back exterior of the house. The area was quiet and empty of servants.

Outside, she found a path leading from the servants' door to the terrace. The flowers and shrubbery were thicker and more disorganized than they had appeared from above. She knelt on the terrace stones and felt all around the plants, moving leaves and peering into the depths. She could not see the ring. At the edge of the terrace bricks the ground sloped slightly; the ring must have rolled down farther. She squeezed between the manor house and the edge of the shrubs to move down the slope, her eyes searching carefully. On the other side of the shrubs was a border of pink and white chrysanthemums interspersed with some pink and purple flowers. A flicker of something shiny caught her eye. The ring lay between the hedge and the orange flowers. She took a few small steps, her eyes focused on the ring. She crouched carefully and plucked it from the dirt. Thank God!

Climbing back onto the terrace, she examined her slippers. In her hurry out of her room, she had flung on the white indoor slippers that Miss Lamb had bought for her a few days ago. The worst of all possible shoes to wear in a muddy garden. One wasn't too bad, but the other was probably ruined.

She dragged her feet on the grass as she walked back to the servants' entrance, but her effort did little to clean the slippers. In the small hall, she sat on the bench and scrubbed the muddy one with a boot brush. The brush merely moved the mess about. One bucket had several inches of water in it, so she wet the brush. As she sat again to scrub, a side door to the hall opened and a young maid walked in. Olivia froze, slipper in one hand, wet brush in the other.

The maid's face was all confusion. After a moment of staring at one another, the maid spoke, "Ma'am?"

Olivia swallowed thickly. "I was out for a walk and my slipper got muddy . . . ." Olivia trailed off. There was no possible explanation that was going to work. A true lady would not be found in a storeroom at the bottom of a servant staircase cleaning her slipper. It would never occur to a lady to clean a muddy slipper herself. Olivia could see the young maid looking at her un-lady-like hands. They were scratched and turning red and puffy; she had scraped them on some thorny bush. A lady without gloves cleaning her muddy slipper. Perhaps she would merely think Olivia odd.

The maid reached for the brush and slipper. "I'll do that." Her words were spoken in a strange mix of hauteur and subservience.

"Yes, see that you do," said Olivia, lifting her chin. She wondered whether to dart up the inappropriate staircase or to wander the main part of the house searching for the main staircase while wearing only one mildly dirty slipper. She chose the servant stairs, taking them two at a time. So far, the morning was not proceeding well.

Back in her chamber, fatigue washed over Olivia. The men and any ladies who were going on the hunt would soon be up and breakfasting, but no one expected the ladies not riding out to get up early. She returned to bed.

She dozed, maybe slumbered, until woken abruptly by a scream from somewhere in the house. She lay in bed, heart pounding, and waited for more. No other sound was forthcoming. Had it been a dream? She slid from the sheets and poked her head out the chamber door. No one was about. Perhaps she had dreamed it.

Pulling open the curtains, Olivia invited in the daylight. The air was warm and bright. She opened her wardrobe and studied the gowns available to her. They were all so beautiful. She pulled out a sea green day dress and laid it on her bed. Then she remembered that a maid should be called to help her dress. She rang for one, then moved to her dressing table.

Her clothes had been unpacked and placed in the wardrobe after their arrival, but her bag of personal items (mostly Genevieve's as Olivia's personal items were ragged and worn) had been only been partially unpacked: a brush and comb, rosewater, and lace handkerchiefs were on the table, but her tooth powder and brush and some other items were still in the bag, including an apothecary envelope she didn't remember packing. Was it from Genevieve? Olivia opened the flap and poured its contents onto her palm. Cloves. From Mr. Rambling.

The knock on the door frightened her. She jumped, spilling the cloves into the hairbrush. She tried to pull one out but only managed to move the cloves farther down among the bristles and old hair. She groaned. These cloves would not be going in her mouth. Again, the knock. Olivia sighed. Weren't servants supposed to enter rooms quietly and invisibly?

She wrapped a robe over her nightgown and pulled open the door, surprised to find Philip Lamb in the corridor. His eyes bore wrinkles at the corners and his expression was grave.

"The hunt was canceled. Mrs. Bracknell, the Admiral's wife, died this morning."

"Good heavens!" Olivia exclaimed, inviting him into her room. "Poor woman. She wasn't that old, was she? And she seemed perfectly healthy last night. Did she die in her sleep?"

"Poisoned. She was murdered."

Olivia's eyes widened. "Murdered? Poison? Why? When? How?" She took a deep breath and collapsed on her dressing table chair.

Philip stayed by the door. "This morning, when she was having her tea. There was something in the milk, they think. Her little dog died too, which is why they suspect poison."

Olivia felt nauseated. She had almost gone down to breakfast earlier. She could have drunk of that milk. "Has anyone else become ill? If it was the milk . . . ."

Philip shook his head. "She took breakfast in her chamber, early. A maid found her only a little while ago."

"The scream," said Olivia. "It wasn't a dream."

"Her chamber is below this one. She began sleeping on the ground floor after she injured her knee."

167

"What will we do? Shall we leave? The Admiral can't want a houseful of guests at a time like this."

"We can't leave, of course," said Philip. "We are suspects. The Admiral is the chief constable for the district, though he'll need to call in someone to investigate. He's understandably distraught. I offered to help, as did Kelvil. The local police, which is just a volunteer force, has been called."

"Good God. This is horrible."

Philip nodded.

Olivia shook her head, wishing she'd never agreed to this stupid wager. Regret turned to dread, then to alarm. "I must tell everyone who I am," she said. "I cannot lie to the police."

Philip nodded. "First thing, I should think. We're all to meet in the breakfast room. Knock on my door when you're ready. We can go in together."

He jumped away from the door as it opened. A young maid entered, mumbling an apology.

"Dress quickly," said Philip, shutting the door behind him.

The maid was Abigail, the same girl who had helped Olivia last evening. She was pretty, maybe sixteen or seventeen with thick ginger hair escaping beneath her cap and a sprinkling of freckles on her cheeks.

Olivia asked her how the servants were holding up. She glanced at Olivia strangely.

"Quite well," she answered. "We aren't used to house guests, but there aren't so many of you."

Olivia nodded slowly. Could she be unaware of Mrs. Bracknell's murder?

Olivia was dressed quickly. She let Abigail put her hair in a simple knot.

"If that be all, miss, I'm needed by some of the other ladies."

"Yes, that's all. Thank you, Abigail."

The breakfast room was warm and bright, windows to the east bringing in the morning sunshine. Colorful flowers served as centerpieces, their floral fragrance competing with the scent of bacon. It was inappropriately cheerful.

Mr. Greenpin was the only other guest in the room. As Genevieve and Philip sat beside him, he put away the book he had been reading.

"Beautiful day for a ride," he said, smiling. "Let's hope the sun doesn't hide."

Olivia looked at Philip. He leaned and whispered in her ear. "He wasn't in the stables this morning. I don't think he knows."

"Has anyone else been in to breakfast?" Philip asked Mr. Greenpin.

"I believe we are the first down. No one else has made a sound. I hope they won't be late. The fox won't wait behind the gate." He smiled broadly.

Philip cleared his throat. "Actually, sir–"

Before Philip could explain, Mr. Greenpin's eldest daughter burst into the room. "Is it true? Mrs. Bracknell's been murdered? Emily and Anne said she had been, but I don't know whether to believe them."

Frances Greenpin's face was flushed, almost excited.

The silver slid from Mr. Greenpin's hands, crashing onto his plate. His knife tumbled to the floor. He had gone pale, confusion drawing lines on his face. "Mrs. Bracknell? Unwell?"

Philip answered. "I'm afraid it's true, sir. A maid found her this morning. Her necklace was stolen."

"Her necklace was stolen?" repeated Olivia, surprised.

"Was it a robbery, then?" asked Miss Greenpin. "Mrs. Bracknell surprised the thief?"

Philip shook his head. "That seems unlikely, given that she and her dog were poisoned."

169

Mrs. Greenpin's eyes sparkled. "Ah, yes. If she'd startled the thief, he would have bashed in her head or straggled her. Poison, though. How strange."

Olivia shuddered.

Chiltern entered the room. "The Admiral has asked that you remain in the breakfast room until such time that he can come to you. The other guests are dressing and will be here shortly. If there is anything you need, please ask the staff, and we will accommodate."

Philip moved to the butler and spoke to him quietly. The servant nodded and left the room.

"The Admiral is interviewing the servants in the morning room," said Philip, "although Dr. Goring is trying to get him to relax and lie down. The village police should be here shortly, and–"

He was interrupted by Mr. Greenpin. "Is this all a tease? Explanation, please!"

Philip and Olivia shared a glance. Philip said. "Someone has murdered Mrs. Bracknell and stolen her necklace. It isn't a joke."

Mr. Greenpin muttered gibberish then went silent. His face blanched. Olivia reached out and squeezed his hand to comfort him and was surprised by how cold he felt.

In a few minutes, the rest of the guests arrived, and the breakfast room became noisy with conversation and the clinking of silver.

The widow Bracknell heaped a great deal of food onto her plate and commented that now she need not worry about being locked up at Kelvil's Sanctuary for the Elderly and Infirm.

Olivia studied the guests. Few seemed distressed by Mrs. Bracknell's murder. The Darlingtons came in last with sober faces. With their aunt's death, they must have very little hope of regaining their inheritance. Unless, of course, they had stolen the Emrubdiam of Khartoum. They might be able to live comfortably for many years on the black-market sale of its jewels.

Peter and Jane Darlington sat together at the end of the table, whispering. She studied them carefully. Miss Darlington spoke quietly and at great length. Peter wore his ubiquitous sneer, until Miss Darlington reached the end of her monologue and his eyes sparkled with mirth. She frowned at him.

Olivia turned to Mr. Greenpin.

"Did you write last night? I've heard that poets write at night and last night was such a beautiful one. Just the sort in which one might be expected to find inspiration."

Mr. Greenpin wrinkled his forehead. His face was less pale, but he had been quiet though most of breakfast. He answered in a barely audible murmur, "Tick, tock, writer's block."

Olivia had no idea how to answer that, so she turned to Philip who was talking to the pink twin. When Anne had entered the room, her eyes were red and swollen as if she had been crying. She sat on Philip's right, and Olivia could easily hear their conversation.

"Nana had been sick for a long time, so her death wasn't a surprise, not like Mrs. Bracknell's, and I hardly know, knew, Mrs. Bracknell and I'd lived with Nana my whole life, and I don't understand why the news of Mrs. Bracknell's passing should make me think so much of Nana now." She took a shuddering breath.

The Admiral burst into the room. Dr. Goring and Kelvil followed on his heels.

Everyone looked up, but the Admiral had eyes only for Olivia.

"Who are you?!" he shouted, extending his arm, and pointing his finger at her. His eyes bulged, his face red and

171

blotchy.

Philip stood and answered for her. "This is Miss Olivia Snow, the actress. She was hired to play the part of my sister, as a wager. It was arranged by Mr. Oscar Wilde and Mrs. Markby. It was meant for everyone's amusement, with no ill intent."

Olivia stood. "I'm so sorry for your loss, sir. And I apologize for coming into your home under false pretenses."

The Admiral paid little attention to their explanations and apologies. Continuing to point and now shaking his hand at Olivia, he shouted, "She knew you, you," he struggled for a word and gave up. "Is that why you killed her?"

Olivia's face flushed and she gasped. "No!" she cried out. "Then, confused said, "Yes! I mean, Mrs. Bracknell might have recognized me. I wasn't sure. She said she knew my parents, and Philip didn't think she knew his parents. But either way, I didn't kill her. I promise you. I had nothing to do with her death."

In his anger, the Admiral forgot to breathe, turning his face scarlet. "There's evidence, what. A maid saw you. This morning. You left my wife's chamber by the windows and returned by the servants' entrance."

An eerie silence descended on the room. Every guest, every servant stared at Olivia, convicting her. She realized now that she had been given a role and had accepted it, without having read the full script. The stage had been perfectly set: the guests in the breakfast room eating with expensive crystal and china; the wallpaper in a cheerful rose pattern; the angry husband with the red face; the tearful young maiden being consoled by the handsome prince; the universally disliked hostess, murdered; and the interloper, who had entered their midst, committed a crime, and who would now be taken away.

"I didn't go into her chamber," Olivia said weakly. "I

dropped a ring from my window and went to the terrace to retrieve it." She slid the ring easily off her finger. Their eyes stared at her, full of disdain and disbelief.

Philip took the ring. "It's Genevieve's," he said, looking at everyone. "It's our family signet." He held it out for everyone to see, then returned it to Olivia.

"It's too big. That's why it slipped off." Olivia slid the ring effortlessly on and off her finger to demonstrate.

Olivia turned to Philip and saw in his eyes something better than what was in everyone else's. He was confused, but he had not yet condemned her.

"Whoever killed Mrs. Bracknell did it for her jewels, yes?" Olivia pleaded. "I don't have her jewels. Search my room, search my things, search my person for God's sake. You'll see. I've not taken anything."

Admiral Bracknell was unconvinced. "Chiltern, lock this woman in the nursery. No, wait, take her to my study; I'll interrogate her immediately. Kelvil and Goring, search her rooms. She may have hidden the necklace elsewhere, but we'll find it, what."

Olivia turned to Philip and whispered, "I didn't do it. You must believe me."

"I promised to protect you, and I will."

Olivia followed Chiltern out of the room without making a scene. The scene had already been made.

Philip debated whether to accompany Miss Snow for her interview with the Admiral or whether to follow Goring and Kelvil who planned to search her rooms. Kelvil whispered to the doctor, then smirked. Philip didn't trust that man. He followed them up the stairs to Miss Snow's chamber.

An empty apothecary envelope lay atop her dressing table.

Kelvil and Goring shared surprised glances. "She didn't hide the evidence very well," said Kelvil.

Philip objected. "It could be for anything. Headache. Nausea. She lives above an apothecary. If she had poisoned Mrs. Bracknell, she certainly wouldn't have left it out like that."

"You wouldn't think so," said the doctor, smelling the envelope and handing it to Kelvil.

"Clove?" asked Kelvil after sniffing. "That isn't poisonous, is it?"

"It has a strong scent. It could have been placed in the envelope to mask the evidence of a poison," said the doctor. "Or the lady could have it for toothache."

Philip grabbed at the envelope. It was empty, with a strong scent of clove. He tossed it back onto the dressing table. "We should leave this to the police."

Kelvil crouched and looked beneath the bed.

The doctor said, "I don't believe he plans to call for the

police."

"Not call in the police?" said Philip, outraged.

Kelvil stood and glared at the doctor. "He'll call in the police."

"She's innocent," Philip said to the two men.

Kelvil moved to a side table and opened a drawer. "I've no reason to believe otherwise." Turning, he looked to where the doctor and Philip stood. "Aren't you here to help search the room? To prove her innocence?"

Philip opened the wardrobe, pushing through gowns, feeling into pockets.

A thorough search found nothing more. No poison. No necklace. As they prepared to leave, a maid appeared at the door, returning a not-very-clean slipper. The three men stared at the slipper, evidence of Miss Snow's early morning excursion.

Philip's face reddened.

"She's innocent," he proclaimed. The two men and the maid stared at him, wordless.

Olivia followed Chiltern down a long corridor. When they'd nearly reached the end, he opened a door and ushered her inside. Without saying a word, he shut the door.

The Admiral's study was brighter than she expected, with large windows on two of the walls. A third wall was made up entirely of bookshelves. There were some books, but much of the shelving displayed those odd ship-in-a-bottle enigmas. In the center of the room was a large mahogany desk, deluged with papers. The Admiral was not an orderly man. Olivia had started walking toward one of the windows when she heard the door open behind her.

Pointing his pen at her, the Admiral asked, "Now, what's your real name?"

"Olivia Snow, sir," she said. "I am truly sorry for coming here under false pretenses. You see, it was the idea of –"

The Admiral interrupted, shaking his head and huffing. "I don't care about all that, what. I just want you to answer my questions."

"Yes, sir," Olivia answered meekly.

He pointed to a chair for her and he sat behind his desk.

"How did you know my wife?"

"I didn't know her, sir."

He shook his head. "Don't pretend, child. She told me she recognized you. So, I ask again, how did you know my wife?"

Olivia swallowed thickly. "I met your wife for the first time yesterday, when I met you. She told me later that I look like my mother. I presume she knew my mother, sir, but before yesterday, I had never seen your wife."

"Umm. Hmm. I see." He offered Olivia a gentle smile. "Not so hard, what?"

The Admiral's change of mood seemed like a good thing, but Olivia remained guarded.

In a pleasant, curious voice, the Admiral asked, "How did your mother know my wife?"

"I don't know, sir. I imagine it was before I was born. When my mother married my father, her family and friends gave her up. They thought she had married beneath herself– and them."

Olivia paused, but the Admiral nodded his head, urging her on.

"My father had been my mother's music tutor."

The Admiral leaned back in his chair and laughed deeply, rubbing his hands together.

"Jolly good!" he said. Just as quickly as his laugh had come, his eyes turned dark. "Was this murder revenge for my wife having slighted your mother?"

Olivia's blood chilled. "I didn't kill your wife. I told you, I didn't know her before this weekend. I had no idea she knew my mother."

"Just the answer one would expect from a murderess," said the Admiral, smiling and winking at her. "Chiltern!"

Olivia jumped at his loud call. The door opened and the butler, who must have been standing just outside the door, walked in. "Take Miss Snow to the nursery and lock her in, until I can decide what to do with her."

Chiltern led Olivia up two flights of stairs, showed her into the nursery, and locked the door, all without saying a word. Olivia dropped to her knees, buried her face in her hands, and cried quietly. Her stress and fears eased as the tears fell. Calmly, she dried her face, stood, and straightened her skirts. Succumbing to emotion would not help. If she were going to get out of this trouble and return to Etta, she needed a clear head.

She examined the nursery-turned-prison-cell. As prison cells, she could have done far worse. On the top floor of Hudson House, the nursery was like her garret apartment, only much nicer. The roof slanted from ceiling to floor, with several large windows cut into the slant. The room was narrow and long, about three times as long as her apartment. Olivia stood and walked the length of the room. The Admiral and Mrs. Bracknell did not have children, but the former occupants of the house must have done.

One side of the room contained a small cradle and a sturdy wooden rocking chair, the type used by a nurse maid to rock a baby to sleep. The other side of the room was arranged as a school room. Olivia walked to the nursery side and opened a large chestnut wardrobe which took up most of the wall at that end. About five pinafores of different sizes hung in the space. She pulled the largest down and held it up to her chest, pleased with the size. In a drawer, she found an old, wrinkled mobcap. Wrapping the cap in the pinafore, and folding them small and flat, she secured the bundle beneath her skirts. One never knew when one would require a disguise.

Opening the drawers on a small dressing table, she found a comb with half its teeth missing. On the other side of the room, she ran her finger through a thick coat of dust on a child's desk. There were three small desks. On the wall was a map of the world, and below it a small bookshelf containing a single volume. She leafed through the well-worn primer. It was of a level for Etta and Sam. Her heart squeezed at the thought of Etta.

Returning the book to its shelf, she strolled to one of the large windows. The day was still bright and cheerful. She pulled at the window, but it stuck. She bent her knees for better leverage and pushed up, to no avail.

"Trying to escape?"

The voice was so unexpected that Olivia shrieked in surprise. Turning, she found Peter Darlington standing in the doorway. He smiled in a way she did not care for and shut the door as he entered the nursery.

"I was trying to get some fresh air," she answered.

"Allow me," he said, crossing the room quickly.

They shuffled awkwardly as Olivia tried to move out of the window box and Peter tried to move into it. He finally stepped to the side to allow her out, but not without brushing his body against hers. In one strong pull, he had the window up. Fresh air blew into the room.

Olivia didn't thank him. She felt uncomfortable, and vulnerable. She wasn't certain he had locked the door behind him, but he might have done.

"The fresh air makes a difference, but I'm certain that given time your own sweet breath would have filled the room." Peter's laughter was soft and strange and gave Olivia goosebumps. She backed away from him slowly. His steps were quicker.

Just then, the nursery door opened and Chiltern entered, carrying a silver tray with teapot and china cups.

"Admiral Bracknell has ordered refreshment for Miss Snow," Chiltern said. The butler chose his steps carefully, moving between the two and causing Mr. Darlington to step backward. "Excuse me, sir. Shall I place it here, Miss?" He looked at Olivia as he spoke, placing the tray upon one of the small desks.

"Yes, thank you, Chiltern."

The butler straightened. The three stood for a moment

with no one speaking.

Chiltern turned toward Mr. Darlington and tipped his head slightly. "Sir, the Admiral would like to see you in the breakfast room."

Peter Darlington mumbled under his breath and left the room without looking at either of them.

When the door shut behind him, Olivia sighed with relief and sank onto the small chair beside the desk-table. "I would pour you a cup, Miss," said Chiltern, "but I'm afraid the pot is empty."

Olivia raised an eyebrow.

"When I saw Mr. Darlington climbing the stairs to the nursery, I thought you might appreciate a chaperon."

"He's lucky you arrived when you did," Olivia said bravely. "Another two minutes and I might have broken this chair over his head."

Chiltern smiled, started to speak, hesitated, then started again. "You won't know this, but I was a footman for the Darlingtons when your mother lived with them. You look like your mother; I recognized you as soon as you entered Hudson House. I heard about the fire which killed your father, and I'm sorry."

"Were you? Thank you," said Olivia. "I miss my parents every day."

Chiltern's face fell. "I didn't realize your mother had died too. My condolences."

Silence hung in the air, then Chiltern nodded slightly and moved to the door. Before leaving, he stopped. "I will send up a maid, to keep you company."

"I didn't kill Mrs. Bracknell." Olivia felt it was important that he believe her.

"Of course not."

"Thank you," she said, relieved by his confidence in her. "Do you have any idea who might have done it? It will be difficult to prove my innocence if I remain locked in here."

Chiltern paused, considering.

"I wouldn't worry overly, Miss," he said finally. "The truth will out."

"I wish I could believe that. Do you think you could talk to the servants, find out if anyone saw anything unusual? Anything that might help me?"

He nodded and left the room. She lifted the heavy silver pot, balancing the weight. It would make an excellent weapon, should Mr. Darlington return.

Philip found the Admiral in the breakfast room, eating and chatting with the doctor. Despite having suddenly become a widower, he seemed chatty and at ease. When Philip declared Miss Snow's innocence and the need to contact the police, the Admiral broke into a fit of giggles.

"Why contact the police, when it is so obvious that Miss Snow is guilty?" said the Admiral, laughing so hard he nearly tumbled from his chair. He straightened and began eating with gusto.

Dr. Goring crossed to Philip and spoke quietly. "He was sobbing heavily only a few moments ago. I gave him some brandy, but I believe the shock of his wife's death has given him a nervous complaint. I've been trying to get him to retire, to no avail."

The Admiral waved his fork and said, "You look like two men hatching a plan. It better not have anything to do with me. I'm not a child, what. I won't have people telling me what to do."

Philip had been on the verge of telling the Admiral to go to his chamber and relax. He now realized the futility of it. He would let the doctor deal with the Admiral. His first duty was to Miss Snow.

"I would not presume to tell you what to do, sir," Philip said with as much humbleness as he could muster. "I merely came to proclaim Miss Snow's innocence. Do I have your permission to talk to Miss Snow and to the servants? Someone may have seen something."

The Admiral chuckled. "Go to it, Lamb. You'll no doubt uncover what it's all about." He looked at the doctor and winked. Goring looked nervously between the two men.

As Philip turned to leave, the doctor whispered in his ear. "Go to Miss Snow. Make sure she's comfortable."

At the Benbow Inn, sunlight poured through a crack in the curtains. Genevieve wiped the sleep from her eyes and slid out of bed. Having had no nightgown, she had slept in her shift. The rug beneath her bare feet was ratty and when she stepped off it, the worn floorboards were sticky. She quickly slid on her stockings and did what she could with her gown. A glance at the mirror showed that her hair was a bird's nest, but there were no combs or brushes, just the pins she'd removed the night before. Where was Lily?

Genevieve looked out the window. The sun was high. What time was it? How late had she slept? Returning to the mirror, Genevieve patted down her hair and pinned it into place as best she could.

The door opened and a maidservant entered. "It's about time. I tried and tried to wake you. If you hadn't been breathing, I'd have given you up for dead."

Genevieve shook her groggy head. Not a maidservant. Lily, dressed as a maidservant.

She laid an ugly black dress on the bed.

"Why are you dressed as a maid?" asked Genevieve.

"We can't very well walk around town in our evening gowns. I made friends with Bitsy, the char-girl." Lily pulled at her apron. "She lent this to me and found an old mourning gown of her mum's for you." Lily indicated the dress on the bed.

"That dress is for me?" giggled Genevieve. "It's so ugly!"

"I know," said Lily, "but I couldn't very well tell her that could I? She's sharing with us, and it isn't like she has a lot to share."

Genevieve frowned. "Well, I only have to wear it until we get home."

After Genevieve donned the uncommonly ugly mourning gown, they joined Oscar in the taproom for breakfast. The innkeeper's wife left to refill the teapot and returned with another plate of scones.

Oscar raised an eyebrow at Genevieve's costume. "Who died?" he asked.

"My dresser, if she sees me in this," said Genevieve, her eyes laughing. "I can't believe I slept so late. What must Mrs. M be thinking? I hope she hasn't alerted my mother."

"She won't have," said Oscar, sipping daintily from his cup. "Lily wired Mrs. M early this morning."

Genevieve turned to Lily. "You've been busy. What did you tell her?"

"That you spent the night with me. It was a wire, so I kept it short," said Lily. "The real trouble will be my mum. I wired her too, but it won't help. I may never be allowed to leave her sight again. And just so you know, you slept so late that we missed the early train. The next one isn't until three."

Genevieve waved her hand. "Sorry. I'm a very deep sleeper. No matter, we'll be back at Mrs. M's for dinner."

"Hopefully," said Lily, frowning.

Genevieve tilted her head.

"Lily is concerned about our financial situation," Mr. Wilde said. "I told her not to worry. You are wealthier than the royal family and the railroad barons together."

"Maybe not that wealthy," laughed Genevieve, "but my family is–"

"But do you have any blunt with you?" interrupted Lily. "Blunt we can use to pay the innkeeper and buy railway tickets?"

Genevieve looked back and forth, from Lily to Oscar.

"I don't carry my wealth with me."

"I told you!" said Lily. "He lost nearly all he had playing cards, and I used my last penny on the wires."

"Well, that cannot matter," said Genevieve. "The inn-keeper can send the bill to my father, and as for the railway–"

Oscar put his hand on her shoulder. "My dear, the inn-keeper isn't going to send a bill to your father. He thinks you are Olivia Snow, the actress. If you request delayed payment, he will assume you are skipping on the bill and call the local constable."

"But . . . ."

"Actresses don't have a reputation for being honest."

Lily piped in. "Olivia does. Everyone knows she's honest."

"Not everyone. Certainly not this innkeeper," said Oscar, leaning back.

"Well, let's not worry yet." Genevieve opened her bag and dropped three coins onto the table. "What have you got, Mr. Wilde?"

Oscar dug around in his pockets, finding several coins and a crumpled two-pound note.

"How far can we get on that?" asked Genevieve, finishing her second scone.

Oscar and Lily looked at each other doubtfully. "Not enough for the rooms," said Oscar. "If we run away from the innkeeper and ride parliamentary to London, we may have enough."

A princess isn't going to ride parliamentary," scoffed Lily.

"I don't mind that," said Genevieve, "but we cannot run out on the innkeeper."

The three sighed.

"Might be we could sell something," said Lily, removing her necklace, a faux-silver chain with a faux-silver cross.

Genevieve looked at Oscar, then down at the large emerald engagement ring sparkling on her finger.

Lily set her precious item on the table. "How much do you think I could get for this?"

Oscar shrugged. "It's no use, my dear. A town this size isn't going to have anywhere to sell precious jewelry."

"You're wrong about that. There's a jeweler's just down from the telegraph office."

"Is there?" Oscar raised an eyebrow at Genevieve.

"Put your necklace back on, Lily," said Genevieve. "I'll take in my engagement ring."

Lily's mouth dropped open. "You couldn't!"

"I'm not going to sell it. I'll use it to get a little loan. It's what ladies do when they are running short of pin money. The jeweler will make me a little loan, with the ring as collateral. Later I will return, pay back the loan, and get my ring back."

"Brilliant!" said Lily, smiling and on her feet. "Let's go."

An older woman entered the nursery, followed by the butler carrying a large trunk with the help of a footman. They set the trunk against a wall and the footman left.

"This is my sister, Dotty," said Chiltern. "She'll keep you company."

"Thank you. What's in the trunk?"

"I've no idea. The Admiral said to bring it here."

In her late fifties or older, Dotty had rosy cheeks and laughing eyes.

"Shall we see what's in the trunk?" Olivia asked.

"Help yourself. I'd best do the mending." Dotty sat herself down in the rocking chair and got right to work.

In the trunk, Olivia found a dozen of Mrs. Bracknell's puzzle boxes and several neatly packed traveling suits. He's packing up her things already, Olivia thought, unnerved. She closed the trunk and sat.

"What's in there?" asked Dotty.

"Some of Mrs. Bracknell's things."

Dotty nodded as if that were the most natural thing in the world. "So, you're Miss Spenser's daughter, are you? When Chiltern said you was, I could hardly believe it. My brother adored your mum. It nearly broke his heart when she ran off with your dad.

Olivia sat in shock as the woman explained that she had been the lady's maid for a woman named Miss Duncan, who had been a good friend of her mother. Miss Duncan eventually married an American and left England.

"Wanted me to go with her," said Dotty, "but what would I do in America, I ask you?"

Olivia smiled. "You knew my mother?"

"Saw her all the time. Miss Duncan were best friends with your mum and Miss Darlington."

"Miss Darlington?" Olivia asked. Jane Darlington could not be more than a few years older than her.

"Mrs. Bracknell now. Born Miss Hortense Darlington, then Mrs. Wilbur Whitehart and now Mrs. Archibald Bracknell. Her the least lovely and the best married."

"Do you suppose my mother had taken her friends into her confidence? Or was it a great surprise when she ran off with the music tutor?" Although Olivia knew the story of her parents' romance, she had never considered how others might have been involved.

Dotty hooted. "A total surprise! Miss Duncan were shocked! Everyone was. For weeks, it was all they could talk over. Miss Duncan studied with Mr. Snow too. I saw him come in the house once or twice. Very handsome. Very polite. Oh, but Miss Darlington were angry. Your mum'd been staying with the Darlingtons, so it looked bad that she ran off when she was with them. Not that there was anyone to complain. Your mum wasn't but a ward."

Olivia knew her grandparents had died when her mother was young. Although she knew her mother had been moved in and out of the houses of relatives and friends, Olivia knew few details of her mother's early life.

Dotty continued, "And then to become the wife of a music tutor. That must have been a bit of a change. No more fancy houses and servants. She had a child who could play music and was invited to all the best houses. Even to Buckingham Palace, I heard. Little Girl Mozart, they called her."

Dotty's mouth fell open, and she dropped the knitting needles and sock she'd been darning into her lap. "That'd be you, wouldn't it? Little Girl Mozart all grown up. Do you still sing?"

Olivia laughed. "I've been known to grace the stage of a certain music hall, but I've found that the theater earns more respect, if not more coin."

Dotty shook her head as if unable to believe everything. "Miss Snow the actress. You're a might bit famous, isn't you? And your mother? How is she?"

"My mother passed."

"Oh, isn't that a shame. I lost my own mum when I was your age. It's a hard thing on a person."

Olivia nodded but didn't say anything. She felt that the loss of her mother had been worse than other people's losses. She had no father. No aunts or siblings. Olivia and her mother had been good friends–well, until that last year when her mother had acted like a love-struck débutante and Olivia was busy singing in music halls, and then making the transition to the theater. The worst was that her mother's death had been so easily preventable, if only her mother hadn't been so gullible.

"Was it the elder Mrs. Bracknell what invited you?" asked Dottie.

"Invited me?"

"No disrespect, but the younger Mrs. Bracknell don't normally invite actresses to Hudson House."

"Oh. Right. No, neither Mrs. Bracknell knew I was me. I mean – You haven't heard?"

Dotty shook her head, her eyes curious round circles.

"I was hired to pretend to be Mr. Lamb's sister. There was a wager among some of the ton to see if I was a good enough actress to fool the party.

"Well, that's hardly a fair wager with you lookin' so like

your mum, and Mrs. Bracknell bein' her good friend."

Olivia shrugged. "No one made that connection. And now, here I am locked up for murder."

"You're locked up for what?" asked Dotty, leaning toward her, brow wrinkled.

"For the murder of Mrs. Bracknell. I didn't–"

Before Olivia could finish, she saw the effect of her words on Dotty. The woman's face lost all its color, and her hand moved to her chest, as though trying to help her to breathe. She leaned back in her chair and closed her eyes.

"I'm so sorry," Olivia said. "I thought you knew."

Dotty's face grew even more pale. She breathed softly and didn't open her eyes or speak.

Olivia jumped from her chair and looked about the room. "Can I get you a glass of water? I'll call for Chiltern." She dashed to the door, but it was locked. She returned to Dotty and put her palm against her cheek.

Dotty opened her eyes and from the light in them, Olivia could tell nothing was seriously wrong. Olivia sighed in relief, her stomach unclenching.

"I hadn't heard," Dotty said softly. "What happened?"

Olivia told the story, from her point of view: explaining about the dropped ring, her search for it, the scream of the servant, the poisoning of Mrs. Bracknell and her little dog, the theft of the necklace, the Admiral's accusation in the breakfast room, and her internment in the nursery. By the time she finished, Dotty's coloring had returned, and her jaw was set in determination.

"There's the Admiral's odd valet Foxmore, not a man I'd trust with the silver, and Davey's lost more than he can pay playing dice. He's got a good heart, but a man can be backed to a corner," Dotty said. "And those twins that are guests have been up to no good. There's been more than an idle bit of gossip about them. I've not paid it much mind, but I'll be askin' downstairs for the details."

"They think the poison was put into her milk," said Olivia. "Do you know which servant would have taken it to her? Who might have had an opportunity to poison it?"

"Mrs. Bracknell takes her breakfast early, before we eat. She wakes hungry and don't like waiting. Gwen always eats quick like, so she can take Mrs. Bracknell a second pot of tea." Dotty gasped. "Was that when she was found? By Gwen?"

Olivia didn't know who had found the body. "Did anyone do anything unusual this morning? Did you see anyone where they shouldn't have been?"

"Let me think." Dotty slowly rocked her chair. "Things wasn't normal, what with all you visitin' and the mornin' hunt. The stable hands weren't at breakfast. Abigail got called up just as she was settin' down. Chiltern came late to eat."

The door opened and Philip entered. Olivia was flooded with a sense of relief, a response that surprised her. In truth, what could he do to help? But his serious, confident face was comforting. There was something about him that felt right, eased her sense of doom. It never hurt to have a rich, powerful person on your side.

Philip found Miss Snow composed, sitting in a child's chair, chatting with an elderly maid who was engaged in repairing the toe of a thick woolen stocking. She rocked in her chair as she worked, a basket of mending at her feet.

Taking a small chair opposite Miss Snow, Philip said, "Tell me what happened outside this morning. What did you see when you went to retrieve the ring?"

Miss Snow wrinkled her brow. "I didn't see anything. I was looking for the ring. I'd memorized the place where it had fallen from the window. When I was outside, I kept my eyes on the terrace bricks and the garden plants."

"You didn't notice the French windows separating the terrace from Mrs. Bracknell's chamber?" Philip asked.

She shook her head.

"Pity. You might have had a chance to see what happened. If Mrs. Bracknell had still been alive when you were there, she could not have helped but see you. Her breakfast table faces the terrace. I wonder if she had the doors open or closed."

"I'm sorry," said Miss Snow. "I don't remember any doors. If Mrs. Bracknell had been watching me, she didn't say a word. She may have already been dead." Miss Snow shuddered.

Philip lay a comforting hand on her shoulder. "Don't worry. I won't let anything happen to you. You are innocent, and I will prove it."

Miss Snow relaxed under his touch and offered a half-smile. "Thank you."

"I vowed to protect you, Miss Snow." A strong emotion passed through Philip, the desire to hold her, to comfort her, encircle her in his arms and protect her.

Miss Snow stood and walked to the window. She stared out for a moment before asking, "What do you know of the Darlingtons?"

"Miss Jane Darlington cares a great deal for her horse. I'd say she's honest and kind-hearted."

Miss Snow cocked her head. "Indeed? Well, Peter Darlington is a bad sort. If the Admiral had been the one murdered, I'd suspect Peter. He detests his uncle. But who would want Mrs. Bracknell dead? It seems like a thief could have taken the necklace without harming her."

Philip watched quietly as Miss Snow paced and spoke, "The twins adored the necklace, and one of them appears to adore the Admiral as well."

Philip said, "I hardly think–"

"When I was looking at the Bracknells' collection last evening, the Admiral brought the twins into the room and one sat on his lap. They seemed quite comfortable together."

Philip wrinkled his forehead. "I doubt either of those young ladies could commit murder."

"Maybe. Or maybe it was the Admiral. He's already packed away some of her things," Olivia said, indicating the trunk.

"What?"

Olivia opened the trunk. "These must be her clothes. They are her size and style. And I know these are her boxes because Mr. Darlington told me about them last night."

Philip picked up the smallest of the puzzle boxes. "I used to have one of these as a child." He turned the box slowly and carefully, feeling each crack and panel.

"It feels like there's something inside." He shook it, and there was the clacking of an object knocking about on the inside of the box. "Albert and I sometimes passed notes back and forth using our puzzle boxes." Philip studied the box carefully. "This one's tricky. I don't see how to open it."

Olivia sighed heavily; it was almost a sob. Philip transferred his attention from the puzzle box to her and chastised himself for being so easily distracted. Without thinking, he slipped the puzzle box into his jacket pocket.

"It's overwhelming, isn't it?" said Olivia, shakily. "How will we prove my innocence?"

"I'll prove your innocence."

Olivia moved with him to the door. They stared at one another, neither saying a word. Philip struggled against the desire to hold her.

"I won't let anything happen to you."

He took her hand, and instead of kissing it, as he had intended, Philip leaned quickly forward and kissed her cheek. Fighting the impulse to hug her, he slipped from the room.

The Benbow Inn was about a quarter mile outside a village. The sun shone softly, without much warmth, but the air was clean and clear. More like Monaco than London. Genevieve could almost smell the sea in the air. They walked by a few small cottages, chickens clucking in back gardens, and finally reached the village.

Lily pointed across the street. "There's the telegraph office. The jeweler's a few shops down."

The two waited as a farmer with a wagon and then a country dandy in a phaeton rolled by before crossing the street.

They passed a tea shop and the smell of baked goods. Several tables were taken with villagers sipping tea, eating cakes, and gossiping. Genevieve paused at the window and then walked slowly on. Next was the telegraph office, where Lily had been earlier. Genevieve paused again.

Lily stopped and looked back at her. "What's wrong?"

Genevieve chewed her lip. "What if he doesn't hold it for me? I've never actually used something to get a loan from a jeweler. I know ladies do it at their favorite shops. The jeweler doesn't sell the collateral, because he wants to keep their custom. But this man won't know me. He could sell my ring for far more than the loan I want."

"Then we'll sell my necklace," said Lily. "Maybe we can buy it back, maybe not. It don't matter."

Genevieve pondered the problem, staring into the telegraph office. Below the front window was a table with forms and an ink pot and stylus. At the back of the room, an elderly woman stood at the counter, talking with a wire agent. They looked to know each other well. He laughed and counted out money. The woman took the bills, patted his cheek, and turned toward the door.

"I know what we can do!" said Genevieve, hopping in place.

"What?" asked Lily.

"You'll see." Genevieve held the door open as the elderly woman left the office. She ushered Lily inside and walked up to the counter.

Genevieve smiled at the agent. "Is it possible to send money through the wires?"

The telegraph agent was only a few years older than Genevieve, with a half-grown mustache and too much macassar oil on his hair.

"Indeed, Miss." He cleared his throat. "It's called a money transfer. You give the money to an agent at one office, say where and to whom it is to be sent, then the recipient of the money can pick it up at the other telegraph office."

Lily gaped. "How does the money go through the wire?"

The young man chuckled. "The money doesn't move. The money you give this station stays here, and the other station gives out its own money. The stations have an agreement and the money will be replaced. There is a fee involved for the person sending the money, of course."

"One moment," said Genevieve, pulling Lily across the room.

Lily stumbled but hardly noticed. "I had no idea people could send money like that. Are you going to wire your family for money?"

"Not my family. I don't want them to know what we're

doing. I'm going to ask Mrs. M for the money she owes me. I won the wager, right?" Genevieve pulled a telegraph form from a stack on the table. "Here, help me compose the wire. We don't have much money, so it will need be short."

After much debate and many scratched-out messages, they came up with: G fooled many STOP won wager STOP wire winnings now STOP Lily

"Why is it from me?" asked Lily as they crossed the room.

"You were the judge for the wager," said Genevieve.

She handed the mostly-filled form to the agent. He went over it with them, double-checking the message, the amount and Mrs. M's address in London. "And your address?" asked the agent, indicating the part of the form that Genevieve had left blank.

"We'll wait," said Genevieve.

The agent frowned. "I'll send the telegraph immediately, but there's no way to know how long it will take for it to get to your friend. The London office might be busy. They might not have a boy ready to run the telegram. And it is impossible to predict if your friend will be home to receive the message."

Genevieve sagged. "I see."

"We're staying at the old post inn," said Lily, turning to Genevieve. "Do you remember the name? The Dented Inn or something like?"

"The Benbow," said the agent, pointing to the line on the form for Genevieve to fill in. "Bunbury"

Genevieve looked up. "This is Bunbury?"

The agent nodded and pointed to the form. "Bunbury."

Genevieve wrote the word, chewing her lip. "Do you know a woman named Agnes Daubeny? She's nearly eighty and in poor health. She's my fiancé's aunt."

The young man shook his head. "I've lived here all my life. I don't know anyone by that name. But if she's ill, she may be at Kelvil's Hospital. People come from all over for his cure."

"That must be it," said Genevieve. "Can you tell us how to get there? Do you think I'd have time to visit her before the wire arrives?"

"Might be. It's not more than a mile or two out." He gave them the direction, and they took their leave.

Out on the street, Lily asked, "Should we tell Mr. Wilde what we're doing?"

Genevieve looked the way they'd come, and the opposite way, toward the hospital. Shaking her head, she said, "We won't be long."

The two crossed arms and headed out of Bunbury on the old hermit road.

✍ *Thirty-Ninth Chapter* ✍

Olivia berated herself. As much as she'd criticized her mother for being stupid about "her prince," Olivia had made an even worse error. Yes, she'd agreed to this stupid weekend for the money, but the real reason had been Philip. She'd liked the look of him. His flirting outside her apartment had been charming. The news that he was "old fashioned" had made her want to know him better. Now, she might hang from the gallows, and why? Because she'd followed a charming man into a hornet's nest. Stupid!

The nursery was quiet and peaceful, which gave an unreal quality to her predicament. Was a murderer roaming the house? A gentle breeze blew in the window and Olivia crossed the room to look outside when a crisp knock sounded at the door. Dotty woke and the two looked at each other. Before either of them moved or said a word, the door opened and the Admiral walked into the room. He was a large man, made larger by the small items in the nursery.

His eyes fell on Olivia. He smiled and looked so glad to see her that she could only assume the true murderer had been found and he'd come to apologize.

He turned his head toward the rocking chair and nearly jumped when he saw Dotty.

"Leave us," he said to her.

"I'm a chaperon, sir," replied Dotty, her features firm.

His face purpled, as it had in the breakfast room. "Don't

be impertinent. By Gad, if I–"

Wanting to stop him from entering a rage, Olivia said, "It's all right, Dotty. I'll be fine."

"See, the lady says it's fine. Jolly Good. Off with you." The Admiral's face cleared and he offered Olivia a generous smile.

Frowning and moving slowly, Dotty picked up her basket of mending and left the room, leaving the door wide open. The Admiral harrumphed at this and shut the door.

"Do you have good news?" Olivia asked.

"Could be, could be." The Admiral crossed to Dotty's rocking chair and sat down. He rocked in large swoops and smiled like he was pleased with himself, smacking the soles of his shoes to the floor and halting the motion of the chair. His crooked smile made Olivia's hair stand on end.

"Over here my dear," he said. "Come, sit on my lap and let's talk this thing over, what?"

Olivia wrinkled her forehead, moving no nearer. The two stared at one another.

"Come on, dear. I won't bite," he said, opening his arms.

"I'd rather not," said Olivia. "I'm quite comfortable as I am."

The Admiral frowned and shook his head. "Don't tell me you didn't enjoy sitting on your father's lap and telling him all your troubles."

It was such an odd thing to say that Olivia was temporarily speechless. Her hopes for good news evaporated. The Admiral was a strange man; dangerously strange, one might say.

She answered, speaking slowly. "I did when I was five. If my father were still alive, I'm certain I would have given it up by now."

The Admiral's face flashed red. Standing and waggling his finger, he said, "We could have worked this out, what.

Now are you going to come sit with me or not?"

"Not," Olivia said clearly, turning her eye to the silver teapot which was within easy reach.

He huffed and puffed and seemed completely at a loss. Moving his mouth to speak, he spluttered and then waggled his finger and slammed the door as he left.

Outside of town, the old hermit road curved into a wood, hiding the sun. In the shadows of the trees, the air was cool. Genevieve was grateful for the long sleeves of her ugly black dress.

Lily hurried nervously. "It's creepy here," she said. "Do you think there are wolves?"

Genevieve laughed. "If there are, they are more afraid of us than we are of them."

"I don't know," said Lily, shuddering. "I'm terribly afraid of them."

"Let's skip," said Genevieve. "It will warm our blood, and one cannot be afraid when one is skipping." She took her young friend's hand, and they skipped down the center of the road.

Lily giggled and Genevieve broke into laughter.

After a few minutes, they slowed, out of breath. The road curved again and the trees thinned. Soon, fields stretched out to both sides of their path. The sun had disappeared and dark clouds covered the sky.

"It looks like rain," said Lily. "Do you think we should turn back?"

Genevieve frowned. "It can't be much farther. We're probably better off continuing on. I don't think we'd make it back to Bunbury. Look, there's the sign."

They turned and followed the drive. In the distance, they

could see a long brick building and many out buildings with the drive continuing on to stables in the back.

The wind picked up, nearly blowing off Lily's cap. She held it tightly to her head and said, "I think we'd better run."

The dashed down the dirt drive and up the few stone steps to the door. A woman in her mid-forties opened the door for them, just as the rain unleashed.

"That was lucky!" gasped Genevieve.

"Just in the nick of time," agreed the woman ushering them into the dry, dimly lit interior. "I'm Mrs. Hollis. How can I help you?"

They stood in the modest-sized entrance hall. A large window above the door let in the dim grey light. Rain beaded on the glass. Several rooms hid behind closed doors and a large wooden staircase led to the upper floor. It looked more like a boarding school than a hospital.

Genevieve said, "I'm here to visit my fiancé's aunt, Mrs. Agnes Daubeny."

The woman wrinkled her brow. "Mrs. Daubeny, you say?"

Genevieve nodded.

"Follow me." Mrs. Hollis led them across the hall to a small dark room. As they entered, she lit two table lamps, their light bouncing off the yellow rosebud wallpaper and changing the ambiance from grim to cheerful.

Mrs. Hollis said, "Your fiancé's aunt's name is not familiar to me, but I'll check the records. My daughter would know right off, but she's in town getting supplies."

She disappeared and Genevieve walked to the sitting room windows which were charmingly bordered by yellow chintz curtains. Water droplets raced in twos and threes down the pane, making clear paths against the fogged glass. Genevieve turned to Lily. "It doesn't seem much like a hospital, does it? Basil's aunt isn't going to be here. This is turning out to be a faradillo. We should have stayed at the inn. What happens if the money arrives, and we aren't there to receive it?"

Lily sank into a large soft chair, sighing happily. "We can stop at the telegraph office on the way back. It shouldn't be a problem."

She closed her eyes and leaned her head into the cushions. Genevieve roamed the room, looking at knickknacks, picking up a ceramic cherubim, paging through a book of poetry.

After a few minutes, the door opened and a serving girl backed into the room, pulling a tea cart. "Mrs. Hollis said to bring this to you and to tell you she'll return shortly." The girl straightened, her large belly pulling against her pinafore. Genevieve's eyebrows went up. It was rare to see a servant still working when so advanced in a pregnancy.

"Thank you," said Lily, moving dishes from the cart to the table in front of her chair. Her mouth watered at the simple bread-and-butter sandwiches. She hadn't eaten since early in the morning.

Genevieve sat across from Lily and poured the tea. Sighing, Genevieve leaned back and looked out the window. "I wonder how long the rain will last."

Olivia sat in the child-sized desk, staring at the scratched surface, thinking of Philip. He seemed capable. Perhaps he could get her out of this mess. What exactly did he think of her?

The scratch and clank of a key in the lock was followed by the shuffle and footfalls of two young male servants entering the room.

"We're to bind you and take you downstairs for transport to town," said one. The other took her wrists and began to tie them with a long linen strip.

Olivia's pulse quickened. "Did the Admiral say to do this? Where is he? Where is Mr. Lamb?"

They ignored her, and she tried to pull her hands away, but the boy had a firm grip. Working together, they bound her wrists securely, although they were relatively gentle about it.

They stood on either side of her as they descended the staircase. Olivia's heart pounded. She tried to calm her breathing. If she were taken from the house, how could she prove her innocence? What would become of her? Where was Philip? Where was Chiltern?

The air outside was cold. A small cart was parked in front of the house and its driver argued with the Admiral, saying that he did not like the cart. The Admiral waved away his objections.

Olivia spoke to the footman on her right, a boy of probably no more than fourteen, "Could I have my shawl or–"

Before she could finish, the Admiral called to her guards. "There you are, what. Bring her down, bring her down." They each took one of her elbows and guided her down the front steps to the drive. "Tie her to the cart, here. A dogcart for a dog, what!" He laughed cheerfully.

The servants hesitated and looked at each other. The pause was short-lived and they gently urged Olivia into the cart, tying her bindings to a small ring in the corner.

Olivia begged, her head turned over her shoulder so she could see the Admiral. "Please, don't send me away. I haven't done anything. I'm innocent. Where's Philip Lamb? You can't do this! Please!"

The Admiral smiled and waved pleasantly as if saying good-bye to a traditional guest who was leaving in a traditional manner.

The cart rocked as the driver climbed up front. He made clicking noise to the horse and the cart rolled.

Olivia made one last plea. "I'm innocent, sir! The murderer is still here. You may be in danger!"

He laughed, waved one last time, then turned his back and walked into the house. The two footmen followed close behind.

I should have sat on his bloody lap, thought Olivia, furious.

She stopped struggling and sank to the floor of the dogcart. Although cleaner than one would expect, the dogcart was stinky, uncomfortable, and unsteady, especially with her weight all on one side. The cart was meant to carry dogs to a race or hunt. She sat awkwardly on the bare wood, her arms tight against the ring in the corner, grimacing as each rut in the road knocked her against the wooden boards.

From the backward view, Olivia watched Hudson House

grow smaller and then disappear as they turned from the long drive onto a road. She wished one of the footmen had been allowed to go back for her shawl. The air was cool, patches of fog hanging in the lower fields. The sky was a dark steel grey and thunder rumbled in the distance, though it might have been the sound of railway cars banging at the station.

Soon they entered a thick but small wood, where the fog wrapped around the heavy-leafed trees. The wet cold air was hard to breathe. She found the wood ominous. Having spent her life amid the cobblestones and traffic of London, she did not trust the English wilderness.

Faced to the rear and watching the road disappear in the fog, Olivia did not see the sharp turn at the front. The cart tipped, angled sharply, and rolled briefly on one wheel before going all the way over. The wood panels of the corner in which she was tied split apart and Olivia was thrown into the brush at the side of the road. Her hands were still tied with the metal ring dangling from the linen strips.

The groom had also been thrown but landed on his feet, his hands wrapped in the reins. Cursing and staggering, he tried to slow the horse who dragged the shattered cart down the road. Before he could look back and see what had happened to the prisoner, Olivia darted into the darkness of the wood.

It would only be a moment before he stopped the horse and returned for her. Olivia had little chance of out running him, with her hands tied and wearing a thick skirt and slippers. The fog would be her friend, she thought, but she didn't want to run thoughtlessly and become lost. Moving only about twenty yards into the wood, she turned sharply and ran parallel to the road, back the way they had come, looking desperately for a place to hide.

The wood had many tall trees, but now that she was

running amongst them, they did not appear so very close together. The forest floor was thick with saplings, shrubbery, and gorse bushes, which snagged at her skirt and slowed her progress. The fog was patchy and not a reliable camouflage. She needed to find a hiding place and quickly.

Behind, she heard the man yell, "Miss Snow! Yeh've got to come back. The Admiral'll 'ave me 'ead. Bloody 'ell!"

Olivia dropped to the ground, slid under a thick gorse bush, and tried to quiet her breathing.

He continued to yell, enabling her to follow his movements by ear. At first, he scrambled farther from her, thinking she'd run deep into the wood. As she began to be relieved by his dwindling voice, his calls grew louder.

"Miss Snow! Miss Snow! If yeh come out, I'll take yeh righ' back. It was to be jus' the loop."

His voice grew stronger; he must be close.

Olivia's heart raced. There was nothing she could do now. If she came out of her hiding place, he would see her for certain.

He stopped calling, but he was now near enough that she could hear the snap of twigs and scrape of shrubbery. She held her breath when she saw his worn brown boots less than five feet from where she lay.

He stood still, uttering no sound. The entire wood was eerily silent.

Olivia felt the urgent need to cough.

The tickle at the back of her throat was impossible to ignore. Her eyes watered. She vibrated her throat to dislodge the tickle, to no avail. It was as though an army of ants were dancing in her esophagus.

Just as she thought her capture inevitable, she heard noise. An erratic tapping echoed across the wood. It was the strangest sound, like a drummer who had lost his beat, tap-tap, then silence, then tap-tap-tap, then a shorter silence, then more tapping. Some were close and others were far away. Soon the entire wood echoed with pitter-pattering. The leaves in the brush above her swayed and bowed, dispersing drops of water onto her face. It was raining.

The tapping was replaced by a crack of thunder. The light dripping became a deluge. The groom let loose a few obscenities and ran back to the road.

Olivia allowed herself a small, throat-clearing cough and felt much better.

The bush moderately sheltered Olivia, so she was not as soaked as she might have been. She waited until the rain eased and then crawled from her hiding place. Moving as quietly as possible, she approached the road cautiously. The broken dogcart lay in the ditch at the side of the road. The horse and driver were nowhere to be seen. Leaning against a tree and sliding to the ground, Olivia let herself cry hard for a short time.

Feeling better, she returned to the shelter of the wood, walking parallel to the road and chewing the linen bindings. The material was well made and strong, but she was soon able to create a small tear. She tried pulling her wrists apart, but the material would not rip all the way through. Ignoring the sodden leaves and mud, she sat and placed her heel against the tear. She pushed and pulled until she felt her arms would pop from her shoulders. Finally, the tear worked its way across a single layer of the material. When it had torn through, the rest of the linen was easily unwound.

It was now time for a transformation. She had once played a pregnant servant girl on stage, and she had nearly all she needed to play one now.

Lifting her outer layer of skirt, she removed the pinafore and cap she had found in the nursery. Pulling at her tight sleeves, she withdrew her arms then tugged her bodice around so she was wearing it in reverse. It fit badly across the shoulders and was tight across her chest. Holding up the overskirt, Olivia slid the small bustle, which normally rested just above her buttocks, to her front. She dropped the skirt and the bulge looked very odd. Raising the waist of the skirt and the height of the bustle, she put on the pinafore, which hid and slightly flattened the bustle, giving her an expectant look. She pulled the pinafore tight across the belly, so as not to look too far advanced in her "pregnancy."

Next, she ripped the linen binding into strips. She unpinned her completely ruined hair, and formed two simple plaits. She pinned them on her head and tied them up with one linen strip. She placed the mobcap on her head, adjusting the thick blue ribbon to hold the cap on tightly.

Making certain the pinafore hid most of the green of her day dress, and with the blue ribbon on her cap, she transformed from an aristocrat with green eyes to a simple maid with blue. Walking with her legs a little more apart than normal gave her the stable gait of a sturdy woman.

She would knock at the back door of Hudson House and report as extra kitchen staff for the weekend. It wasn't a perfect plan, but it was a start. The best way to prove her innocence would be to reveal the actual murderer, and to do that she needed to get into the house.

The rain had cleared the fog, and the sky had become a lighter and more friendly grey. When she exited the wood, the sun shone brightly and the wet meadow grasses sparkled like diamonds. A lane cut across the main road, heading east. She hadn't noticed it from the cart. A sign at the turn indicated Kelvil's Sanctuary for the Elderly and Infirm.

Olivia hesitated.

No one at the hospital would recognize her if she stayed out of the way of Mr. Kelvil and the doctor. Maybe this would be a better place to hide. Servant gossip moves readily between houses. She could ask questions and perhaps learn the identity of Mrs. Bracknell's murderer. She would need to if she were ever going to get her life back.

Before Olivia had been whisked away from the manor, Philip contemplated what his next action should be. He couldn't believe one of the twins would have killed Mrs. Bracknell, but his own certainty might be a blindness. Olivia knew women better than he. Philip looked for the Greenpins and learned that the three sisters, disappointed that the day's hunt had been canceled, had gone riding. He asked a groom who was sweeping out a dogcart if he'd seen which way the girls had ridden. The young man pointed, and Philip set out on horseback to find them. The sky was overcast, and the wind carried the scent of rain. He hoped the Greenpins had not ridden far.

Reaching the top of a small hillock, he caught sight of the girls gathered by a small brook at the edge of a copse. One of the twins sat on a large stone, staring into the stream. The older sister and the other twin were arguing. The horses, untied, grazed nearby. Philip made to wave at them but stopped, realizing that if he came at them from the other side of the copse, weaving through the trees, he could listen to their conversation. He retreated from the top of the hillock, skirted its edge, and dismounted. Hobbling his horse, he walked surreptitiously through the trees.

The splashing and bubbling of the brook made stealth unnecessary, but also made overhearing the sisters' conversation difficult. He was nearly upon them before he could hear the eldest sister, who was saying something about jealousy. Philip tried to remember her name. Florence? Francine? Frances, yes Frances. He had no idea what the twins were called and couldn't tell them apart.

The twin laughed. "Jealous? Don't be absurd. I've got plans for someone else. Besides, the Admiral is repulsive. Lord knows why she fancies him."

Philip wondered who "she" was. The other twin? It was hard to imagine her fancying the Admiral. She might fancy his money, though.

"It's the attention," said Frances, bending a small tree branch until she could grasp a large green leaf, which she plucked and absentmindedly tore into small pieces. "Father never gave us enough attention. It's why you are what you are and why I am what I am."

The other snorted.

Frances turned back to her. "Well, the question is, did he kill his wife or not? I don't see how he can have been talking marriage to her, if he wasn't planning to get rid of his wife."

The twin shrugged. "Does it matter?"

Frances looked outraged. "I don't want her marrying a murderer, regardless of his wealth. What stops him from killing her if he finds someone else he prefers?"

"With my skills, I can make certain he never prefers anyone but us."

"You're disgusting."

Thunder rumbled. Philip studied the darkening sky, then returned to where he'd tied his horse. Riding back around the copse and to the top of the hillock, he looked down at the sisters. They were in the same general area.

Philip called to them.

The twin nearest Frances was the first to look up. She waved at Philip and said something to her sisters. The twin on the rock also waved. Frances headed in the direction of their horses.

Philip dismounted and walked his steed down the hill. "A storm is imminent."

Thunder boomed in reply.

"I don't want to go back!" said the twin sitting on the rock. "I can't bear to be in that house with Mrs. Bracknell being dead. I wish Father would let us go home."

"Father tried to leave," said Frances, "but the Admiral talked him into staying. If you want to leave, you should use your charms on the old man. It's my impression you can get him to agree to anything you want."

She glared at Frances who, struggling to maintain control over the three horses, did not notice.

"What's this?" asked Philip.

Frances looked at him with irritation. "Here, you're supposed to be good with horses. Take this one." She handed Philip a rein and led the other two horses to the rock.

Frances climbed the rock, then mounted her horse. The twin who had been talking to Frances shimmied up the rock and sat next to her sister, putting her arm around her, and whispering in her ear.

"I'm not going!" said the girl who had been on the rock all along. She slid away from her sister.

"Suit yourself," said the other twin, standing and mounting her horse from the rock.

"You shall get very wet," said Frances, who then galloped off.

The twin sitting on the rock continued to pout, looking from Philip to her sister.

The mounted twin laughed. "Don't be a ninny. It's going to rain."

"Oh, all right!" she said. She signaled for Philip, and he led her horse to her. She slipped gracefully onto the saddle. Despite her reluctance to return to Hudson House, she drove her horse hard, catching up with Frances. The other twin rode warily, and Philip stayed by her side. The wind had picked up and black rain clouds followed close behind them.

"How'd you get paired with that actress woman?" She had to shout to be heard above the wind.

"Through my sister," Philip answered. "Genevieve made a wager. I never should have agreed. It was a terrible idea, and now look what's happened."

"Maybe the actress planned it all along," she said. "Clever way to get into a house full of jewels. If Mrs. Bracknell hadn't recognized her, she might have pulled it off."

Philip shook his head, although as his companion kept her eyes in front of her, she couldn't have noticed. They were riding quickly now, trying to beat the storm. Philip shouted, "Miss Snow had nothing to do with the murder or theft."

They made the stables just as the rain began. Frances and the other twin were disappearing inside Hudson House. Philip and his companion handed their horses to a groom and stood at the stable door. The rain fell in heavy sheets. Philip pulled off his jacket and offered it to her. She took it and tilted her head coquettishly.

"We can wait out the storm here," she said, stepping close and throwing his jacket over their heads. Her forehead knocked against his jaw. What the hell? thought Philip. He stepped away quickly, out from the protection of the barn and into the rain. His jacket fell to the ground, one sleeve in the mud of the yard. Leaving the jacket, he dashed through the rain.

A footman opened the door, pretending not to notice the strangeness of Philip's wet, jacket-less appearance. He went immediately upstairs to change and plan what to say to Olivia. The Greenpin girls were obviously innocent. Their conversation pointed to the Admiral as having a clear motive. The more Philip considered it, the more likely it seemed. The

Admiral's reluctance to give up his duties as Chief Constable and call in the police were understandable if he were the guilty party. The "theft" of the necklace could be a ruse.

He changed out of his wet clothes, then went to speak to Olivia to tell her what he'd learned from the Greenpins. The door to the nursery was open and Olivia no where to be seen. Philip returned to the first floor and checked her bed chamber, but it was also vacant. At the end of the corridor, he talked to a maid who was putting away linen in a closet, but she didn't know anything.

"Ask Chiltern," she said, pointing down the staircase to where Chiltern was briskly crossing the large hall.

"Chiltern!" Philip called, descending the stairs several at a time. "Where is Miss Snow?"

"In the nursery, sir." When Philip pointed out that she wasn't, Chiltern frowned.

A tall young footman who'd been standing by the front door stepped forward, his face flushed. "The Admiral had us tie Miss Snow to the dogcart, and Jack drove her to the gaol in town."

Shocked, Philip turned to Chiltern, who also looked appalled.

"Where's the Admiral?" Philip asked the boy.

The lad pointed down the corridor. "In his office."

Furious, Philip marched to where the boy had pointed and threw open the door. The Admiral sat in a plump velvet chair reading a newspaper.

"Why have you sent Miss Snow to the village gaol? You–"

"Don't get yourself all worked up, Lamb." The Admiral laughed. "She'll be back."

"Sir, I think you'd better come." This was spoken by Chiltern who appeared in the door. The Admiral and Philip followed him to the front entrance where a sodden groom stood dripping, creating a puddle in the entrance hall.

"The cart flipped," he explained. "I tol' yeh it weren't fer people. It flipped and the lady ran away."

"Was she hurt?" Philip asked.

Simultaneously, the Admiral asked, "Where was this?"

"I don't think she were hurt. She ran off quick enough. It were in Abbott Wood, that spot where the road jogs sudden-like. The cart didn't make the turn."

Philip sighed. Running away would make her look guilty.

The driver continued, "I yelled fer 'er and looked in the wood, but when the rain started, I came back."

Philip's heart sank. Olivia must be drenched and cold and afraid. He had failed utterly in his duty to her.

The Admiral barked at the groom for his incompetence.

"I'll find her," declared Philip. Outside, the heavy rain had stopped and the sky was clearing. He had a boy saddle the horse he'd ridden earlier. It threw up clods of mud as Philip galloped down the lane. His voice was silent, but his heart called out to her. She couldn't have gone far, he thought. He would not be able to forgive himself if anything happened to Olivia.

The ruts and potholes in the road leading to Kelvil's Sanctuary for the Elderly and Infirm were filled with water and mud, but the scenery was pastoral and fresh from the recent storm. As Olivia maneuvered around the puddles, she tried to decide on a course of action. She could ask after a distant relative, or she could be in search of work. Her sodden muddy clothes did not speak well for her, but even respectable people become wet in the rain.

The road led to a long, low building of red brick with large friendly windows. It seemed a good building for its purpose. Fruit trees lined the path and Olivia pulled down a ripe apple. Stepping into the shade of the tree, she ate the crisp tart fruit thankfully. It must be nearly noon, and she'd eaten little at breakfast. She threw away the core and continued down the path.

The long building had a door on the side, which looked appropriate for servants. Olivia wiped her hands on her pinafore, straightened her appearance the best she could, then rang the bell.

She waited, wondering whether to ring again, when the door opened. The woman was a healthy forty or fifty, with a stout form, dimpled rosy cheeks, and grey curls escaping from a mob cap. Her smile was friendly and open. "Got caught in the storm, did you? Come in. We'll dry you out."

Olivia followed her inside, through the entrance hall to a

small office. The woman bustled about, clearing books and papers off a chair, and signaling Olivia to sit. "We've been surprisingly busy this morning. My daughter's gone and the doctor's out, but I'll help the best I can." She sat behind the desk. "Right. I'm Mrs. Hollis, cook and housekeeper. My daughter would normally get you settled, but she's in town. She manages the girls and the babies."

It was obvious she expected Olivia to know what she spoke of, so the actress nodded.

Dipping a pen in an ink pot Mrs. Hollis asked, "Name and age?"

Olivia cleared her throat and gave the name she'd decided upon earlier; the age she invented on the spot. "Daisy Evans. Eighteen."

Without looking up, Mrs. Hollis scratched on her paper and asked, "When's the baby due?"

The question surprised Olivia. She touched her hands to her fake belly and considered how best to answer. Her bulge was not large; she could be perhaps five or six months. "Late November, early December," she said, hoping that seemed reasonable.

"Any family or others who might be helpin' to pay your board and such?"

This interview had Olivia baffled. Mrs. Hollis obviously thought she was pregnant and was here because she was pregnant. Was it a home for unwed mothers? Kelvil had described it last night as a retreat for the elderly and infirm. A script was so much easier to work with. Olivia wrung her hands and hesitated before answering. "No. I've no money."

Mrs. Hollis looked up kindly and said, "Don't you worry. It's not required, but it does help when it comes." She lay her pen on the desk and asked, "So, how much do you know about what we do here?"

"Very little," said Olivia honestly.

"Our elderly patients pay, and we have a few wealthy benefactors. Girls like yourself do most of the work. We match you with a patient and you'll be her caregiver. You take her on walks, you help feed her, you read to her, whatever she wants or needs, including cleaning messes and what not. We've a doctor who keeps them in health and handles medication. We call you the granddaughters and they are your grandmothers. Any questions?"

Olivia shook her head.

"When your time comes, we'll have the doctor in for you. You and the babe can stay together for two weeks, then we'll decide what comes next. The older babes go to a nursery and some girls stay to work there. Other girls do cooking or heavy housework. Some work elsewhere and send money back. Some stay with their grandmothers. Your work will depend on what we need and your own skills. We are not an orphanage–you cannot leave your child with us and disappear, do you understand?"

Olivia nodded.

"Good. What work have you done before?"

"I was in service. Worked my way up to chambermaid."

Mrs. Hollis nodded, unsurprised. "You'll need to sign this contract, saying you'll either work for us, or send money to us to pay for the care of your infant. We aim to keep mother and child together as much as possible. Can you agree to it?"

Mr. Podgers the cheiromantist was certainly correct about being forced into deceit. She would prefer not to lie, not to sign a contract with a fake name. But she wasn't pregnant, so she wasn't taking advantage of these people, not really. She was wanted for a murder she did not commit. If re-captured, she could very well hang. What choice did she have?

Olivia looked across the desk at Mrs. Hollis and her grey,

smiling eyes.

"Yes," Olivia said, her voice full of gratitude. "I'm that much thankful you'll help me."

Mrs. Hollis nodded and scratched pen against paper. Finally she turned the paper and pushed it toward Olivia. "I'll need your mark, just there."

She took the pen and wrote Daisy Evans.

Mrs. Hollis stood from the desk and led "Daisy" from the room. "We'll get you in to some dry clothes and you can meet your grandmother. Your arrival is in good time, as we had a new lady arrive this morning. The doctor got her checked in, and I haven't met her yet. He hasn't bothered with the paperwork, so I can't tell you nothing about her."

They climbed a narrow staircase with creaky wooden steps until they reached a long dark corridor with many doors.

"These are the granddaughters' rooms," Mrs. Hollis explained. "This used to be a boys' school before my son-in-law bought it. These were the teachers' rooms. Larger than servants' quarters, but not at all extravagant."

She opened a door to a small clean room containing two thin beds, a large dresser, and a dressing table with no mirror above it.

"You'll share with Sally. She's due a month before you; a nice girl, although she's got a bit of a temper. Get out of those wet things; I'll have some dry clothes brought to you."

She closed the door, and Olivia let out a long sigh.

✦ Forty-Fourth Chapter ✦

Genevieve and Lily had finished the tea and sandwiches eons ago, but Mrs. Hollis had not returned. The rain had stopped and the sun was out. Lily turned from the window.

"What should we do?" she asked Genevieve. "If only there were a bell or pull rope or some way of calling a servant. I believe we've been forgotten."

Lily walked to the door and peaked out. Genevieve joined her. The corridor was empty. They walked a few steps and came to the entrance hall. At the sound of footsteps, Lily looked up, to see Mrs. Hollis coming down the stairs.

"Oh!" she said, seeing Genevieve and Lily. "You must think I've forgotten all about you." She hurried down the last few steps and put her hand on her chest to slow her heavy breathing. "A new granddaughter arrived, and I had to get her registered and settled, and then Mrs. Pennypacker fell and her granddaughter couldn't get her up, and . . . but that doesn't concern you. Your aunt isn't here, I'm afraid. I don't know how you could have been so misled."

Genevieve shook her head. "It is my error. Thank you for the tea, and for giving us a dry place to wait out the rain."

Lily could tell that Mrs. Hollis was harried and had many things to do. She was impressed with how the woman remained mostly calm, ever friendly and kind.

"I hope the rain holds out for you. Good day!" Mrs. Hollis

called, waving from the door.

As they set off down the lane, Lily asked, "Do you think we'll catch the three o'clock?"

"Only if the money is waiting for us," said Genevieve, and the two hurried down the lane.

When the sky outside his chamber window grew dark with clouds, Oscar laughed aloud, imagining Genevieve and Lily in their borrowed garb and ill-coiffed hair soaking wet from their walk back to the inn.

When Genevieve and Lily had not returned for lunch, Oscar imagined the two were waiting out the storm in some cafe. He ordered a sandwich and a pint and sat in the taproom.

When the sky out the window cleared, he ordered another pint and waited for the sound of their voices at the inn door.

When a group of young men gathered in the taproom and offered to buy Oscar a pint, he accepted. When they invited him to a game of darts, he joined them.

When Oscar heard a familiar voice at the inn registration desk, he peeked out the taproom door in time to see Genevieve's fiancé, Basil Daubeny, signing the register, a well-dressed lady by his side. The two climbed the stairs together and disappeared into one of the inn's chambers.

The clothes Mrs. Hollis brought for Olivia included a simple grey home-spun, stockings, a large white pinafore, and a white mob cap. She assumed this was the dress of all the granddaughters and it suited her needs well. She left the bustle tied to her front, then put on the home-spun and pinafore. Mrs. Hollis had not brought her shoes, so she was forced to wear the damp slippers she had come in.

Once she was dressed, Mrs. Hollis turned her over to a girl named Ruth, a former "granddaughter" now working in the infirmary. Ruth was quiet and stern, telling Olivia only what she thought she would need to know to do her job. When Olivia tried to gossip, asking questions about other girls and the people of the neighborhood, Ruth kept quiet and offered nothing.

Olivia learned that the granddaughters' rooms were on the upper floor of one wing and the grandmothers' rooms on the upper floor of the opposite wing. The chambers were identical in size and layout, but the elderly patients had the rooms to themselves and nicer furnishings. On the ground floor, under the granddaughters' rooms, were a library, con-servatory, three sitting rooms, and the large dining room. In the center was Mrs. Hollis's office, Mr. Kelvil's office, and a waiting room. Under the grandmothers' chambers were the infirmary, the doctor's office, and the doctor's personal chambers. The kitchen and pantries were on the ground floor off the dining room. Ruth showed her each and every cupboard and closet as well as the wares kept inside.

Finished with her duty, Ruth gave Olivia back to Mrs. Hollis who was shuffling papers in her office.

"Now, let's introduce you to your grandmother. She's in the blue sitting room," Mrs. Hollis said, leading Olivia down the corridor. "I met her myself when you were dressing. A very nice lady and younger than most of our grandmothers. Her arrival took me completely by surprise. I didn't realize she was coming–my daughter left me no note or paperwork. She came with the doctor early this morning and so while Ruth and I rushed to get her chambers ready, he got her settled. I'm not certain what her complaint might be. Some of our grandmothers seem healthy but have relapses, and so it is nice to have a doctor at hand."

By this time, they'd reached the sitting room and Mrs. Hollis opened the door. Olivia followed her inside.

Sitting on a flowery divan beneath a deep blue wallpaper was the last person Olivia expected to see.

Mrs. Hollis said, "Mrs. Bracknell, may I present the girl who will be your granddaughter, Miss Daisy Evans."

Mrs. Bracknell looked up and smiled. She was alive and well and doing cross-stitch in the blue sitting room at Kelvil's Sanctuary for the Elderly and Infirm, her little terrier tugging at her skirt.

As Philip rode the horse down the lane, he considered where Olivia might have gone. According to the stable boy, Abbot Wood was just past the turn to Kelvil's hospital. Would she seek refuge there? She had disregarded all of Philip's warning to stay clear of that man the night before. As he neared the turn, he saw two women up ahead of him. One appeared to be a woman in mourning, and the other might be her daughter or her maid. It was hard to tell from the distance. Should he ride on and ask them if they'd seen Miss Snow? As they entered the shade of Abbot Wood, they began skipping. Odd. No, he would see if Olivia had sought shelter at Kelvil's hospital. He turned his horse and rode down the lane.

"Did you bring my trunk?" asked Mrs. Bracknell.

Olivia walked slowly to the divan, keeping her eyes on Mrs. Bracknell's face.

"Is it still in the wagon?" asked Mrs. Bracknell irritably. "Because if it is, they can–"

"You're supposed to be dead!"

"You don't have it, do you?" She sighed heavily. "Yes, I'm supposed to be dead. Were you fooled? It was Archie's idea. When he heard that you and Mr. Lamb were going to try to fool us, he wanted to fool you. Were you fooled?"

Olivia gaped.

Mrs. Bracknell chortled. "I wanted to use tomato sauce and feign a bloody murder scene, but Archie and Chiltern over-ruled me. Poison is so boring, but sneaking out without anyone seeing was a bit exciting. Was everyone fooled?"

Olivia was livid. The hostess hadn't spent a minute thinking how this would affect her guests. Olivia remembered Mr. Greenpin's ashen face, his daughter crying over her breakfast, Dotty's near heart attack.

"Archie made it into a wager, of course," Mrs. Bracknell continued. "The country is mad with gambling."

A wager, of course.

"Who knew?" Olivia asked.

"We kept it secret the best we could, as we weren't certain who might give it away. The doctor was the one who told us about your charade and helped to hide me. Chiltern and my maid were the only servants we told. They helped me leave the house. Archie didn't want to tell my niece and nephew, but I insisted. I'm their last relative, you know. Were the people who knew convincing? How did everyone take it? Who was accused? No one has come to tell me anything!"

"Did Mr. Lamb know?" Olivia asked, hoping that he had not. His concern for her well-being had seemed so genuine. She remembered his worried eyes, the creases on his forehead, the way his lips had felt against her cheek.

"Oh, no!" answered Mrs. Bracknell. "He and you were trying to fool us, so we tried to fool you. Did we?" She lifted her little dog onto her lap and ran her fingers through his fur.

Olivia was relieved but also annoyed. "How long were you going to pretend to be dead?"

Mrs. Bracknell shrugged. "Until Archie comes to get me. I hoped he'd be here by now. I'd like to be home for dinner. I've been rather dull. Please, tell me what happened."

Olivia shook her head and stood, irritated. The charade planned at Mr. Wilde's salon had been silly and stupid and perhaps she shouldn't have taken part in it but this second charade was far worse. Pacing the room Olivia considered how to react, which of her emotions to display. She glanced at Mrs. Bracknell, who stared at her, face eager. The little dog also stared, its head tilted as though waiting for her response.

"I was the one accused," Olivia said waving her arms with emotion. "Your husband had me locked up, then tied me to a dogcart to take me to gaol."

Mrs. Bracknell looked startled. "Locked up? Where?"

"In the nursery."

Mrs. Bracknell's whole body relaxed, and she let out a slow breath. All of which annoyed Olivia even more.

"I thought I would be hanged," Olivia explained. "I could see no way of proving my innocence. On the way to town, the cart overturned and I was thrown. I escaped into the wood and made my way here."

Mrs. Bracknell tut-tutted. The terrier turned its eyes on its owner.

"My dear, I am so sorry. Is that why you are calling yourself Daisy? You believe you're hiding from the police? I do apologize. I shouldn't have trusted Archie. In truth, it was the fact that I don't trust him that convinced me to take part in this stupidity. Tell me, how did the Greenpin twins handle the news of my death?"

"Excuse me?"

"The twins. How did they handle my death?"

Olivia didn't see why that was important. She tried to remember. "Anne was upset. At breakfast, she rambled on and on about her grandmother who had died. I'd say she was the most distressed of everyone."

Mrs. Bracknell frowned. "And Emily?"

Olivia shook her head. "I don't remember."

"They are tricky girls. It's hard to know what's real and what's not."

That was certainly true.

Olivia realized of a sudden that she didn't need to return to Hudson House. She could take a train to London this very day and be done with the whole ridiculous weekend. Her anger melted away, replaced by a blissful relief.

Mrs. Bracknell rubbed her little dog. "I think my husband is seducing one of those girls, or perhaps it is the other way round. There have been too many whisperings and caught glances and people not being where they should."

Olivia no longer paid attention to the woman, instead wondering how much a ticket to London would cost. Perhaps Mrs. Bracknell would give her the blunt for a ticket.

Mrs. Bracknell continued. "I've wondered if this whole charade wasn't staged to remove me from the house for the night. And you, poor girl. I wonder what Archie's plan was. Tying you up and taking you to gaol. What was he thinking?"

"Would you loan me the money for the fare to London?" asked Olivia. "If it's all the same to you, I'd rather be away."

Mrs. Bracknell's eyes lit up. "Of course. Excellent idea. We'll take my carriage into town and I'll drop you at the railway station. You'll easily make the three o'clock. Then, I'll return to Hudson House and see what my husband is up to."

As Philip approached Kelvil's Sanctuary for the Elderly and
Infirm, he watched a wagon being unloaded of goods. The
servants carrying in the supplies were surprisingly all young
women in various stages of pregnancy. The person manag-
ing the unloading was a young woman in a straw bonnet
with a large brim tied with a ribbon beneath her chin. Her
grey woolen cloak was damp from the rain, and the hem of
her practical blue dress was muddy. She turned at the sound
of his arrival.

"Hello!" she called cheerfully. "Are you here on a visit?
Johnny, take this gentleman's horse to the stables." The driver
of the wagon, a man in his fifties with a white bristle beard
and a sodden bowler came and took the reins.

Philip followed the woman into the entry where she removed her cloak and shook the water from it.

"Pardon me," she said. "We got caught in the rain." She
turned as she removed her cloak and saw his face for the
first time. "Good heavens!" the woman said. "It's Mr. Lamb.
What a delightful surprise! What brings you to our sanctuary? But let's not talk in the entryway. Come into the office."
She put her hand on his shoulder and ushered him through
a door on their right.

Philip recognized her as the maid from his London boarding house whom Kelvil had ruined. She had apparently not
committed suicide. She was older by several years, with

more flesh on her figure, a happy blush to her cheeks, and an air of confidence. Philip had no idea what her name was.

She offered him a seat and sat behind a desk shuffling papers. "I didn't realize we had a relative of yours. That's why you're here, I assume? You aren't here to see one of the girls?"

Ignoring all of her questions, Philip asked, "How did you come to work here? When I returned to the boardinghouse that autumn, and you and your mother were no longer there, I feared the worst. One resident said you'd killed yourself."

Her eyes grew wide. "Killed myself? Whyever would he say that? Oh, because Alfred had left for a few weeks? My mum was that worried. But I knew he'd gone home to tell his own mum about me. She didn't like it at first, but she came to the wedding. And it all changed when she got ill. I'm a bonny nurse, as is my mother. Then Alfred thought up the idea of the hospital-sanctuary. Mothers-to-be are good caregivers, and we can make certain they stay active and healthy while waiting for the babes to be born. So many young girls are tossed onto the streets. We've been able to support the place with donations and the fees from the elderly patients. My mother-in-law was the first patient, and I was the first girl."

Philip had a hard time reconciling Kelvil with the man she was describing. He had married her? Set up a hospital for the elderly and girls in trouble? Something was wrong, but he could not decide what. As she talked, her eyes gleamed with enthusiasm, and Philip was reminded of Olivia and his reason for being there.

"I'm seeking a young lady." He paused, realizing he didn't have a good story for what had happened to Olivia and why he should be seeking her. He couldn't possibly say that she was wanted for murder. "My sister and I were staying at Hudson House," he extemporized, "and we had a fight. She took off, just before the storm. I'm not sure where she is, and

I thought maybe she'd ended up here. She's stubborn and will probably hide from me, but I'd like to apologize."

Mrs. Kelvil's eyes softened.

Philip continued, "She is most likely wet and a bit lost. She is young, in her early twenties. She has dark hair, is very pretty." Philip tried to think how else to describe her. "She's a city girl; she doesn't know the country at all. Have you seen her?"

Mrs. Kelvil shook her head. "I was in town all morning, so I couldn't say if she came here. I could ask–"

She had begun to stand when the door opened and an older woman entered the office talking.

"Jennie, we've a problem – oh, excuse me. I didn't know you had someone with you."

Jennie. That was the name Philip had been unable to remember.

"Mother, this is–" began Mrs. Kelvil.

Philip stood and offered Jennie's mother his hand. For some reason, the name of the cook at the boardinghouse, who now stood before him, came instantly to mind. "Mrs. Hollis, it's lovely to see you."

"Mr. Lamb!" said Mrs. Hollis, her eyes widening with a smile. "What a pleasure."

"Mother, Mr. Lamb is looking for his sister who is in trouble–not the kind of trouble our girls are normally in– she's a city girl who's lost. Is that right?" Jennie asked, looking at Philip.

Philip nodded.

"Did she stop here this morning?"

Mrs. Hollis held her hands in the air. "I've seen lots of young ladies this morning! It's been a whirlwind of activity. I've hardly had time to breath. First there was two young ladies asking about an aunt who isn't here. They came together from the train."

"My sister would have been alone," said Philip.

Mrs. Hollis nodded. "Daisy arrived alone. Former chambermaid."

"It would be just like my sister to use a false name. What does Daisy look like?" asked Philip.

"What does Daisy look like?" Mrs. Hollis asked herself. "Let me think. Average looking, I suppose. Brown hair? Brown eyes? Average height? Six months or so gone with child."

Philip shook his head. Olivia was not average looking, and certainly not with child.

Mrs. Hollis turned to her daughter. "I paired her with the new lady– I wish you'd warned me to expect her. I'd no idea. I put her in a sitting room and got Phoebe to clean out a patient chamber for her."

Philip stood. "Thank you for your time. I see you have a lot to do."

Jennie Kelvil stood quickly and walked him to the door. "I'm sorry we couldn't be of help. I'm sure your sister will turn up."

"Do you mind if I talk to your grounds staff?"

"There's just the grooms and the gardener," said Jennie. "In the stable, there's Johnny, who took your horse, and his grandson Mickey. Don is the gardener. If she was wandering around outside, one of them might have noticed."

Neither Johnny nor Mickey had seen Miss Snow, and after thirty minutes of hunting for the gardener, Philip learned nothing from him either. He was disappointed, but not surprised. If Olivia were hiding, she'd hardly show herself so easily. Returning to the road, Philip headed for town. He walked into every shop, looking about, and asking after Olivia.

At the telegraph office, Philip learned that a lady matching Olivia's description had been in. Relief washed over

Philip, his tangible joy surprising the agent.

"Did she seem well?" Philip asked.

The agent paused. "Well enough. Her friend seemed more worried, although once they'd sent the telegram they both seemed happy enough."

Philip's heart sank. Olivia wouldn't have a friend with her.

"Did it seem as though she knew the friend well? Is it possible they had just met?"

The agent frowned. "I suppose it's possible."

Philip interrogated the agent, becoming more and more frustrated by his vague answers. He seemed to change his mind about everything he said.

A queue had grown behind Philip.

"I'm sorry," said the agent, "I can't tell you more. But you can talk to them yourself. They are waiting at the Benbow Inn for a response to their telegram.

Philip turned and saw the queue behind him. He thanked the young man and left the office. He doubted the lady could be Olivia, but he headed to the inn.

After dropping the actress at the railway station, Mrs. Bracknell drove the Victoria carriage out of town and to the next village where she sold the horse and bought a young, fresh mare.

She wondered which would be the best way to approach Hudson House. Crumpet sat on the seat beside her, the little dog's head resting on her lap. She petted his head, the contact softening her anger.

When she'd been sneaked out of the house in the morning, the butler had neglected to put her carefully packed trunk into the wagon. She'd ended up at Kelvil's without the puzzle boxes, without her clothing, without any of the things she needed. Mrs. Bracknell had begged Kelvil's servants to send for the trunk, and although they agreed to, nobody had. They bustled about, carrying tea trays, mopping up messes, caring for the forgetful old fools. Mrs. Bracknell had gone so far as to pay a boy to drive to Hudson House and grab the trunk, but he hadn't been able to find it. He was told the butler was unavailable, and the footmen turned him away.

Well, she would have to sneak in herself, grab the trunk, and be off.

Olivia paced the railway platform. She smiled at a woman who stood with a young girl, two bags by their side. The girl looked eagerly down the tracks, though there were at least ten minutes until the train would arrive. Olivia had no luggage and was once again wearing the sea green day dress she'd put on that morning–this time without the pinafore and with the bustle in the proper location. The skirts were still damp and dirty from her time hiding in the wood. In one hand, Olivia held her train ticket. Her empty hand clasped and unclasped. All the other clothing, everything that had been loaned to her for the week-end by Genevieve was still at Hudson House. As was Philip.

After Mrs. Bracknell had agreed to take her to the station, everything had happened quickly. It wasn't until she had the ticket in hand and was waiting for the train that she began to have second thoughts. She pictured Philip. His charming smile on the train. His cheeky words in her chamber. His worried eyes in the nursery. His kiss on her cheek. She felt a pang in her chest.

Reaching the end of the platform, Olivia turned and continued pacing.

A serious relationship with him was out of the question. He was the son of a princess. She was an actress. Even if they continued to see one another, it would only turn out like the Earl. Olivia chewed the inside of her cheek. Well, not like the Earl. Philip was an honorable man. As such, he would never pretend to court her. They would never see one another again. The heaviness in her chest deepened.

Reaching the other end of the platform, she spun and continued pacing.

She shook her head. Forget the romance. Was it good behavior to disappear as she was about to do? To get on a train and leave him to deal with the Admiral and Mrs. Bracknell and all the rest? Would Mrs. Bracknell properly explain where Olivia had gone? Would Philip understand? He'd been so serious about "protecting" her. Would he worry? She pictured him on the train tomorrow, all alone. What would he tell Genevieve? What would he think of her?

Olivia stopped in the middle of the platform. To her left was the walkway that led through the ticket building and beyond, to the road to town.

"There it is!" called the girl on the platform.

Olivia felt the ground tremble beneath her feet, heard a whistle and the chug of the approaching train. Moving quickly, she threw her ticket into a bin and headed for Hudson House.

Genevieve and Lily stood in the telegraph office queue.

"Where did all these people come from?" asked Lily.

Genevieve shrugged. Her feet hurt and she was tired and hungry. She said a small prayer in French that Mrs. M would have sent the money and that it was waiting for them.

When they arrived to the front of the queue, the same young telegraph agent stood behind the counter. He looked surprised to see them.

"Has there been a response yet?" Genevieve asked. "Did she send the money?"

"Not yet," he said. "We'll send a boy as soon as it arrives."

Genevieve smiled wearily.

"There was a man here, looking for you."

"A man?" Genevieve looked at Lily.

Lily laughed. "Oscar probably wondered where we'd gone."

The agent said, "I said you were waiting at the Benbow Inn."

Lily and Genevieve both laughed. "And so we will be. Thank you."

As the telegraph office door shut behind them, they heard the whistle of a train.

"No!" wailed Lily. "The 3:00! We've missed it!"

"Oh, Lily," she said, hugging her young friend. "Don't worry. It isn't the end of the world."

"You don't know my mum. It might be the end of the world for me."

"Yes, she must be worried for you. But you are fine, and when she finds that out, she'll be thankful."

Lily didn't feel any better. Genevieve did not know her mother's temper. The two walked arm in arm toward the inn.

There were several people waiting to register at the Benbow Inn front desk, so Philip entered the taproom and ordered an ale. He surveyed the room and almost dropped his glass when he spotted Oscar Wilde playing cards with a middle-aged man.

"Now this is a surprise," said Philip. Oscar looked up as Philip set his ale on the table. Oscar's eyes, cloudy with drink, showed no surprise at seeing Mr. Lamb.

"Philip Lamb," he said. "This is Mr. Rogan, the innkeeper. I invited him to play so I could erase my debt, but when I win a hand he serves me an ale."

From the slurring of his words, Philip could tell that Oscar had won several hands.

Philip felt Mr. Rogan assess him: his tailored clothing, his expensive accent.

Philip pulled out the empty chair and sat. He ignored the innkeeper and spoke to Oscar. "What are you doing here? Have you seen Miss Snow? Have you heard about what's happened at Hudson House?"

Oscar tilted his head. His eyes flicked nervously. He shook his head, then looked, with surprising lucidity, at Philip. "I'm here absolutely by accident. In fact, I have no desire to be here. Have you any money? If you give me some blunt, enough to pay this man, I promise to leave."

The innkeeper eyed Philip. "Two rooms for one night,

breakfast for three and a single ale. I don't mind who pays."

Philip frowned at the innkeeper and spoke to Mr. Wilde. "There's been some trouble at Hudson House," he said, not wanting to mention the murder. "Miss Snow left, and I'm looking for her. You haven't seen her, have you? I thought maybe she'd come to this inn."

Mr. Wilde pulled a cigarette case from his pocket, then fumbled trying to open it. The case fell on the table twice. Philip grabbed it and held it open for him. Oscar slowly took a cigarette and carefully struck a match. Taking a deep drag, he waved out the match. It wasn't until he'd blown smoke above Philip's head that he spoke.

"I haven't seen Miss Snow since she left London. Has she won or lost the bet? Because I could use the blunt. Just enough to pay this man and return to London. What do you say?"

Philip glared at Oscar and stood to leave. "If you see Miss Snow or hear anything about her, send a message to Hudson House. That might be worth some blunt." He uttered the last word with contempt and hurried away.

"He wasn't very friendly," the innkeeper told Oscar when Philip had left.

"And I admire him for it. I thought he was the sort of man who tried to please everyone. I see I was wrong."

The innkeeper stared silently at Oscar before leaving for the kitchen.

Oscar pulled Philip's half-full glass of ale across the table and took a sip. He looked up to see Basil Daubeny staring at him. Oscar offered him a half smile.

Basil spoke to his female companion and then strolled across the taproom.

"Oscar Wilde," he said in a false chipper voice. "What brings you to Bunbury?"

"An abduction," said Oscar.

Basil raised an eyebrow. "Is that so?"

"Indeed, but not to worry. The abductee is safe and apparently of no concern to you. Who is this lady that does concern you?" Oscar eyed the lady who stood just outside the taproom, watching them.

Basil laughed falsely. "My sister, Mrs. Julia Cardew. She won't enter the taproom, and we are about to leave or I'd introduce you. We're here to see my aunt, you know. Now we're off to borrow a farmer's wagon. Too far to walk. Good day." Basil tipped his hat and dashed to his "sister."

Oscar watched them skeptically. He was certain he'd

never seen the woman before. He doubted they were here to visit an aunt. If they were siblings, he would eat his cravat. He looked around the room to make just such a wager and was disappointed to see that the room was empty.

Olivia recognized the turn where the dogcart had flipped and broken. As she walked along the road, she gazed into the wood where she had hidden from the driver. She remembered how she had been afraid, desperate. It had all been a gag, a wager. It seemed a lifetime ago. As she followed the road out of the wood, she heard the clopping of a galloping horse. She stepped to the side of the road and stopped to watch the horse and rider pass.

The horse slowed to a trot. The rider had dark hair. A strong, straight posture. The horse stopped, and Philip slid from the saddle.

"Olivia!" The emotion in his voice astonished her. She heard relief and astonishment, joy and – euphoria? Was she imagining that?

"Philip," she whispered. Before she knew what was happening, he had thrown his arms around her. She relaxed into his hug. He felt safe and strong and she didn't want him to let go. Except that she couldn't breathe. And his wool jacket was damp and smelled like horse.

"Philip," she gasped.

He let go.

"Forgive me," he said. "I thought . . . I didn't . . . ."

She laughed.

He smiled. "I've been so worried. When the driver said you'd run away, I didn't know what to do. It made you look guilty, although I am certain of your innocence. Then there was the thunderstorm, and no one else would go looking for you, and . . . ."

Olivia cocked her head. "They haven't told you? You don't know?"

"Know what?"

She grabbed his arm. "Philip, Mrs. Bracknell isn't dead. I went to Kelvil's hospital and she was there. It was all pretend. A charade. They knew about our wager before we arrived and decided to fool us."

Philip's expression went from confusion to astonishment to anger.

"How could they– You were so afraid. I was so–"

Olivia tightened her grip on his arm. "I know. It was another stupid wager. When I found out, I was so angry. I let Mrs. Bracknell take me to the railway station, and I almost left without returning to Hudson House."

He turned to her. Their eyes met and held.

"But you didn't leave," he whispered. "Why did you come back?"

"It seemed unfair to abandon you."

He took her hands and held them, then slowly raised one to his lips. "I was so worried," he said. He cleared his throat and dropped her hands. "Do you want to return to Hudson House? I could take you to the railway station. You could still leave."

"The last train has gone. Let's return to Hudson House and laugh as though the joke is funny. We can eat their food and sleep in their beds and return to London in the morning."

He smiled and touched her on the chin. "If that is what you want."

Philip helped her onto the horse and got up behind her.

The innkeeper's wife was behind the front desk when Genevieve and Lily returned.

"It looks as though we'll be staying another night," said Genevieve. "I hope our rooms are still available."

The innkeeper's wife made some marks in a large notebook.

"Is there a private parlour where we could take tea? A large tea, with sandwiches and cakes and whatever else you can offer?" Genevieve asked.

She eyed them skeptically but nodded and led them around the staircase to the private parlour. The room was small but clean. It had one long table, with a bench along the wall and three chairs opposite.

Before she left, Genevieve asked after Mr. Wilde. "In the taproom," said the innkeeper's wife. "Would you like me to send him to you?"

"Yes, please," said Genevieve, sinking gratefully onto one of the chairs. Lily had already appropriated the entire bench, lying down its length.

"Finally, someone I expect to see," said Mr. Wilde, entering the parlour with a slight stagger.

"We've had quite the adventure," said Lily, not sitting up.

Genevieve explained, "We sent a telegram asking Mrs. M to wire us some money. And I discovered that we are in Bunbury, which is where Basil's aunt lives."

Oscar raised an eyebrow. "Indeed?"

"Yes," Genevieve continued, "So I decided to try to find her, which was ridiculous and caused us to walk all over the countryside."

"You don't look wet," said Oscar, pulling out a chair and sitting.

"We waited out the storm at a hospital."

Oscar raised his other eyebrow.

"Then we returned to the telegraph office, but the money hasn't arrived. We heard the 3:00 train, which we've missed. I've told the innkeeper that we'll have to stay another night."

"Not necessarily," said Oscar.

Lily sat up. "Did you find some money? Win at cards? We could hire a carriage."

"Don't be ridiculous, I never win at cards." Oscar took his time opening his cigarette case, removing a cigarette and lighting it. After he had exhaled a stream of smoke, he spoke. "But your brother could probably get us home."

"My brother?" said Lily. "He's six and in London–"

"Not your brother. Genevieve's brother."

Genevieve cocked her head. "Which brother?"

"Mr. Philip Lamb was in the taproom less than an hour ago. I didn't give away that you'd been abducted and spent the night with me."

Genevieve opened her mouth, but Oscar held up his hand.

"I didn't say a word to him about you. He doesn't know you are here, at least not from me. But if you are inclined to secure his aid, he is staying at Hudson House. Three miles distant."

"He's here? The Admiral lives here?" marveled Genevieve.

"Olivia's here too?" asked Lily.

Oscar squinted at the wall above Lily. "I didn't see Miss

Snow," he said. "Only Mr. Lamb. I asked for money, but he refused. Hopefully, he won't refuse you."

Genevieve was on her feet. "I'll send a note. We can pay the bill and take a carriage to London. You'll be home to your mother tonight, Lily!"

Lily squealed.

Genevieve dashed out the parlour and returned a moment later. "I was at the front desk asking for note paper, when a man came in asking for directions to Kelvil's hospital. Apparently, Hudson House is just beyond. He's going to give us a ride. Grab your bonnet, Lily. You can help me convince Philip to send us home."

She dashed out, Lily on her heels. Oscar finished his cigarette, astonished to find himself once again alone. He cheered considerably when the innkeeper's wife arrived with a tray of cucumber sandwiches.

"My favorite," he said, taking three.

The wagon turned out to be only slightly larger than a dogcart. The driver did not appear to be happy with his two additional passengers. He grumbled something to the effect that they could sit in the back. A very pregnant girl sat on the bench and flinched when the man took the reins and sat beside her. Lily and Genevieve hurried to the back and pushed a trunk and handbag to the side.

"That way," said Genevieve, pointing and cheerful. "Take the High Street straight through town. It isn't far."

Lily tried to make herself comfortable in the uncomfortable wagon. It was dirty and rickety and driven by a grumpy man who didn't want them there. She wished she were already in London.

They rolled through town and onto the old hermit road. Genevieve guided the driver through the creepy wood. At the turnoff to Kelvil's Sanctuary for the Elderly and Infirm, he stopped.

"You can walk from here," he said over his shoulder.

Genevieve stood in the back of the wagon. "But you promised to drive us there."

"It's late and I've changed my mind."

"But I'm not certain how far it is, and we're terribly tired," whined Genevieve. The girl sitting next to the driver looked at her sympathetically.

The driver turned away from Genevieve and his voice thinned. "You can walk from here and be glad you got this far."

Genevieve flushed. "You agreed to take us to Hudson House."

"We can walk," whispered Lily, pulling on Genevieve's arm.

"If you wait until I unload Jane, I'll give you a ride back to town," said the driver, with a nasty laugh.

"No, we're getting out," said Lily, as she tugged Genevieve down from the wagon bed.

Genevieve scowled as the driver set the horses to motion, toward Kelvil's and away from Hudson House.

Lily put her hand on Genevieve's shoulder. "It's not like we don't know how to walk. Besides, once we get to your brother, we won't have to walk no more."

Genevieve snorted. "I don't like being treated like that. What a pig!"

Lily shrugged and the two set off.

Philip slid off the horse and helped Olivia down. A groom took the horse and the two walked out onto the lawn where the Greenpin sisters played croquet with the Admiral. Mr. Greenpin sat on a wicker lawn chair, a notepad in hand and a glass of lemonade nearby.

The Admiral clapped his hands at their approach. "By jolly you found her! Good for you, what! Our little murderess has been captured!" The Admiral's laugh was deep. He darted glances at the twins to see their reactions.

"Thank God!" Emily said. "I am that relieved, aren't you Anne? I've been worried all day she would sneak up on us and slit our throats."

Olivia stared, unsmiling. She hadn't trusted them before, but now she felt a deep dislike for the twins.

Philip approached the Admiral. "Surely you have given up the charade?"

Olivia kept her distance from the group but called out. "Mrs. Bracknell must have returned."

"From the dead?" whispered Anne, her face white like new milk.

Emily laughed. "Is she meant to be haunting us, then? It would be just like her."

Frances frowned at her sisters and stepped toward Mr. Lamb. "Why'd you bring her back here? Surely she should be in the town's gaol?"

"It was a charade," said Philip. "Mrs. Bracknell wasn't murdered. She isn't dead. She was hiding at Kelvil's hospital."

"Mrs. Bracknell should have returned by now," said Olivia. "Haven't you seen her?"

At the disbelief in the Greenpin faces, Olivia pleaded to the Admiral. "Tell them, sir. Tell them it was a hoax."

The Admiral looked flabbergasted. His eyes darted about. "I don't know any such thing. My wife was poisoned this morning."

"Did you see Mrs. Bracknell?" Emily asked Philip. She stood close to him, closer than comfortable. He took a step away and turned to Olivia.

"She's alive!" called Olivia, panicking. "She dropped me in town. She was driving a Victoria carriage. Her little terrier sat on the bench beside her. She said she was returning to Hudson House. Maybe she stopped at Kelvil's to get something. But she's alive!"

The Admiral and the Greenpins looked at her skeptically.

From his wicker chair, Mr. Greenpin muttered, "Ghost . . . most . . . toast."

"Mr. Lamb!" called a voice. Miss Darlington hurried from the direction of the stables, her pudgy, short frame waddling, her face bright and happy. "She's much improved! The bran mash and water have sent the colic packing. I can't thank you enough."

Miss Darlington joined the group, shaking Philip's hand and beaming.

"I'm happy to hear that," Philip said, looking awkwardly at Olivia.

"Miss Darlington," said Olivia, dread turning to hope. "Mrs. Bracknell said you were in on the charade. You know that your aunt wasn't murdered. Please, tell everyone."

Miss Darlington blushed. "I wasn't for a minute in favor

of it. I kept quiet, that's all. I'm glad it's over. Nasty business."

"See?" said Olivia. "It was a charade."

Anne's mouth fell open.

Emily turned on the Admiral, angry. "Your wife isn't dead? You've lied to us?"

The Admiral laughed awkwardly. "Fooled you, what! Great gag!"

"That's appalling!" said Frances. "Come, Papa." She pulled her father up from his chair and led him toward the house.

Philip took Olivia's arm and walked with her across the lawn.

"I'd prefer not to leave your side for a second, but I'll let you change for dinner. Promise me you won't leave your chamber until I knock on the door. I don't trust the Admiral or anyone else in this house."

"Promise," said Olivia. Not because she was worried about her safety, but because she wanted him by her side too.

The old hermit road curved to the left and sloped down. To the right, a long drive disappeared in a small wood. There were no signs or markers of any kind. Genevieve and Lily looked at the lane.

"This lane must go to Hudson House, don't you think?" asked Lily. "It wasn't supposed to be far past the hospital."

Genevieve chewed her lip. "Maybe we should stay on the road past the curve. If nothing there looks like Hudson House, we'll come back to the lane."

Past the curve, the two could see a short drive at the bottom of the hill. A small carriage and a farmer's wagon were parked in an open area off the drive. A man and two women stood by several large stacks of wooden boxes. They were close together, looking at something one of the women held. They moved apart, suddenly. The man grabbed the older of the two women, who shrugged him off.

Genevieve paused, staring. "That looks like Basil. And if that older woman is his aunt, she's healthier than I thought."

The older woman put what she'd been holding in her handbag and pulled out a pistol. The man and the other woman backed up, knocking over a stack of boxes.

Not boxes, bee hives.

The bees swarmed. The man who looked like Basil fell to the ground. The younger woman swore. Horses whinnied and pulled against their leads. A dog yipped. The older woman, swatting, hurried to the small carriage, climbed up, slapped the reins, and drove down the lane, away from the road. She disappeared as the lane curved and went up.

Dashing down the hill, Genevieve yelled to Lily, "Run to the wagon and be ready with the reins." As she ran, Genevieve unpinned her widow cap's lacy veil and covered her face with it as protection from the bees.

By the time Genevieve reached the-man-who-looked-like-Basil and the lady, they had stood up and were swatting at the bees. The woman had a jacket, a high collar, gloves, and a large hat that kept her mostly protected. The man, who was indeed Basil, had fared worse. His hat had fallen off when he'd bumped into the bee hives and he wasn't wearing gloves. His neck and head were covered with stings.

"Quickly, quickly," said Genevieve, pulling at Basil but talking to the woman. "Get him into the wagon."

The woman looked up, startled, and nodded.

"Genevieve?" said Basil, hobbling to the wagon.

"Yes, surprises all around. We can talk about that later. We need to get you help. Does this lane go to Hudson House? Should we try for the hospital?" asked Genevieve.

"Hudson House is better," said the woman. "Basil will be fine. We need to follow Mrs. Bracknell." Genevieve could not help but notice how beautiful she was and that she had used Basil's Christian name. What was he to her, that such intimacy came naturally?

Lily held the reins nervously. "I've never driven a wagon," she said.

Genevieve looked at the woman who was helping Basil into the wagon and then back to Lily. With only a little hesitation, she said, "I'll drive," and climbed up beside Lily.

The lane climbed a small hill and then Hudson House and its buildings were clearly visible. The lane came in from the rear, so they drove up behind the stable yard. Before

Genevieve had stopped the wagon, the beautiful woman had jumped out and yelled at a stable boy.

"Where's Mrs. Bracknell?"

The boy pointed, saying. "Ma'am drove the carriage to the back gardens. Didn't want no help."

The beautiful woman was off, running, without waiting to hear more.

Genevieve climbed down and met Basil at the back of the wagon, where he sat on the edge. His face was swollen with more than a dozen red blisters. She put her hand to his forehead.

"You're warm. We need to get you inside. Some cold compresses or something. Pull out these stingers." She pulled one from his neck. "Do you know the people here?"

Basil shook his head. "Not really. The butler." He slid to his feet. "We should hurry to the house. Julia might be in danger. What a disaster I've made of this."

Genevieve frowned. Julia. He was using her Christian name as though they knew one another intimately.

She answered, "Quite possibly. Can you walk?"

Basil nodded and leaned on her.

"Here," she called to the stable boy Julia had yelled at. "This man is hurt. Help us get him into the house."

The boy helped shoulder Basil and led them to a back door of the large estate house. Lily shuffled nervously, a few steps behind.

Philip closed the door of his guest chamber and sat on the bed in relief. Miss Snow was safe. She was innocent. They would soon return to London, away from this crazy place. Exhausted, he lay on the bed. As he turned, a sharpness dug into his side. Mrs. Bracknell's puzzle box was in his jacket pocket where he had absentmindedly dropped it that morning.

He studied the box and set his mind to solving the puzzle.

After about ten minutes, he realized that the eye of the decorative bird was a pin that could be slid into an unobtrusive hole on the side corner. Click. One of the side panels opened. With a little maneuvering, he was able to slide open the box.

Inside, he found his Lamb family signet ring. He stared at it, trying to understand what he was seeing.

Olivia dried her face and looked in the mirror, feeling glad to be clean once again. She'd removed the damp and dirty day dress and stood in a fresh shift. Her hair was down, brushed and smooth on her shoulders. The cake of soap she'd used on her arms and face left its scent of fresh lilac. Rather than wait for the maid's help, Olivia swept up her hair in a simple bun, leaving strands to fall on either side of her face.

She studied the gowns in the wardrobe, wondering which would be appropriate for a dinner among scoundrels. Should she dress in style and beauty as to make them in awe of her? Should she dress informally, to show how little respect she had for them? Perhaps she shouldn't think of the Admiral and his guests at all. She should dress to impress Philip. Which gown would he find most attractive?

Olivia jumped at the sound of a gunshot and a scream. They came from the back garden. She dashed to the window. The pane was open and she could smell the acrid scent of gunpowder. Below, on the other side of the flower beds where she had lost the ring that morning, stood Mrs. Bracknell, Chiltern, and a woman Olivia did not know. In one hand, Mrs. Bracknell held a rope tied to a trunk, the trunk that had been in the nursery. In the other hand, she pointed a pistol at Chiltern and the woman. Mrs. Bracknell backed slowly away from the two, dragging the trunk toward a horse and small open carriage which stood in the middle of the lawn. Her limp and cane were gone.

Mrs. Bracknell spoke, but Olivia could not make out the words. She imagined it was something to the effect of, "Stay where you are." The Admiral's wife walked slowly sideways, toward the carriage, flashing her eyes between the two people, the horse and carriage, and a group of stable hands who had congregated at the edge of the yard.

The widow Bracknell stepped out from behind a large shrub. The older woman was behind and out of sight of her daughter-in-law. The widow walked with steady steps toward a garden ornament display. The marble pieces were meant to look like Roman ruins. Two tall columns, two short columns, fake rubble, and several faux-decayed statues of gods. The widow easily lifted a short marble column and sneaked behind Mrs. Bracknell.

Olivia gasped. The widow moved quietly and quickly and smashed the column against her daughter-in-law's head. Mrs. Bracknell crumpled to the ground. Chiltern sighed and sank to his knees. Olivia watched in wonder as the mysterious lady dashed forward and took up the pistol.

From the corner of her eye, Olivia saw movement and glanced across the side of the house. Philip was looking out his window.

"Did you see what happened?" Olivia called to him.

Philip nodded. "But I don't understand. One minute."

His head disappeared into his room and a moment later a knock sounded on her door. Olivia opened the door a crack, saw that it was Philip, let him in, and closed the door behind him.

"I didn't believe the weekend could become more –" Philip stopped speaking when he realized Olivia was not fully dressed. Olivia realized it at the same moment.

"What must you think of me?" she said, blushing. "I would not normally– I was so shocked by the gunshot–"

Philip nodded, keeping his eyes on the floor and moving toward the door. "Yes, as was I."

Before he could open the door, a knock sounded.

Olivia jumped. "Who could that be?"

Without lifting his eyes, Philip whispered, "I can't let you be found with me, here, like this."

He shrank to the floor and scampered beneath the bed. When he was completely hidden, Olivia took a deep breath and asked, "Who is it?"

"Lily," said Lily's voice.

"Lily!" Olivia repeated, shocked. She pulled open the door to find her dear friend standing in the corridor, dressed in dirty servant garb. "What are you doing here? And what are you wearing?"

Lily pushed into the room and shut the door.

"You will not believe what has happened to me."

ᴏᴏ *Sixty-First Chapter* ᴏᴏ

Everyone had an opinion as to the best cure for bee sting. Basil lay on a long sofa in the front receiving room, sleeves rolled and arms exposed, a medical experiment. The Admiral said to leave the stings alone: everyone knew that bee venom was a curative for rheumatism.

"But Basil doesn't have rheumatism," said Genevieve, applying a handkerchief of ice to his swollen red face.

Cook waved the Admiral away and applied butter to Basil's neck. A footman appeared behind the sofa and set an onion upon three stings on his arm, but when Basil screamed, Genevieve told the footman to leave.

An elderly maid suggested vinegar and baking soda, and Basil held out the arm that had been burned by the onion. A crowd gathered to watch the ingredients bubble. Basil sighed in relief.

There was some sort of clamor from the back of the house. The servants and Admiral dashed out the door, leaving Genevieve and Basil alone.

Genevieve removed the cold, wet handkerchief from Basil's forehead and looked at him. His face was nearly unrecognizable. The right side was far worse than the left. His right eye was swollen shut. His right cheek was bloated so that his mouth puckered down and his pencil-thin mustache looked askew. His forehead was pocked and swollen as well.

"Please," said Basil, grabbing her hand and directing the

cold handkerchief back to his face. "The ice feels wonderful."

Genevieve held it gently against his skin.

"My dear Basil. It appears I have quite the wrong impression of your aunt. Is she the older woman who pushed you into the bees, or is she the young and beautiful woman?"

Basil laughed, then flinched at the pain.

"Neither."

"Do you have an Aunt Agnes Daubeny?"

"No, but–"

Genevieve removed the palliative handkerchief.

She asked, "Every time you said you were visiting your aunt? You were visiting. . . Julia?"

Basil twisted so that he sat up in the sofa. His face grimaced in pain and he held his right arm close to his chest. "Not every time. Let me explai–"

"No. Don't speak." Genevieve turned her back to him. She looked at her hands. At her emerald ring. Her mouth puckered into a small frown. She slid the ring from her finger. "I release you. I don't know why you would propose when–"

Basil spun Genevieve around and kissed her. Briefly. With a great deal of pain.

"Ahhhh!" He groaned and grabbed at his face. Genevieve smirked. Gently applying the ice to his cheek and mouth, she guided him back to the sofa.

"Sit down, you rascal, and explain yourself. I've no idea what you've been doing."

Basil lay down gratefully.

"It's all to do with the jewel robberies."

"It does, does it?" said Genevieve skeptically.

"I work for Scotland Yard, secretly, although I suppose not so secretly any more."

Genevieve scoffed. "If you think an unbelievable story more likely to be believed, you are sadly mistaken."

"There was a string of thefts in Northern Africa, all done

in the same way. Then in France. Then on the ship *Ville de Naples*. Then in England. There were two main suspects: your brother Philip and Admiral Bracknell."

"Philip! How ridiculous."

"He was in all the right places at the right times," said Basil. "He was one of the few first-class passengers aboard the *Ville de Naples* who did not lose any items."

"He lost the Lamb family signet ring," said Genevieve.

Basil cocked his head. "He did? He didn't report it."

Genevieve shrugged. She chewed her lip. "So you got close to me to get close to Philip?"

Basil nodded. "I searched his rooms, but never found anything."

"Our relationship? It was pretend?"

Basil grabbed Genevieve's hand and held it between his own, which were over-warm.

"I tried to be rude. I tried to be dismissive. I tried to protect my heart and yours. When Philip stopped being a suspect, I needed a way to disappear from your life. My sister suggested asking you to marry me. She was certain you would refuse. She believed you were only teasing your other beaux by appearing to like me."

Genevieve half-laughed. "I only accepted because my brother told me I couldn't marry you."

"You don't love me?" asked Basil.

"As much as I like displeasing my brother, I must admit that I do not love you, Basil."

Joy spread across his face. "Thank goodness!"

Genevieve wrinkled her brow. "You don't want me to love you? I thought you were in the midst of declaring your love for me."

"Yes! I love you," said Basil, the one eye not swollen shut beaming happily, "but I don't want you to love rude, selfish Basil. I want you to love the real Basil."

Genevieve pouted playfully. "And who is the real Basil?"

"I want to show you. Will you forgive my deceptions and allow me to court you as I really am?"

Genevieve paced back and forth. "And Julia? Who is she? What does she know?"

"Julia has known everything since the beginning–she's been my ray of light and sanity. Scotland Yard recruited her before me. She narrowed down the suspects to Philip and the Admiral. She's been visiting Hudson House, talking to the servants, searching for the stolen goods. She enlisted the help of the butler, Chiltern, whose son is a policeman. It was difficult for her to travel alone, so I sometimes came with her. We posed as husband and wife. Every time I had to visit my 'aunt,' and keep–"

"Husband and wife?" interrupted Genevieve, holding her palms in the air in disbelief. "In what way did you pose as husband and wife? At the Benbow Inn? Did you stay there together?"

Basil cocked his head, confused. "Yes. That's where we stayed. It was better to be husband and wife than–"

"So this is the real you?" Genevieve threw the ice-filled handkerchief at him, hitting him in the chest. She slid off the engagement ring and threw that as well. It soared over the sofa and hit the wall behind him.

The only one of Basil's eyes that could widen, widened.

"Genevieve? Why are you angry?"

Genevieve shook her head and waved her arms. "I'm not angry." She stomped her foot. "I'm shocked. Aghast. Offended." Facing him, hands in tight fists at her hips, she said, "If you can pose as husband and wife and travel with–"

"My sister. She's my sister. Julia is my sister. I said that at the beginning, didn't I?"

"No! You didn't!" Genevieve's pout turned into a delightful smile. "The beautiful woman is your sister?"

Basil nodded. "Hopefully she's captured Mrs. Bracknell and found the stolen jewels. I should be helping her."

Genevieve leapt the few steps between them and threw her arms around Basil, kissing him on his head, his nose, his cheek, his lips, until he cried out in pain.

"And then the young, pretty lady jumps out of the wagon and goes chasing after the lady with the pistol," said Lily, "and I help Genevieve get her fiancé into the house. I asked some bloke where you were, and he told me to check here. And that's what's been happening."

Lily sat on Olivia's bed, kicking her heels against the side. Olivia watched the worn boots, certain they would connect with Philip at some point. The bed skirt had rustled several times, when Lily explained how Genevieve had been kissed by an ogre and abducted by an oaf, but Philip had not revealed himself.

"What an exciting adventure you've had," said Olivia. "Your mother is never going to let you out of her sight again."

"I know!" said Lily. "Here, let me help you with that." Lily left her seat on the bed and buttoned the cuffs of Olivia's long sleeves. While Lily had told her story, Olivia had donned the brown traveling suit, hoping to leave as soon as they'd eaten. Perhaps before. They would have to get Lily and Genevieve back to London. The Admiral must let them have a carriage.

"Shall we dress you in something better than what you're wearing?" asked Olivia, looking through the wardrobe for something small enough for Lily.

"Nah, I've gotten used to this," said Lily. "I'm more comfortable in these rags than in something fancy I might ruin."

"Are you certain?" said Olivia, pulling out the morning

gown she had planned to wear on Sunday.

A knock sounded at the door. "Genevieve, maybe?" said Olivia, moving toward the door. Before she got there, it opened and a footman stood at the entrance. "Miss Snow, a woman has arrived–"

"Don't mind me!" Lily's mother pushed her way into the chamber, an infant in one arm and two children on her tail. The startled footman looked at Miss Snow with apologetic eyes.

"She's a friend," Olivia said, smiling.

The young man bowed and slipped out the door.

"You two young ladies have a lot of explaining to do!" said Mrs. Rambling, her face an angry red.

"Look at this room!" said Sam running in circles in the wide space between the bed, dressing table and window.

"It's bigger than our whole garret!" said Etta, twirling around.

Mrs. Rambling transferred the baby from one arm to another.

"Here, I'll take Theo," said Lily. The baby started crying as soon as he was securely in Lily's arms.

"He's hungry. Always hungry," said Mrs. Rambling, sitting on the bed and undoing the buttons on her chemise. "I'll feed him, and you explain yourselves. I've been that worried, I have."

"Oh, no!" said Olivia shaking her head. "Lily just spent the past half hour telling me how she got here. She can tell that story to you on the road to London."

"How did you find us?" asked Lily, handing the baby to her mother.

"I went to Mrs. Markby's house, of course. It was where you said you were havin' dinner. I never heard of no dinner going into the next morning. The lady told me she'd got a telegram, sayin' you'd spent the night and would be home soon. So I went home, worried and angry, but what could I do? Mid-afternoon, and still no word, I went back to Mrs. Markby. She was out, so I waited. When she come in, she says she don't know nothin', but then she sees the telegram you sent, asking for money."

Mrs. Rambling shifted the babe to her other side without pausing the story. The jiggling of her weight on the bed caused Olivia to look at the bed skirt behind which Philip still lay. She hoped he wasn't being crushed.

Mrs. Rambling continued, "Mrs. Markby wanted to send the money, but how did we know it was you? Then we noticed the town name, Bunbury, where the telegram was from. Mrs. Markby let me take her carriage, with a driver and everything."

"You've got a carriage we can all go home in?" asked Olivia, her face a smile.

"Not everyone, but it's big enough for us and you."

"But the telegram agent didn't know we were at Hudson House," said Lily, trying to follow her mother's story. "He was to send the money to the Benbow Inn."

Mrs. Rambling nodded. "That's what he told me. So I went to the inn. Very nice lady runs that inn. She was none too pleased with how you kept her waiting for payment. I paid what you owed and more. No one can say a Rambling doesn't pay what is owed. She told me you'd ridden in a cart to Hudson House, so here we come."

She buttoned her chemise, threw a cloth over her shoulder, and burped the baby. Her eyes landed on Lily. "I may have answered your questions and done all the talking, but don't think I've forgotten who's in trouble."

"We were trying to get home!" said Lily. "Honest! Miss Lamb was abducted, so we had to help her."

Etta pulled on Olivia's sleeve. Olivia turned to her little sister and noticed that Sam lay half under the bed, only the bottom half of his legs exposed.

Etta said, "Why is there a–"

In a loud voice, Olivia said, "Lily and Ruby, I need you to go downstairs. Explain to Genevieve that we are leaving and get the driver of your carriage ready. It's late. Also, ask a footman to find the Admiral. We'll get everything worked out and get everyone home this evening." As she spoke, Olivia pushed them out the door. Lily looked at Olivia in confusion and Olivia stared at her to help.

"Come on, Mum. I'll introduce you to Miss Lamb and her fiancé. If he is still her fiancé, which I very much doubt."

Olivia shut and locked the door.

Sam sat cross-legged on the floor. "I didn't say nothin'. He told me not to, and I didn't."

Etta lay on her stomach, looking under the bed. "Who is he?"

Philip crawled out, rumpled and dusty. "My name is Mr. Philip Lamb," he said, shaking their hands formally. "I thank you very much for waking me. I was playing hide and seek with some friends and fell asleep."

Etta giggled.

"Hide and seek?" said Sam. "You?"

"It's very embarrassing. Please don't tell the others that I fell asleep," said Philip, crouching down so he was close to eye level with the children.

"I won't tell," said Etta, her eyes sparkling in amusement.

Olivia tried hard not to laugh.

"You know who I am," said Philip, "but I don't know who you are."

"Sam Rambling," said Sam.

"Henrietta Snow," said Etta.

Philip looked at Olivia when he heard the young girl's name.

Olivia nodded. "I pretended to be Henrietta because it's

271

my little sister's name."

"Your sister?" he looked at Etta closely, her wild red curls, her freckled nose, her mischievous smile. His eyes dropped to the chain she wore around her neck. "My God!" he exclaimed, reaching for the signet ring.

"No! It's my father's," said Etta, pulling out of his reach and darting across the room. She climbed onto the dressing table chair, watching him over the chair back.

Philip stood and looked at Olivia. "Who is her father?"

Olivia sighed. "I don't know. My mother never said. She called him her 'Prince Charming.' He promised marriage and disappeared when she got pregnant. She always believed he would return–the ring was supposed to be proof of that. She died in childbirth."

"Mama told Olivia to name me Henrietta," said Etta.

"His name may have been Henry," said Olivia. "I'm named after my father, Oliver."

"My brother was called Henry," Philip said softly. "She looks just like him."

Olivia studied Philip. "Your brother? Henry? When did he die? How?"

"Crossing the English Channel. He had important news for us, which he never delivered. He wasn't on the passenger list. It took months to discover what had happened to him."

"Come here, Etta, dear," said Olivia, pulling Etta into her arms. "Let him look at your ring. It's a lamb, not a dog. This man, Philip Lamb, might be your uncle."

Etta looked at him skeptically. She let them remove the chain from her neck, then scrambled down and stood with Sam.

"He's the prince," said Sam. "Remember? Livvy was going to spend the weekend with a prince? If he's your uncle, that makes you a princess."

"Does it?" Etta asked Olivia. "Am I a princess?"

"I don't know what it means," said Olivia, suddenly realizing what it could mean. The Lamb family would want Etta. They would take her away from Olivia.

"It isn't the same, is it?" said Olivia. "The signet is different."

"No. Yes," said Philip, breathless. "This is most certainly a Lamb family signet." He pulled the ring he'd recovered from the puzzle box earlier and showed them both to Olivia.

She took them in her hands, Etta's ring with the chain. Philip's ring. They were identical Her stomach dropped. If only Etta's emblem had been the funny-looking dog she'd always imagined it to be.

Olivia took a deep breath. "They're identical." She draped the chain and ring around her little sister's neck, saying, "We should be downstairs with Lily and Ruby, figuring out how to get home. It's much too late for the two of you to still be awake."

"It's not late," said Sam.

"I'm not tired," said Etta.

Olivia guided them out the door, not meeting Philip's eyes.

Before she could leave, he grabbed her hand. "What happened? Your face went from happy to sad in an instant. The change was obvious even to me, and I'm not good at reading people."

Olivia pulled her hand away and pointed Sam and Etta downstairs. "Lily and Ruby should be in that room, where the servant just came out. I'll meet you there."

The two ran down the stairs.

Olivia turned and looked Philip in the eye. "She's my sister. I've raised her myself, hidden her from gossip, tutored her, fed her. If she's a Lamb, what happens to her? What happens to me?" Olivia's voice cracked at the last question. Her eyes filled. Philip took her hand, rubbing her knuckles with his thumb. "I've spent all day thinking of you, searching for you. When I found you, I thought, 'I'll never let her go.' As I lay beneath the bed, I planned how I would court you. I will woo you. I will make you feel about me the way I feel about you."

Olivia looked up and into his eyes. His earnestness shined like a beacon. "I already do," she said.

He leaned toward her, and she leaned toward him.

He smelled of brandy and some foreign spice.

She smelled of lilac and champagne.

Their kiss was warm and pleasant and lasted until they heard voices below.

"She's up there!" shouted Sam, "Kissing the Prince!"

Epilogue

Philip wove in and out of the crush until he reached Olivia. He handed her a glass of champagne and looked at the crowd surrounding Genevieve.

"She's doing it again, isn't she?"

"It's a good story," said Olivia, sipping at her champagne, "and it shows that Basil isn't who everyone thought he was. She is rectifying his character."

Philip wrapped his arms around his wife's waist. "And you don't feel the need to rectify my character? Genevieve says my reputation is for stuffiness."

"Hush. She's almost finished."

"And then the Admiral's mother, hits Mrs. Bracknell with a marble column. Boom! Down she goes," said Genevieve, waving her arms. "Knocked unconscious and carted off to gaol. The widow Bracknell said she'd wanted to do that for years!"

The crowd around her laughed.

"Basil's sister suspected the antique puzzle boxes. That's where Mrs. Bracknell hid the stolen jewelry. Puzzle boxes are nearly impossible to open, but Basil, here," Genevieve put her arm around her fiancé, "He's a whiz at that sort of thing."

"Not fair," Philip whispered in Olivia's ear. "I opened more than half of them."

Olivia slapped him playfully on the arm.

A young man in a purple waistcoat spoke. "But I don't understand about the Emrubdiam . Wasn't it a gift from her husband? It wasn't stolen."

"It was stolen!" replied Genevieve. "Mrs. Bracknell stole it in Cairo, but she didn't have a puzzle box to hide it in. She put it in a shoe and the Admiral found it. His memory is so terrible that he thought he'd bought it. He wrapped it and gave it to her as an anniversary gift. Imagine her shock when he presented it to her in a crowd of people! She needed to deal with it right away. They'd already planned her fake murder, so she thought she could have the Emrubdiam disappear too. She hoped the guests would forget about it. If they said anything, she would deny that the Admiral had given it to her. He would never remember."

"Did he marry the twin?" asked a young woman.

Genevieve laughed. "Nearly. His mother got him out of that.

"And Mr. Wilde?" said the man in the purple waistcoat. "I heard that you returned to London and forgot about him."

Genevieve covered her mouth in embarrassment, then waved her hand. "We did! Mrs. Rambling paid for the food and the inn, but no one told Oscar."

It was two days before anyone realized Oscar Wilde was still at the Benbow Inn in Bunbury. It was another two months before he would speak to any of them. Not that they noticed, wrapped up as they were in their own ridiculous affairs.

"The Lambs are moving up in society," Oscar said to his mother, reading *The Times*. "Philip Lamb is to marry an actress. The young Miss Lamb is engaged to a policeman. How proud their parents must be."

"Isn't it romantic?" warbled his mother.

"Our standards are falling, Mother."

"We're Irish, Oscar. We don't have standards."

"What next?" cried Oscar, turning a page and rustling the newspaper. "Shall the king of England marry an American divorcée? A prince of the crown marry a commoner from Reading? If the quality don't marry quality, who will?"

"Pass the sugar. Are you wanting a princess yourself? I dare say you could have interested the young Miss Lamb if you had behaved properly."

Oscar scoffed. "If she'd had the slightest interest in me, she would have remembered I was stuck at that inn."

Lady Wilde turned away so that her son could not see the smile on her face.

"I had to learn of the whole episode from the papers. Not a one of them came to tell me."

"Stop whining," chided Lady Wilde. "Miss Snow came on several occasions and you pretended not to be here."

"Third time's the charm. She didn't come a third time."

"I told her you were being a baby and that you would visit her when you'd grown up. More tea?"

"Yes, please." He held out his cup.

"I think it was best you were left at the inn. You might have died of an allergic bee reaction if you'd been with them."

"Or fallen in love. Everyone seems to have fallen in love. That would have been far worse than death by bee. You are right, mother. It was good I stayed at the inn. And it gave me the time I needed to start my next play."

"You haven't told me what it is about."

"This whole affair. People pretending to be other people. People falling in love with people they don't know. I've swapped names and changed genders and altered most of the story line."

"Sounds wonderful. What are you calling it?"

"I don't know yet. I was thinking of calling the main

character Ernest and playing with that."

Gazing at an advertisement for shoe buckles, Lady Wilde replied, "That's nice. It's important to be earnest."

Acknowledgements

This story took more than ten years from beginning to end. Many people helped me on this journey, and I'm going to forget some of you. For that I apologize.

First, my book club of dear friends who through the years have given their reading time to my many stories including this one: Kathryn Blakeman, Sherri Hefferan, Nancy Huspeni, Margaret Konkol, Michelle Konkol. For your support, suggestions, and ability to catch typos, I thank you!

To my dear friend and artist Sally Powell, for your feedback, support, and love.

To amazing author and beta-reader Tinney Heath. Your advice has been a blessing.

To the students of Per Henningsgaard's Book Editing class (WR 461/561) at Portland State University in the winter term of 2014. Your comments and suggestions changed the direction of this story, increasing the silliness factor. Thanks for pushing me to focus on a tone when I was wobbling between several.

To the Aspiring Authors of Stevens Point writers group members including Karen Bezella-Bond, Jim Pollack, Bev Scott, Jacqui, and others whose names I forget (so sorry!). Your wisdom and poetry greatly improved my early drafts.

To my more recent writing group, Karen Bezella-Bond (I can't mention you enough!), Kerry Ames, Nicolas Kubley, Christine Sommers, and Mark Thwait. You may not have read or helped with this story, but our regular meetings helped me think of myself as a writer and pushed me to put pen to paper (or fingers to keyboard).

To my family: Andy, Craig and Tom. Your love is what keeps me going.

And, finally, to my mother. She was there at the beginning, reading each chapter as I wrote it, levitating me with praise, urging me to write faster, correcting British faux pas, asking questions, making suggestions. I did not write fast enough. When you died, this novel nearly did too. Wilde Wagers is what it is today because I wanted a story that would have made you laugh. A story to where people like you and me (and there are many of us, right?) can escape when the world becomes dark. I miss you, Mom. This story is for you.

Historical Notes

Oscar Wilde is the name of an actual historical person as are a few other names in this story. You should not assume that anything in *Wilde Wagers* is an accurate representation of the real Oscar Wilde, other famous people, England, London, British English, or the nineteenth century. I did some historical research in the early days, but this novel took many different directions and went through many drafts. In the end, I decided that for *Wilde Wagers*, silly entertainment was more important than historical accuracy. I hope you agree.

About the Author

Elizabeth Caulfield Felt is a senior lecturer in English at the University of Wisconsin, Stevens Point. She is the author of the fictionalized autobiography, *Syncopation: A Memoir of Adèle Hugo* and a co-author of the children's mystery *The Stolen Goldin Violin*. She is currently working on a series of steampunk fairy tales. Learn more about her and her writing at

http://elizabethcaulfieldfelt.com

www.ingramcontent.com/pod-product-compliance
Lightning Source LLC
Chambersburg PA
CBHW050148120726
47903CB00002B/544